THE AGENT RUNNER

A NOVEL

SIMON CONWAY

Arcade Publishing • New York

First North American Edition 2017

This is a work of fiction. Names, places, characters, and incidents are either the products of the author's imagination or are used fictitiously.

Arcade Publishing books may be purchased in bulk at special discounts for sales promotion, corporate gifts, fund-raising, or educational purposes. Special editions can also be created to specifications. For details, contact the Special Sales Department, Arcade Publishing, 307 West 36th Street, 11th Floor, New York, NY 10018 or arcade@skyhorsepublishing.com.

Arcade Publishing® is a registered trademark of Skyhorse Publishing, Inc.®, a Delaware corporation.

Visit our website at www.arcadepub.com.
Visit the author's website at www.simonconwaybooks.com.

10 9 8 7 6 5 4 3 2 1

JAN 0 6 2017

Library of Congress Cataloging-in-Publication Data

Names: Conway, Simon, 1967- author.
Title: The agent runner : a novel / Simon Conway.
Description: First North American edition. | New York : Arcade Publishing, 2017.
Identifiers: LCCN 2016034631 (print) | LCCN 2016040988 (ebook) | ISBN 9781628725995 (hardcover : acid-free paper) | ISBN 9781628726138 (ebook)
Subjects: LCSH: Intelligence officers—Great Britain—Fiction. | Great Britain. MI6—Fiction. | BISAC: FICTION / Espionage. | FICTION / Suspense. | FICTION / Thrillers. | GSAFD: Suspense fiction. | Spy stories.
Classification: LCC PR6053.O5143 A73 2017 (print) | LCC PR6053.O5143 (ebook) | DDC 823/.914—dc23
LC record available at https://lccn.loc.gov/2016034631

Cover photo credit: iStockphoto

Printed in the United States of America

For Sarah

"Round the decay
Of that colossal wreck, boundless and bare
The lone and level sands stretch far away."

Percy Bysshe Shelley, "Ozymandias"

THE AGENT
RUNNER

1

Old Misgivings

April 2011

It was midafternoon when Ed Malik arrived in Jalalabad to catch the *Sabre Express* back to Kabul. Transport was an American Black Hawk with dark green camouflage. As it fuelled, he sheltered from the wind at the edge of the landing site, squatting in the dirt in flip-flops and tatty *shalwar kameez*, with the tail of his black turban drawn across the bridge of his nose.

He'd been summoned to the British embassy for what the ambassador chose to refer to as a "fireside chat," and as usual, it provoked in him a mixture of resentment and unease. Waiting with him, and similarly disguised, was his bodyguard, Dai Llewellyn. Built like a prop-forward, Dai was a fair-haired, soft-voiced Welshman with a way of moving that never seemed hurried and a core of gentleness that a life of violence seemed to have left untouched. Ed and Dai had known each other since Iraq in 2003, when they shared a billet in the *Big Brother* house, the SAS villa in downtown Baghdad, and they had been together in Afghanistan since 2006. There were several occasions that Ed could point to when Dai's actions had, in all likelihood, saved his life, and Ed was careful to treat him with the utmost courtesy.

The Black Hawk lifted off ten minutes later. Strapped into a bucket seat, Ed stared through the cabin doors at the patchwork of green fields and plantations in the broad valley below. On the starboard side he could see the snow-capped mountains of the Hindu Kush in the distance. It was too noisy to speak or be heard and, lulled by the vibration, he soon fell asleep.

When he woke up, the sun was hot in his eyes. Looking down through the open door, he could see the helicopter's shadow running over crumpled brown ridgelines. It was said that you could still find the bleached bones of British soldiers scattered in the gullies and barren washes. Every time Ed flew over, he couldn't help but reflect on the fate of his fellow countrymen there during the disastrous retreat from Kabul in 1842. Eighteen thousand soldiers and civilians slaughtered in the winter snow by Pashtun tribesmen.

Dai nudged him, offering a paper bag full of dates. He took one, its flesh like sweet chewable leather.

At Sarobi, they dipped down into the gorge briefly before climbing again. He could see the churning serpentine of the Kabul River and beside it, on the narrow and winding road, trucks ablaze with reflected light, full of ammunition and other supplies to maintain the NATO presence. It was difficult to imagine the current military adventure in Afghanistan ending as badly as the first Afghan War, but ten years on from the most recent invasion it was becoming clear that Britain's fourth war in Afghanistan would end with as few political gains as the first three.

The Black Hawk came in to Kabul abruptly, swooping down from the ring of grey mountains that trapped a layer of smog over the city. They landed on an earth strip at the edge of the airport and the helicopter taxied on its road-wheels to a hard-standing in a storm of white dust.

Ed jumped out into a hot wind laced with sand.

There was an armoured Land Cruiser waiting for them in Car Park B and an Afghan police pick-up joined them as they passed the old MiG-21 on a concrete plinth at the entrance to the airport.

"Straight there?" Dai asked.

Ed nodded.

The Kabul traffic was the usual slow-motion free-for-all. It was sunset before they arrived at the British embassy and Ed began the laborious process of negotiating his way through the blast-wall chicane and the air-lock entry system.

Inside the control room he found a sleepy watch keeper as pale as a cavern-dwelling fish and a water cooler dispensing chilled Malvern water. He drank several cups. The watch keeper informed him that the ambassador was running late.

Ed kicked off his flip-flops and sat down on bright blue modular seating to read a long-out-of-date *Economist* magazine. The control room smelled of floor wax and toner, odours of the NATO presence.

Within half an hour, the ambassador arrived. He looked Ed up and down.

"Christ man, you're not Kim astride the gun Zam-Zammeh."

"It's good to see you too, sir."

Ambassador Chetwynd-Marr was a vain man of patrician bearing with a grey widow's peak and lousy teeth. He was a Classics scholar and an Arabist with a working knowledge of Pashto.

"I know that something significant is under way," he told Ed, "and if it's going to turn into a disaster, like these things often do, I don't want to be the one to say, 'If only you'd told me I could have warned you.'"

"Thanks for your concern, sir."

The ambassador was well-known for his deft command of hindsight. He was invariably wise after the fact, though rarely before it. Known to his staff as "Old Misgivings," he was mocked behind his back by the younger diplomats, who shook their heads while imitating his ponderous voice: "Of course, I always had misgivings . . ."

"I want to be part of a winning strategy here, Edward, not a losing one."

"We all want that, sir."

"Look, I don't want to have to ask for you to be sent home," he said in a sympathetic tone. "I'm a reasonable person. It's just that things are volatile right now, and I think I need to know what's going on over on the other side. Pakistan, I mean. I need to know the identity of your agent."

Unlike many of his fellow MI6 officers, Ed Malik did not regard spying as a profession of cold betrayal. He saw it as one of careful trust building. He believed that you couldn't run an agent without trust on both sides. Of course it was limited, and of course there were things you kept from each other. There were necessary lies. That was understandable. But if you were considering whether or not the information being passed to you was of vital national interest, you needed to know that your agent had been trustworthy in other matters. And the agent, for his or her part, needed to know that you weren't going to chat about what they'd just told you. What was said was protected and—above all else—the agent's identity was protected. That was the code he lived by, and he didn't like to have it challenged. It was one of the reasons he avoided Kabul whenever possible.

"I can't do that," Ed replied.

"Why not?"

"You know why not. We have an agreement when we recruit people. We don't talk about them to anybody."

"Don't you think I'm trustworthy?"

"No, actually, I don't."

"What do you mean?"

"You wouldn't be able to resist bragging about it."

The ambassador's memoir was the worst-kept secret in Kabul. In a year or two he'd be strutting his stuff at every literary festival in Britain and spouting off on the *Today* programme first thing in the morning.

Chetwynd-Marr spluttered. "With one phone call I could have you on the next plane back."

"No," said Ed. "By all means, make the call, though."

The ambassador's eyes narrowed. "I knew something was going on. You're hiding something from me."

"I can't discuss it."

"At least let me see the intelligence reports first."

"You see all my intelligence reports. They don't get circulated in London without it saying whether the ambassador agrees or disagrees."

"You're sure about that?"

"Absolutely."

It wasn't true, of course. The intelligence that Ed was "sitting on" was known to only two people outside of the top floor at Vauxhall Cross: the prime minister and his foreign affairs adviser, who'd had it stove-piped directly to them in a "red-jacket" folder. He could imagine the consternation on the ambassador's face if he told him the truth.

2

Turning Nightingale

Edward Henry Malik was thirty-five years old, a former British Naval Intelligence officer and, by profession, an MI6 agent runner. Like his predecessors in the Great Game, the "tournament of shadows" fought between the Russians and the British in Afghanistan in the nineteenth century, he preferred to use guile rather than weapons to achieve his aims. But there was an impulsive and at-times-violent streak in him too, times when his voice lowered and his fists became his means of exclamation.

He was tall and slim with broad shoulders, and his chest tapered to a narrow waist. He had curly black hair and dark, knowing eyes with long lashes. His smile was tight-lipped—half courteous and half suspicious. A career in intelligence had taught him to play his cards close to his chest, to look and listen first. As a result, he had few friends. His colleagues hardly knew him at all.

For four years he had been isolated by an operational firewall, running an agent code-named *Nightingale* inside the Directorate for Inter-Services Intelligence—ISI—Pakistan's nefarious

Hydra-headed spying agency. It was the ISI that was credited with driving the Soviets out of Afghanistan and creating the Taliban to fill the void. It was the ISI that had provided shelter to remnants of Al-Qaeda since their defeat in the aftermath of 9/11. And it was the ISI that had picked the Taliban up off their knees in 2006, pressed fresh weapons in their hands, and sent them back into Afghanistan to battle with the Crusaders.

The ISI treated Afghanistan, particularly its Pashto-speaking lands, as its own personal fiefdom, and if you wanted insight into the current insurgency, you needed an asset inside the ISI.

It had been almost impossible to establish a decent network of reliable informants in Afghanistan. Just as in Iraq, there were too many local agencies, most of them penetrated by the enemy, too few sources, and not enough secure locations to meet.

When the break came, it was a result of unforeseen events that required a swift response, and not in Afghanistan. It was March 2006 and Ed got a call on the secure phone at the Kabul embassy telling him to get on the next available flight home. He rode back in the cargo hold of an RAF Boeing C-17 along-side coffins carrying the bodies of two infantrymen killed by a roadside bomb in Helmand. At Brize Norton, he side-stepped the cortege and strode across the tarmac to a waiting police car. He was driven north on the motorway, hurtling up the fast lane with lights and a siren.

Ed spent the journey studying the contents of the MI5 file he'd been handed. A surveillance operation initiated by one of their people in an Oldham mosque had uncovered the existence of a small cell of ISI officers, who were up to the same things as MI5, monitoring the activities of jihadi talent scouts in Oldham and Manchester who were recruiting local kids for specialised training in madrassas in Pakistan's tribal areas. The ISI cell had been under surveillance for several months now.

The file included detailed biographies of the cell members and their friends and relatives as well as a summary of their activities. It was the first time he saw a picture of Nightingale: a grainy black-and-white photocopy of the passport photo on his visa application. But you could tell he was good-looking, with a square jaw and chiselled cheeks and a curved bow of a mouth. *You're a spoiled young man* was Ed's first thought. There were other photos of course, of clandestine meetings, of pick-ups and casual encounters, with Nightingale at the centre of attention and everybody around him smiling as if they felt some kind of gravitational pull. They must have fallen over themselves to confide in him. *What a carefree life it must be for this spying lark,* Ed thought, followed by a sharp retort: *now it's all going to be very different.*

At the back of the file was the transcript of a phone intercept. A panicked call made by Nightingale from an address in Oldham to a number in Islamabad just over fifteen hours ago. According to GCHQ, the calm and unhurried voice on the end of the line in Islamabad belonged to the "Hidden Hand"— Pakistan's legendary spy of spies—Major-General Javid Aslam Khan.

The lights and siren were switched off as they approached Oldham.

Ed was dropped off on the Lees Road, half a mile short of his destination, and walked in. He was the right skin tone for the neighbourhood. He turned into Gibraltar Street. The carcass of a Victorian mill dominated the skyline. The single-storey redbrick bungalow was at the end of a shabby cul-de-sac. Frosty blades of grass were pushing up through the cracked tarmac of the carport and the curtains were drawn. He knocked on the door.

A white woman opened it. She was not tall, about five-four,

he estimated, late twenties with auburn hair cut in a sensible bob and a determined look on her face. She was wearing practical clothes: black jeans, canvas sneakers, and a fleece.

"Come in."

He stepped inside. It was chilly. She handed him a pair of latex gloves, which he snapped on. "How is he?"

"Like a sulky child," she replied. He registered her Yorkshire accent. "What do you want to do first?"

"Show me the body."

He followed her down the hall to the bedroom.

The body on the bed was cold and rigid. His back and buttocks had the blue-cheese-mould patina of stagnant blood, livor mortis. Ed realised why it was so cold: they must have turned off the heating in an attempt to preserve the body for as long as possible.

"Cause of death?"

"By the looks of it, he choked on his own vomit. They were smoking heroin." There was a fold of discoloured aluminium foil beside the bed and a lighter. "I'm told it's almost impossible to kill yourself smoking heroin."

"Bad luck then. A nasty surprise."

She nodded. "He says he woke up alongside him."

"That's when he made the call?"

"That's right. He woke, found the body, and called Islamabad. He was told to sit tight until midnight tonight when a clean-up crew would arrive and he would be given a fresh set of instructions."

Ed looked at his watch. They had three hours.

"What about the other members of the cell?"

"They've gone quiet. No calls, no web traffic, and no movement."

Nightingale had made the call and, subsequently, word had gone out to the rest of the cell to stop whatever they were doing and wait. Khan was known for caution. He didn't want to waste a clean-up crew on a trap. Nightingale hadn't liked that, of course; he'd objected in the strongest terms. *You can't leave me here with a dead body.* But he'd been told to put a sock in it, to sit tight and wait.

"Where is he?"

"He's in the kitchen. We've been moving him back and forth between the kitchen and the living room all day."

Nightingale was sitting at the kitchen table with a blanket around his shoulders and a cup of sweet tea in his hands. He'd had fifteen hours to work his way through the full gamut of emotions—despair, anger, outrage, bitterness, and resignation.

The other MI5 officer was standing with his back to the sink. He was tall and broad-shouldered, wearing Lycra cycling shorts and a waterproof jacket. There was a cycle helmet on the sideboard beside the kettle.

He nodded to Ed. "Now say hello to the mystery man who's come all the way from Kabul to have a chat."

Nightingale grunted and continued to stare into his cup of tea.

"I'll take it from here," Ed told him. He waited while the two MI5 officers went through into the living room and then sat at the table. Ed placed his hands down with his fingers splayed, a pianist centring himself before a recital. He resisted the urge to rub his face. He remembered his training: on first meeting an agent, appear calm and carry yourself with author-ity. *Be gnomic. Be Desi Yoda.* Sweat prickled the back of his neck. He wished he'd had an opportunity to shave.

"I have to make a decision," he told Nightingale in a con-versational tone. "I have to decide whether to call in the police, or do nothing and let your people clear it up."

That brought his head up: wide-eyed, eager as a puppy. It hadn't occurred to him that he might walk away from this. Later, Ed would pinpoint that as the moment when he first decided that Nightingale was a lousy spy, his face so expressive you could watch each and every thought unfold. Later still, he would revise his opinion: Nightingale's thoughts were so random and grandiose and scattergun that they served to disguise his true feelings. Maybe he wasn't such a bad spy after all.

"If I bring in the police, you'll be arrested and you'll probably go to prison, your cover will be blown and your relatives will no longer be welcome here. The Prevention of Terrorism Act already gives us wide powers, but we won't be in any way constrained by it." *Keep your voice as flat as an oil spill*, Ed told himself. "Let me spell that out for you. Any members of your family here in the UK will suffer. Your cousin will be kicked off his chemical engineering course at Imperial and deported. Your aunt in Gloucestershire will almost certainly lose her job at the solicitors' firm. There will be no more summertime visas for your mother and father. And the money they have been squirreling away for the day when Pakistan becomes uninhabitable will be seized and made forfeit. As for your wife, does she know you bat for the other side? I think we'll let her know. That's just the start. We'll think up whole new ways to inconvenience you while you're waiting on remand. I can guarantee you won't like your cell mate and he won't like you."

Nightingale's face was ashen and his lower lip wobbled, the tears welling up in his eyes. He rubbed them with the backs of his hands.

"It's a bummer, isn't it?"

"What do you want?" Nightingale said.

"I understand you are about to be recalled. I understand you have been offered a new position with the ISI's Afghan bureau."

"How do you know that?"

Never answer a direct question.

"I think at this point you have to assume that we know everything about you," Ed told him. "In fact, we know you better than you know yourself."

"What is it you want from me?"

"It's simple, really. We want you to go back to Pakistan as planned. We want you to take up your new job in the Afghan bureau. We want you to go on working for Khan, but we want you to work for us, too. In return for a regular flow of information, we'll guarantee your cousin finishes his course and there won't be any problems for your family. We'll even add to the pot of money your parents have stashed away and we'll offer you and your whole family British citizenship and police protection for life."

"You want me to spy on Khan?"

"Exactly. We want to know what he's up to in Afghanistan. We want the whole picture, warts and all."

"I don't have any choice, do I?"

Then he smiled, his tears forgotten. That was Nightingale for you; he was too devil-may-care to be blackmailed, and although his family struggled to maintain their lifestyle, it wasn't about the money either. For him, it was about the excitement. If being a secret agent was a thrill, how much more thrilling to be a double agent?

Four years of clandestine meetings followed, in ditches and graveyards scattered across Afghanistan, anywhere sufficiently distant from prying eyes, and often only for a few minutes. Nightingale provided Ed with information that allowed coalition forces to successfully disrupt attacks, smash insurgent networks, and counter the flow of weapons and bomb-making materials over the border. And if at times it had seemed as though the information provided by Nightingale was partial—the smashed networks were invariably those considered the most independent of the ISI and the disruption of bomb-making materials didn't result in a significant reduction in the number of explosions—and that Nightingale might in fact be a triple agent—an ISI plant receiving guidance from

Islamabad—Ed could put his hand on his heart and say he had expressed his suspicions to London and had been told, in no uncertain terms, to keep his opinions to himself. For four years Nightingale had been referred to by London as "the gift that kept on giving."

But now, in a surprise move, Nightingale had returned to Pakistan and been given a new posting, an off-the-books surveillance operation in the ever-so-quiet garrison town of Abbottabad. Ed recalled the last time they'd met: a month ago in Kandahar, in the cemetery behind the chaotic bazaar known as the Chowk Madad.

"I'm getting close to something that will interest London," Nightingale had told him in his familiar high-handed way. Over the years it had become his favourite way of baiting Ed. Acting as if there was someone *important* in London who was his *real* handler, and Ed was little more than a conveyor of messages, the opposite of Ed's suspicion that Nightingale was little more than a conveyor of messages himself. After four years of secret meetings, they behaved towards each other with the sly hostility of a long-married couple.

"Khan's got something hidden away up in Abbottabad, right under the noses of the joint chiefs. Something mega-secret. There is a house under permanent surveillance. I think I can wangle my way up there."

"You need to be careful," Ed cautioned him, not for the first time.

"I met someone. They call him Noman. He's something big in SS Directorate, so he's got a finger in every pie. The thing is, Ed, he's got the hots for me, big time. He's a beast. You should see the way he looks at me. He can't wait to get his hands on me. He can hardly control himself."

"And you're going to let him?"

Nightingale was defiant. "Why not?"

"Because I forbid it," Ed told him. "Your focus is on

Afghanistan and imminent threats to UK security. Whatever the ISI is up to on home soil is outside our remit."

Nightingale pouted. "All right, all right," he said. "I'll stay well away."

You encourage them to cheat and lie, Ed thought, *and they do it to you as well.*

It was two weeks later that Nightingale got back in touch, via a dead drop run by the Intelligence cell at the embassy in Islamabad.

I was right! It's the Big Kahuna!

3

The Surveillance Operation

Waking, Noman thought he could smell sulphur. When he raised his head, the poison struck: thirst, nausea, and a barbed pain behind the eyes.

Tumultuous dreams.

For as long as Noman could remember, he had been dreaming about the annihilation of the world. As a child it was often an earthquake: abysses yawned and mountains rose and fell. As a teenager, it was more often than not a flood or a zombie apocalypse. Then in 1998, in operations *Chagai-1* and *Chagai-2*, Pakistan detonated six nuclear devices in Balochistan, and another dream was folded into the mental gravy: an atomic explosion over a desert city; first a shockwave that demolished houses and factories, after that a fireball rolling outwards to the horizon, melting car tires and searing human shadows into the asphalt. And last of all, the mushroom cloud, rising and spreading and hanging silently over the desert.

Ka-fucking-boom.

His eyes were smarting, and his vision was watery. There was a thin layer of acrid black smoke hovering just below the

ceiling. It took him a few moments to realise that the neighbours were burning their rubbish again.

When he turned he felt the warm body beside him, naked
and face down. He reached out and ran his fingers down the
young man's spine and over his smooth, round buttocks. When
he first woke he had not been able to remember who it was. The
touch of his skin brought recollection. Tariq.

He slipped out of the bed and padded across the tiles
towards the chair where he had discarded his clothes. He did
not want to wake the boy. Tariq's amused and knowing smile,
his peppy moves and jaunty over-confident quips, all of which
seemed so attractive the night before, might provoke violence
in him now in the slough of the morning. Noman had always
been ruled by extremes: shamelessness and shame were the
roots of his emotions.

Reaching the chair, he realised that his clothes were not
where he had expected to find them. He squinted at the floor
with his eyes still smarting, but they were nowhere to be seen.
He must have left them in the next room. Naked, he went out
through the bedroom door into the unfinished space beyond.

The house belonged to a major who taught on the Technical Graduate Course at the nearby Kakul Military Academy.
Similar in function to Sandhurst or West Point, the academy
provided training to officers for the Pakistan Army. The major
had been "encouraged" to find temporary accommodation elsewhere. The house was a new-build, located in the Bilal Town
suburb of Abbottabad: an ugly, flat-roofed, three-story struc-
ture constructed of unrendered cinderblocks that had been put
up to replace a house destroyed in the 2005 earthquake.

At the centre of the cement floor there was a tap stand and
a bucket. He knelt down, wet his hands at the tap, and rinsed
his eyes. His head was splitting. When he looked up he felt
three pairs of curious eyes watching him across the room, then
a shudder of indiscriminate rage.

The first set of eyes belonged to a Bandar monkey on a chain. The red-faced monkey had been there last night. It had spun on its chain and shrieked while he bent the boy over a chair. Now it bared its fangs.

The second set of eyes belonged to an elderly, bearded manservant who was squatting beside the camp chair where the deed took place. He was a classic Hazara, flat-nosed and Chinese-looking, with characteristic features inherited from thirteenth century Mogul invaders. The evidence of last night's seduction—the bottle of scotch and the traces of white powder—had been cleared away and the trembling old man was holding up Noman's pressed and folded shirt, jeans, and underpants like an offering at a shrine. Balanced on top of them, like a crown on its cushion, was his gun, a Glock 17.

The third set of eyes belonged to a professional watcher, a young intelligence officer with floppy hair and skinny jeans. His name was Omar, and he was perched on a stool beneath a hide of camouflage netting with a 25–125 times magnification spotting scope on a tripod in front of him. By rights, he should have been watching the neighbours and logging their movements in the army-issue ledger in meticulous longhand, but instead he was transfixed, startled by the sight of the legendary spy-catcher, ruthless interrogator, decorated hero of the Siachen Glacier, and all-round very fucking scary piece of work Noman Butt, kneeling buck-naked at the tap stand.

Like the sleeping boy Tariq, Omar was a Close Observer. There should have been a surveillance team of at least six watchers in the house, but the nature of the job, the absolute need for secrecy, and the requirement to circumvent normal procedures meant there were only these two trendy bhanghra boys from a privileged suburb of Lahore, who looked like they'd stepped out of a nightclub—Tariq and Omar—their ancient manservant, and a bad-tempered monkey.

Beyond the hide was a large window with a view, just visible through the diffuse and smoky air, of the crumpled ochre slopes of the Sarban Hills and the burning disk of the sun. It was a bright day throbbing with malevolent promise.

Noman closed his eyes, gripping the bucket. Murderous fantasies assailed him of destroying them all, of stamping on the monkey and strangling the old man and of kicking the two boys until their organs burst, turning their supple youth to offal.

Instead, he should be praying, pressing his forehead to the rough cement in abasement, earning him the *zabiba*, the permanent thumb-shaped bruise of the truly devout, but it was a long time since he had prayed with conviction. He was ready to sacrifice for Islam, anything short of throwing himself into a cauldron of molten metal, but he struggled to live by it. He felt like death.

"Shit, *yaar*," he muttered. He was still half-drunk.

He took a deep breath, swallowed, and held himself erect. First, a shower. He let go of the bucket, snatched his clothes and gun from the old man and went down the stairway to the room where he'd left his briefcase. He opened it and rummaged around until he found his phone. Five missed calls, all from his fleshy, imperious wife. He threw the phone back in the briefcase, went to the bathroom, and locked himself in.

His hands trembled on the shower lever. Suddenly, he was sick, vomiting into the shower pan. Purged, he sat on the tiled floor with his head in his hands. He was poisoned. He had been poisoning himself for weeks.

He struggled to his feet again. As he stepped into the shower, he caught sight of himself in a mirror on the medicine cabinet and was briefly paralysed by fear and self-loathing.

He closed his eyes and took slow, deliberative breaths. When he looked again, the moment had passed and what he saw was a hard, compelling face with massive angular cheekbones and a stubborn jaw. But that wasn't what terrified the unwary in basement cells. It was all in the eyes; he had mesmeric eyes of blue, scary bowel-voiding eyes, so perfectly blue they went all the way back to Alexander the Great's foray across the Indus, and some said they tunnelled all the way back to Satan, to the very first evil eye.

Pummelled by the cold spray, Noman began to feel like himself again.

He was a short man, with close-cropped hair and a weight-lifter's physique. He was strong, the strength discernible in his legs and shoulders, in his broad neck and in his spade-like hands and stubby fingers.

Noman worked in intelligence, for the Inter *bloody* Services *bloody* Intelligence Agency, or ISI, having come into it from the army and before that, an orphanage. As an officer cadet at the nearby Kakul Academy, he had narrowly missed out on the Sword of Honour, the prestigious award for best cadet, after completing the Long Course in 1994—not bad for an orphan convert from a low-caste Hindu village. It was in the nature of things that the sword was won by the less capable but bet-ter-connected son of a Punjabi officer of the Leadership Caste. After the passing-out parade, the commandant had grudgingly told him that he might even make general one day, provided India and Pakistan didn't immolate themselves with nuclear weapons before he got the necessary crowns and pips.

He had served with the Baloch Regiment in Free Kashmir and been awarded a Crescent of Courage Medal, a significant honour only one down from the Sign of the Lion Medal, which had replaced the British Victoria Cross at the time of Partition and had so far only been awarded to martyrs, which was too high a price for a piece of tin as far as Noman was concerned. He had received the medal for conspicuous gallantry in repel-ling an Indian attack on the Siachen Glacier.

The attack had been a total surprise, even to the Indians

whose mountaintop artillery position was delivered by an avalanche into the midst of a Pakistani Forward Operating Base (FOB). In the sudden chaos that ensued, Noman had killed five Indian soldiers with an ice axe. He'd dug himself out of a hastily excavated snow hole, and they were all over the place. Close to him, Indian gunners were climbing out of a tiny window from an almost fully submerged portacabin bunkhouse that had been lifted out of its cradle of concrete blast walls and surfed the wave of snow down the mountain. They were popping out like champagne corks. He'd gone at it with the axe until he was the only one left standing, and then he'd hacked at the snow until he'd dug out enough to plug the window and prevent any more escaping.

After that, he'd completed the punishing eight-month Special Service Group selection course and gone on to command the Seventh Commando Battalion. From Special Forces he'd transferred to the ISI and served across several directorates, including the Afghan bureau. It was while at the Afghan bureau that he had come to the attention of Javid Aslam Khan, the farsighted hero of the struggle against the Soviets in Afghanistan, the man credited with creating the Taliban and ending the Afghan civil war.

Khan, who was without a son, had taken a liking to Noman, spotting his unscrupulous intelligence and appetite for the work. He chose to nurture Noman's ambition and steer him through the labyrinthine corridors of Pakistani intelligence. He offered him his daughter in marriage. As a result of his patronage, Noman Butt was now in command of the ISI's SS Directorate that monitored the activities of "flagged" groups within Pakistan. That made him the in-house expert on every armed group and extremist faction in Pakistan, from the Federally Administered Tribal Areas to Free Kashmir, from Balochistan to the Punjab.

For five years now, in the SS Directorate's longest-running surveillance operation, a succession of close observers had watched the house next door, logging the comings and goings of a white SUV whose spare tire cover was emblazoned with an image of a white rhino. It was an ugly three-story house, with high-walled balconies that made it look like a chest of drawers with the drawers partly pulled out. The driver of the SUV was an Arab named Abu Ahmed al-Kuwaiti, also known as Sheikh Abu Ahmed, also known as "the courier."

Showered, Noman stepped out of the stall and dried himself. Avoiding the mirror, he checked the medicine cabinet. Nothing. Then he remembered he had some Valium in his briefcase.

He put on his underpants, jeans, and shirt. He stuffed the Glock down the back of his trousers. He dry swallowed a Valium and went up the stairway again. The monkey had retreated to a corner of the room, and the manservant had made himself scarce. Noman stood at the doorway to one of the bedrooms for a few moments contemplating Tariq's sprawled and sleeping body. His anger had dissipated now. Tariq really was a beautiful boy.

"The guest is out in the garden, sir," Omar said.

Excited suddenly, Noman went over to the hide, and Omar slid off the stool to allow him to look through the scope. He pressed his eye to the viewfinder, and the house opposite sprang into high relief, the electronically enhanced lenses bringing the figure of a man in the courtyard close enough to touch. A tall, frail, stooping man shuffling along under an umbrella, his beard shot through with two distinctive white streaks.

In the house next door, under the very nose of the military establishment, lived the leader of the most flagged group of all, the world's most wanted man.

The Sheikh Osama bin Mohammed bin Awad bin Laden.

For all that he regarded bin Laden as little more than a prisoner, and this half-arsed and poorly manned operation as a pointless drain on the directorate's resources, Noman couldn't help but feel humbled and a little awestruck in the presence of bin Laden. The scything airplanes and the plunging towers had often been featured in his dreams.

He watched as bin Laden completed his slow circuit of the courtyard and went back into the house, careful to furl the umbrella before stepping inside. Looking up from the scope, Noman realised that his eyes had filled with tears. Rather than have Omar see him like this, he pretended to study the ledger of observations open on the music stand beside the tripod.

"I'm leaving," he announced after a minute or so.

"Sure," Omar replied and then remembered who he was talking to, "I mean . . . yes, sir! Thank you for visiting."

Noman put on his mirrored sunglasses, picked up his brief-case, and went out into the morning.

4

Apache Commando

Bouncing down one of the narrow dirt streets in his glossy black Range Rover, Noman found his way blocked by a crowd of determined-looking women and howling brats. Beyond them, in a trash-strewn open space, he observed a white tent with a banner announcing a mother-and-child vaccination programme. After pumping the horn a few times, he realised it was futile and reversed up the alley.

Soon he was speeding south on the Murree Road with the windows down and the supercharged V8 engine growling, his hands too busy for driving. Steering through the curves and bends of the national park with his knees, the pine forest rising above him on one side and the ravine falling away on the other, he loosened the tobacco in the barrel of a Gold Flake cigarette and squeezed it out onto his palm, crumbling hash into the tobacco, kneading and mixing before refilling the Flake, twisting it shut, and lighting up. Deep drag.

Hakuna matata, as the Africans would say. No tension.

A welcome jolt to the brain.

He rooted around amongst the CDs on the passenger

seat until he found what he was looking for, a bootleg of Adil Omar's freshly cut track "Paki Rambo." He cranked it up to full volume, and the words rattled around in his head like an unshooable fly:

I'm a junky on a binge and damn I'm so faded
Apache Commando
Put my foot in your asshole

He felt his spirits soar.

The P . . . the A . . . the K . . . the I
Paki Rambo!

Above all, Noman thought of himself as a survivor. Not the lickspittle, ass-kissing kind of survivor who made general these days. He was the opposite—the dogged, undeterred-by-anything, approach-every-task-with-utter-concentration kind of survivor. He knew how to endure, and what it was that got you through. It was a quality that his superiors had recognised and valued in him—there was no job too difficult or too morally compromised for him to accept.

He was up for anything, he thought, anything except facing his wife this sunny morning. Irritated, the mood just as suddenly broken, he pulled over at a roadside café that overlooked the river. He sat in a plastic chair, and they brought him a chai that had been steeped long enough to acquire a rich dark colour and made creamy with full-fat milk.

What I need is a plan, he told himself, *something other than alcohol and drugs and arse to get by on. I'll make a plan.*

Back in the car, he rolled himself another joint. Newly fortified, he set off again. He drove past an abandoned fairground with a rusting Ferris wheel and dropped down into Murree.

He nudged forwards through narrow, crowded streets that were festooned with electrical cables, between market stalls with plastic awnings. Then he was out the other side, with his foot down, on the expressway heading south.

Instead of taking a left towards Rawalpindi—and home—he turned right towards the office.

The ISI headquarters was a sprawling complex of buildings beside a private hospital in the G-5 district of Islamabad. With its neatly clipped lawns and tinkling fountains, it resembled the campus of a well-funded university. The entrance on Khayaban-e-Suhrawardy Avenue was suitably discreet: no sign, just a plainclothes officer with a pistol who directed Noman through a chicane of barriers, soldiers, and sniffer dogs.

He parked the Range Rover outside the central building, dispensed a few drops of Visine in his eyes—nothing to be gained from letting the top brass know you're a waster—and went in, crossing the circular, echoing lobby to the elevators.

Seated in his windowless office, he unpacked his briefcase: two vodka bottles, dirty socks and underwear, Valium, condoms, a couple of wraps of cocaine, and several packs of Gold Flake cigarettes. He stuffed them randomly into drawers. He noticed that there was a memo in his in-tray calling for all serving offices to wear their uniform when in headquarters. He crumpled it up and threw it in the direction of his overflowing wastepaper basket. Next in the pile was a report from a source inside the Swat branch of the *Tehrik-i-Taliban*, the Pakistani Taliban, whose leadership were getting hot under the collar over some girl in the valley who was using Facebook to demand education for women. There was nothing those crazy old goats in the Taliban were more afraid of than a girl with opinions. He scrawled "*Kill Her*" in the margin and then thought better of it and crossed it out. He wrote "*Leave Her Alone,*" thought better of that, and finally consigned it to the wastepaper basket. Let them sort it out.

He spread his hands palms down on the desk. *This is where I begin again*, he told himself. *I reinvent myself. I make my plan.*

He had another shot of vodka.

Back to the in-tray. There was an approach from a *Lashkar-e-Taiba*-affiliated group based in Free Kashmir who had devised a plan to demolish the turbines on the giant Bhakra Dam in Himachal Pradesh.

You had to give it to the Lashkar boys, they always thought big. They had already trained a cadre of fighters in night swimming, cliff climbing, and explosives handling. They just needed help with moving the explosives into India on the Dubai-Bombay run. There was no way the Joint Chiefs would give the green light. They had already war-gamed it. Blowing the dam would likely lead to the collapse of the government in Delhi and might precipitate all-out war. Still, it was a plan worth developing and keeping in a drawer in preparation for an uncertain future. The speed with which the glaciers that fed into the Indus were melting meant that Pakistan was likely to run out of water in the next twenty years. A hundred and eighty million people without a cup of water between them; that exceeded even the most apocalyptic of Noman's dreams. The only possible response to such a situation was to start blowing Indian dams. He wrote *"More Info"* in the margin.

The phone rang.

"Noman?"

"The very same."

It was Major Tufail Hamid. He sounded pleased to hear him. Tufail was Chief of Staff to Khan. He was a lean, neat, unobtrusive man with a fastidious nature and dark pouches beneath his eyes. Like Noman, he had completed the arduous Special Service Group selection course before transferring to the ISI. At one time he had been one of the SS Directorate's most valuable spies. In his final undercover operation his cover had been blown, and he had been tortured for several days in a basement. Now he was the poacher-turned-gamekeeper, nurturing his own position as key-holder to Khan where he once nurtured networks of informants. He wore white gloves to disguise the damage wrought by acid.

Tufail had served under Noman in the Seventh Commando Battalion; it was Noman who got him his first job with the ISI; and after the acid attack, it was Noman who had recommended him to Khan when he was looking for an aide-de-camp. Khan had tentacles that reached into every corner of Pakistan and beyond, and it was good to have a friendly set of eyes and ears in his immediate circle.

"How is the old man?" Noman asked.

"Disappointed," Tufail replied in a brittle, chiding tone. Noman had been expecting the call ever since he made the decision, against Khan's wishes, to visit the surveillance house in Abbottabad. "He wants to meet you for lunch. He's booked a table at Kinara."

"I'll be there," Noman said.

"Good."

"Why don't we have dinner tonight?" Noman asked him suddenly. "Why don't we go to the Cave and eat super nachos?"

Noman loved the Flintstones fakery of the Cave restaurant with its honey-coloured plastic rock walls and glowing stalactites, its mock stone-age façade on the edge of a shopping mall.

Tufail was silent for a moment.

"How are you, Noman?" he asked.

"Not so good."

"Are you drinking?" Tufail asked.

"Maybe."

"You bloody well better be there tonight."

"I'll be there," he said. He meant it when he said it.

5 پ

The House of War

Arriving at Kinara on the south bank of Rawal Lake, Noman was shown to a table in a gazebo with a view across the water. He ordered a Pakola ice cream-flavoured soda. He wished that he could have a beer, something to dull the edges of his headache. Khan came in fifteen minutes late to find him ordering a second Pakola.

"Bring me tea," Khan told the waiter.

Major-General Javid Aslam Khan considered his son-in-law. Seventy years old and lean as a compass needle, he had hard, unforgiving eyes behind thick bifocal glasses.

"How are you, Noman? How is Mumayyaz?"

"She wants a divorce."

Khan looked at him without expression. "That's not funny, Noman."

They both knew that Mumayyaz would never leave him. The only reason Khan was asking was because Noman hadn't been home for several weeks. He'd been on a binge, criss-crossing the country, visiting regional outposts and surveillance operations from Free Kashmir to Balochistan, a tour that had ended close to home, in bin Laden's neighbour's house.

The waiter brought tea. Khan waited until he had left before speaking again. "Tell me about Abbottabad."

Noman thought that Khan almost certainly knew about what happened last night with the boy. In all likelihood, either Tariq or Omar had called Khan the moment he left the house. They were Khan's boys. There was almost nothing that Khan didn't know. It occurred to him that part of the reason he had fucked the boy was as a gesture of defiance. How juvenile and ridiculous that seemed now.

"No change," he told Khan, grudgingly. "Our guest remains confined. A courier comes and goes. They burn their rubbish."

Khan sipped at his tea and looked around the restaurant. Nothing seemed to disturb his air of having his mind on something more important than his surroundings. He carried with him an inscrutable scheme of things next to which Noman's sarcasm often seemed childish.

"I went up there to make sure the operation was being run properly," Noman told him, peevishly. "It is my responsibility as a serving officer."

"You did what you had to," Khan told him.

There were times, watching Noman in action, that Khan felt a tearing inside at the prospect of the torch passing to such a new and unfathomable bearer. He regarded his son-in-law as a man of lavish and prodigal talent, in many ways an admirable fellow. He lived up to the Urdu name given to him in the orphanage, Noman—one who carries all the blessings of Allah. It was his untamed libido and his loud-mouthed swagger that Khan struggled to understand. It was as if, like Napoleon's, Noman's character had been fixed for the lack of a couple of inches, which in conjunction with a shameful past, a brutal upbringing in an orphanage, and a murderous army career had produced a creature more akin to an *afreet*, a demon, than a regular intelligence officer.

Khan was still trying to understand why he had gone to Abbottabad. He didn't give much credit to Noman's claim that it was his professional responsibility, and it was surely more complex than simple boredom or deliberately going against Khan's wishes. It was as if he had gone there to tip his hat, to pay homage to a hero. The last thing Khan wanted was for bin Laden's house to turn into some kind of shrine.

The decision to hide Osama bin Laden in Abbottabad had been taken by a small secretive group of "retired" former ISI officers, Khan foremost amongst them, who had taken on responsibility for bin Laden's welfare after he crossed the border into Pakistan in early 2002. A group chosen because, if it ever came out that they had been hiding him, the Joint Chiefs of Staff would be able to semi-plausibly deny any knowledge of it.

The obvious choice for hiding bin Laden, the tribal areas, was deemed too risky, too volatile. And so it had proved. There were the American drone attacks to worry about, but more than that, too many fighters holed up there had turned against their former masters in the ISI. There was a time when an ISI officer could count on easy access to any jihadi training camp or madrassa on the border, but that was true no longer. It was only three months since the Pakistani Taliban had executed Sultan Amir Tarar, best known as Colonel Imam.

The grey-bearded Imam, who was a guerrilla-warfare specialist and hero of the Jihad against the Soviets, regarded the tribal areas as his spiritual home and the motley gangs hiding there as his children. He was always offering them advice on how to tackle the enemy. It didn't stop them turning against him. They filmed the execution. After a short speech, a masked man shot him five times, four more than looked strictly necessary.

Khan had found himself feeling surprisingly sanguine about the murder.

"These things happen," he remembered telling Noman at the time. "If you feed a crocodile you must be careful it doesn't bite off your hand."

Truth be told, Khan was relieved to have the Imam out of the way. He had become something of a public embarrassment with his outspoken views on the American presence in Afghanistan. The Americans had loved him once, though. George Bush Senior had given him a lump of the Berlin Wall in thanks for bringing the Soviet Union to its knees. But then they had taken against him when they learned he'd been active in Afghanistan after the September 11th attacks, facilitating the movement of Al-Qaeda fighters across the border into Pakistan.

The Americans had a habit of taking things personally.

It amused Noman to think how angry the Americans would be if they ever learned that bin Laden was being hidden in plain sight. The Americans loved it when they were invited to send their generals up to the Kakul Academy to lecture the officer cadets. They jumped at the chance, and they showered money on the Pakistani military, thirteen billion dollars in the last decade. Little did they know that their greatest foe was living quietly just a few hundred metres from the entrance to the academy.

It wasn't a sanctioned operation, of course. The politicians were not informed. It didn't appear on any paperwork. It wasn't discussed over tea and tiffin cake at the Punjab Club. That was why Khan didn't like him going up there. He didn't want to attract any attention. Stay away, he'd said. But Noman argued that since the budget for the surveillance team was buried in an SS Directorate slush fund under his control, it was his duty to keep an eye on the operation.

"Now that you've been, are you satisfied?" Khan inquired.

"No," Noman muttered. "I don't trust those kids you've got up there."

Khan stared evenly at him without comment. Noman could imagine what he was thinking: *If you don't trust them, why did you nail one of them on the job?* There were times when Noman felt a visceral hatred of his father-in-law. He looked away. "I need to do some proper work."

Khan raised a skeptical eyebrow. "Proper work?"

"I want a proper operation to run. Something more than going through the motions." That was what he wanted, something concrete to launch himself at. "I've been looking through open files. I've been thinking about the House of War."

"Forget about it," Khan replied. "It's a tall tale. A story to frighten the Americans."

"I'm not so sure."

The first whisper of the existence of a cell known as *Dar al-Harb*, or the "House of War," had coincided with the much-derided declaration in May 2009, by the then-Prime Minister Nawaz Sharif, that Pakistan's nuclear security was the strongest in the world. An American National Security Agency computer trolling phone lines in South Waziristan had picked up a conversation between two Taliban commanders in which one of them had used the Pashto term *itami*, meaning "nuclear" or "atomic." The House of War had an *itami* device, he said.

A few days later, one of the agency's trawlers intercepted a conversation between two advisers to Baitullah Mehsud, the short, thuggish Pashtun who had assumed command of the Pakistani Taliban. The advisers were overheard discussing an ethical dilemma that had recently come to the fore. Was it permissible under the laws of Islam for the House of War to use its "device?"

The Americans had gone ballistic. They had directed their entire intelligence infrastructure on South Waziristan—wire intercepts, drones, and covert agents. The ISI, when they were eventually informed, had been more skeptical, scornful even. Baitullah Mehsud was a semi-literate gangster with a big mouth, and those he surrounded himself with weren't any better. His experience with bombs was limited to strapping a few pounds of homemade explosives to hapless teenagers and blowing them up in bazaars. The ISI adamantly assured the Americans that no one would be stupid enough to give Mehsud, or anyone associated with him, a nuclear device.

But what was the House of War, and what kind of threat did it pose? In private, the ISI went into overdrive, frantically seeking out information from their network of informants across the tribal areas on this hitherto-unheard-of entity—Dar al-Harb—which was named after the scholar Ibn Taymiyyah's term for those lands that lay beyond Muslim subjugation, and which presumably would be the target of any planned attack. All they uncovered were rumours. It was said of the House of War that its members eschewed all modern forms of communication; that their leader, who was known as Abu Dukhan—"the Father of Smoke"—lived in a cave that could be sealed by a boulder attached to a hydraulic ram; that they were some kind of millenarian Wahhabi death cult; that they enjoyed the financial backing of a world-weary Gulf sheikh; that, above all, they had dedicated themselves to the acquisition and detonation of a nuclear device.

What of Mehsud and his advisers? Surely they knew of the whereabouts of this difficult-to-pin-down group—all summer, thousands of Pakistani troops backed by helicopter gunships swept the Taliban strongholds, picking off forts and hideouts one by one, searching for clues. The number of American drones increased to such an extent that there was a constant buzzing in the air, like mosquitoes that could never be swatted away. Then on August 5, Mehsud was killed in a drone attack on the small town of Zahara, a few miles to the east of the Taliban stronghold of Makeen.

With his death, all talk of *itami* devices ended. Not a whisper. It was as though the threat evaporated into the air. In Washington and Islamabad, they let out a collective sigh of relief. They told themselves that the House of War was a tall tale, an absurd boast by a gang of ill-equipped mountain fighters. But Noman wasn't so sure. In his book, absence of evidence wasn't evidence of absence. Just because people had stopped talking about them didn't mean they didn't exist.

"I'm thinking of going to look for them," Noman said.

"If you go up there, you're signing your own death warrant," Khan told him. "You know what happened to Colonel Imam."

Noman laughed bitterly.

"You think it's funny, ha-ha?" Khan snapped. "Do you know how you look? You're sweating alcohol. I can see your eyes. Do you think people in this business don't know what's going on with you?"

"I'll cease drinking tomorrow."

"Ceasing tomorrow!" Khan shook his head in exasperation. "Always tomorrow. That's funny, Noman. You do that." He put down his teacup. "Come home. Mumayyaz is waiting for you. She loves you very much. Stick with your current responsibilities."

"I need a mission. Work is medicine for me."

Khan leaned across the table and said, "You're protecting the most wanted man in the world. What more do you want?"

"Oh, please," Noman hissed, pushing back his chair. "Bin Laden's a toothless tiger. We both know that. He's a bugbear to frighten the Americans with and to keep the lunch moolah rolling in. He hasn't left the house in five years. You don't need me to keep an eye on him, and you don't want me going up there anyway. Anyone could do it. I need real work."

Khan stared hard at him. "Relax. Sober up. Call me in a day or two, and we'll discuss what you should do." He called for the bill. "Don't go anywhere until you're sober."

They went out to the car park. Khan gripped Noman's sleeve.

"People are watching you," he said. "Evil people who wish you ill are watching you."

"What are you talking about?" Noman demanded.

"You're not amongst friends. You should trust no one except me."

6 ✥

The One-Legged Mullah

Khan spent that evening in Peshawar having dinner with a village mullah at one of the rattletrap gypsy shacks between the Grand Trunk Road and the Kabul River. The mullah was of the Kakar tribe of Uruzgan in Southern Afghanistan. He had joined the Taliban at its inception and served under the warlord Dadullah Akhund, who had a reputation for beheading his enemies. It was said that the mullah had been involved in the massacre of thousands of ethnic Hazaras in the Bamiyan province and that he had also had a hand in dynamiting the Giant Buddha statues.

These days, the mullah scratched a living in the tribal areas. In return for food he performed circumcision rites, officiated at weddings and funerals, and conducted the occasional exorcism. In the recent past, he and Khan had collaborated several times in matters relating to the presence of foreign fighters there. Like most Pashtuns, the mullah was convinced that all good things came from Pashtuns and whatever was bad came from aliens—Americans, Russians, Tajiks, Punjabis, Arabs, Uzbeks, Chechens, take your pick—and like all Pashtuns, he'd been taught since the cradle that to resist foreign domination was what it was to be a Pashtun.

He was a large, intolerant man of few words. With his weathered, outsized features and veins of scar tissue, and his clothes marbled with grease and grime, he looked like he'd been hewn out of the local onyx marble, which only served to make his ill-fitting, pink plastic leg all the more incongruous. He'd lost the original to a Russian anti-personnel mine back in the eighties.

Khan had collected the mullah and his boy from outside a tiny concrete shack in the Tehkal quarter, the filthy flyblown area behind University Road. Khan had tried to persuade the mullah to leave the boy behind, but the mullah was having none of it. "He is my oath," he'd insisted. So they had driven out here, near where the Kabul River meets the mighty Indus. The food was good, and it was relatively quiet this late in the season. If something went wrong there would be fewer casualties.

The collection of shacks and the elderly Ferris wheel along-side them had appeared on the pebble beach when the cold weather lifted, and would last until the river swelled with snow-melt from the Hindu Kush and the gypsies moved again.

The open-sided hut where they chose to eat was strung with fairy lights and had rope charpoys arranged around rick-ety wooden tables. The cook had an orange hennaed beard and grunted in approval when Khan chose the largest amongst several Mahseer with glistening golden bodies and yellow-red fins that were stacked in a white plastic cool box.

While he gutted and cleaned the fish, Khan and the mul-lah and Khan's driver sat on the rope beds. The weary mullah removed his leg and rubbed his stump. The mullah's boy squat-ted on the pebbles at the edge of the light in his ragged black overcoat with the bulky vest beneath it. *This was what it must have been like for Dr. Frankenstein*, Khan reflected. You start out full of optimism, with a belief in progress, you do your best, but it turns out that all you can do is make monsters. It becomes an issue of damage limitation. You hope you can keep them in the fold so they are useful. But you can't control everything you create.

The cook's teenage son brought them a tray with mismatched cups and saucers and a metal teapot. The mullah watched the teenager pouring the tea as if he aroused some dreadful appetite, and Khan felt a shiver of distaste followed by a sudden surge of alarm, which he struggled not to show. What if the mullah's boy was jealous? Was this how it would end, in a fit of murderous petulance? He glanced at the boy. No visible expression. If the boy harboured murderous rage, he was keeping it well hidden. The cook's son finished and went back inside the shack.

I'm too old for this, Khan told himself.

He remembered the first time that the mullah had shown him what was hidden underneath the boy's black coat—a fabric vest packed with a mixture of potassium chlorate and ammonium nitrate and covered in a coating of ball bearings sunk in epoxy resin—he'd felt a profound sense of disappointment. He'd set out to defend Pakistan from those that threatened its borders. Was this where it got you, sharing dinner with a teenage suicide bomber?

There was a lot of talk of helping bring the Pashtuns into the twenty-first century but Khan regarded this as nonsense. His belief was that a more modest goal was advisable. Dragging them out of the Stone Age would make a start.

The reason the mullah was down in Peshawar was to report to the feudal landowner, or malik, who provided him with housing and whose tenants the mullah served. The landowner was no longer able to travel up to his land holdings. His reputation had suffered a terrible blow after an assassination attempt against him, which killed one of his guards. He had left town immediately after the attempt and failed to attend the guard's funeral.

He had been too scared go to the funeral, which was viewed as the worst crime amongst Pashtuns, who valued physical courage above all else. You could not show fear in the tribal areas and remain a malik in anything but name.

The mullah poured his tea from the cup into his saucer and drank from that, slurping noisily.

"There is a situation developing," Khan said.

The mullah squinted at him over the saucer. "What kind of situation?"

"Someone is showing an interest in the House of War."

"As I said they would," the mullah told him.

With Pashtuns, Khan reminded himself, and with tribal people generally, it was a commanding voice and an assured presence that counted. "You know your part in this," he said, sternly.

The mullah shrugged.

"If this individual comes looking for the House of War," Khan continued, "it is possible that he will find his way to you."

"Who is he?"

"His name is Noman Butt. He is a bold, ruthless, and ambitious man. He is not to be underestimated. If he finds you, I want you to make sure he doesn't learn something that might be open to misinterpretation."

"Misinterpretation?"

"We both know what I'm talking about."

"You should have had me silenced when you had the chance," the mullah said.

"Who can say for sure what I should have done?" Khan nodded to his driver, who went and fetched a briefcase from the car. Khan passed it to the mullah, who opened it and stared indignantly, as always, at the bundles of rupees inside. Khan knew that the mullah did not like to talk about money. He did not see himself as a venal man. He lived simply. He did not drink. He did not fornicate, except with the occasional boy, which did not count. He was a crook, but a crook from tradition, not to be thought a fool.

"I will be deeply hurt if you do not accept this gift," Khan told him, in the usual manner.

It had always been said of Pashtuns that they could not be bought—only rented for a while.

"What would you have me do with Noman Butt if he finds me?" the mullah asked, eventually.

"Put a halt to his investigation."

"How do you suggest that I do that?"

"You're not usually this slow."

The mullah eyed him speculatively. "You don't like this Noman very much, do you?"

"My feelings on the matter are not important," Khan said. "My priority is the security of the state."

The mullah nodded solemnly. "The security of the state . . ." He closed the briefcase and set it down by his side.

The cook brought them their fish on a metal platter. It had been dredged in chickpea flour and spices and fried to a golden hue. They sunk their fingers in the succulent flesh and lifted morsels to their mouths. The mullah ate as noisily and messily as he drank, pausing between mouthfuls to wipe his fingers on a pile of freshly baked flatbread. Khan ate sparingly. He found the prospect of sudden death robbed him of his appetite. The boy in the suicide vest did not eat at all. When they were done, the mullah stretched out on a charpoy and Khan's driver passed around a snuffbox.

The mullah was right, Khan thought. It would have been sensible to have killed him when he had the chance. Even though he was paying him, Khan had little confidence that the mullah would do as instructed. His best remaining hope was that Noman gave up on this foolish idea of searching for the House of War.

They dropped the mullah and his boy back in Tehkal and drove back to Rawalpindi. At Hasan Abdal, they left the Karokoram and joined the Grand Trunk Road that stretches for sixteen hundred miles, from Kabul all the way to Chittagong in Bangladesh.

Khan went to bed at midnight, without touching the glass of milk that his daughter Mumayyaz left on his bedside table, as she had done every day since his wife died. There were times when he felt weighed down by mourning—for his beloved wife, for the nobility of the struggle to secure Pakistan, and for the man-child that he never had.

7

Fear and Loathing in the Brandy Shop

His mother was the village whore, and he had no idea who his father was. Now he over-revved a state-of-the art, turbo-fucking-charged Range Rover, jerked off to fisting nuns on a ruggedised Toughbook, and hosed miscreants with a Generation 4 Glock pistol, thank you very much. He scared the living shit out of anyone he pleased to.

Noman Butt was born in a one-room hut in a village of low-caste Hindus. The village sat astride the smuggling route that runs from Afghanistan to the Arabian Sea, and was just a few miles from the shrine to an ancient Sufi mystic, where drumbeats filled the night air, and uncovered women in red spun like dervishes. The soft aroma of hashish and cooked bread wafted through the tiny alleyways and old men with watery eyes sucked on clay pipes.

In the summer, the heat hit you like a five-knuckle wallop. It was on such a day when the temperature reached forty-eight degrees that his mother died. She fell across the door to their hut and trapped him alone inside. He was four years old. It was two days before one of her more impatient and impassioned clients broke down the door. Noman had survived by drinking water from a brass bowl, left as an offering to a Hindu deity.

He didn't know which one.

From the village he was taken to an orphanage and raised as a true believer, though he was never allowed to forget that he came from Hindu stock. It didn't seem to matter that the village had disappeared without a trace after corrupt local officials diverted floodwaters to protect a prominent landowner's fields. It wasn't the kind of past you could so easily erase. There were times when it felt like he carried a mass of Hindu gods on his shoulders, swarming like flies above their sacrifices.

He had stolen their water, and one day they would make him pay the price.

It was after midnight when Khan's chief of staff, Tufail Hamid, found him. He was in a brandy shop squeezed between a boss-eyed whore and a *musth malang*, a filthy, stoned beggar from one of the local shrines who controlled a clutch of giggling, half-naked boys who were gathered at their feet. The *malang* was wearing a dress, with a headdress made from animal skins and feathers like a pagan shaman.

"Tufail!" Noman roared, waving his fists. "*Salem Aleikum!* I want to talk to you!" He batted away the whore's roving hands and shoved her along the bench to make a space. He slapped the wood. "Come here! Come here!"

Reluctantly, without bothering to disguise his distaste, Tufail stepped between the boys on the floor and sat alongside him.

"I waited for over an hour at the Cave," he said.

Noman scrunched up his face. "What?"

"You stood me up."

He nodded slowly. "You're here now."

"What's the matter with you?" Tufail demanded. "What do

you want to talk to me about? Does Mumayyaz know you're here?"

"Don't be such a killjoy." Noman hooked him around the neck and dragged him under his arm in a headlock. He patted the crown of Tufail's head. "Faithful Tufail." He leant close, his mouth next to Tufail's ear. "Evil people are watching me."

"What are you talking about?" Tufail gasped. "Let go of me!"

"Something's not right here. No. No. No. Your boss Khan is up to something."

Abruptly he let go of Tufail, who shook himself and rubbed his neck.

"You bastard."

But Noman wasn't listening. He'd been working himself into a fury over what Khan had told him outside the restaurant. What did the old man mean? Who were these unnamed enemies supposedly ranged against him?

He staggered to his feet, scattering boys in every direction.

"*Mere saath aaiye*," he said. "Come on!"

Twenty minutes later they were sitting on plastic chairs outside a hole-in-the-wall chai shop. Noman was alternating sips of sweet, milky tea and puffs on a cigarette.

"I'm sure you're just being paranoid," Tufail told him once he'd explained.

"He said it!" Noman protested, louder than he'd intended. He looked around suspiciously. There was no change in the tempo of snoring emerging from the nearby line of rickshaws. Satisfied they were not being overheard, he leant forward and repeated the warning, "Evil people who wish you ill are watching you. That's what he said. He doesn't say things without cause."

Tufail gave him a sympathetic look. "Are you a hundred percent positive that's what he said?"

Noman gritted his teeth. "Of course I'm bloody positive."

"It's just that you're not yourself at the moment. You've been filling yourself up with drink and God knows what else."

"You think I imagined it?"

Tufail rocked his head from side to side. "You have a high-pressure job. Maybe the most difficult job in Pakistan."

"I'm not crazy!"

"Calm down!" Tufail reached out with one white-gloved hand and placed it on top of Noman's. "I'm not calling you crazy. I just think you need rest and recuperation." He glanced around. "Leave bin Laden to Khan. It was stupid of you to go up there. You have other fish to fry. What about Lashkar-e-Taiba or the Tehrik-i-Taliban?"

Noman shrugged. "I feel like a naysayer. That's all I do, say no. No, you can't kill this so-and-so or no, you can't blow up that dam. Sometimes it feels like I haven't done anything since Mumbai."

He had always considered the four-day rampage through the city in 2008 as one of the high points of his career. Whispering down the voice-over-Internet into the ear of the gunman Mohammed Ajmal Kasab as he strode through the train station and fired into the crowd at the Metro Cinema had been one of the most voyeuristically exciting experiences of his life.

"Your chance will come again," Tufail told him. "And when it does you'll be transformed. I know you. When you get the bit between your teeth you're unstoppable. In the meantime you need to take it easy." He sighed. "I think you should go home. It will make Khan happy and Mumayyaz too."

"Yes," Noman agreed in a resigned tone.

And so finally he went home.

8

Good Vibrations

Noman drove the blacked-out streets of Rawalpindi's old town, along narrow alleyways of shops with their shutters down, eventually turning into a high-walled cul-de-sac, at the end of which was an archway with a set of wooden doors on hanging stiles with iron straps and white-painted jambs. This was the entry point to the Khan mansion, a large, sprawling affair of many floors and wings and sagging roofs and painted shutters that was spread out over several blocks and seemed to insinuate itself in the spaces between adjacent buildings, like water between rocks in a stream.

He beeped the horn and the elderly chowkidar dragged the doors open and threw up an enthusiastic salute as Noman drove into the small courtyard beyond. It didn't matter what time of night or day he pitched up at the gate, the old chap was always there, grinning like an idiot and stamping his heels together and saluting. The chowkidar was a Christian convert from a much-persecuted Hindu village close to the Indian border, and he seemed to imagine that his lowly status gave him some affinity to Noman. In return, Noman despised the old fool and would have happily got rid of him by now, but the hiring and firing of domestic staff lay in his wife's gift, and she enjoyed the spectacle of her husband's discomfort too much to sack the man. He made a mental note to get the local street youths to beat him up at the first opportunity. In the Swat Valley, when the Taliban were in charge, they'd made Hindus wear red turbans, and Noman regarded that as a good thing. *Make 'em stand out so you can easily herd them together*, he thought.

There were two other cars in the courtyard: Khan's silver Mercedes and beside it, his wife's white Pajero, which she hardly ever used. Noman parked between them and went inside without a backward glance.

He strode down cluttered passageways, brim-full with hat racks, stags' heads and stuffed fishes in glass cases, the legacy of generations of rapaciously acquisitive Khans, and up and down stairs, and along further corridors to the dark-panelled study that was lined with hardback books.

It was in this room that he had first realised his father-in-law's air of learning was a sham. The books all bore the ex libris stamp of a certain Colonel Arthur Neville of the 44th Regiment of Foot, and many of the pages were uncut. It was a gentleman's library, looted intact from the site of the massacre of Lord Elphinstone's ill-fated expeditionary army in the Tazeen Pass at the ignominious end of the First Afghan War in 1842, and its only real use was to provide kindling for the fire in the mild, wet winter months.

By means of a secret lever concealed in the fireplace, he opened a door disguised as a bookcase and entered his wife's apartments. Her bedroom was at the end of a narrow, dimly lit corridor. It was a large and mysterious space, rendered exotic by candles, the centre dominated by a teak four-poster bed with lustful serpents coiled around the columns, and a tapestry scene from Paradise of eager virgins on the canopy.

As he had expected, Noman found his wife Mumayyaz,

en déshabillé, reclining on the bed, surrounded by a litter of unwashed plates and cups, rifled magazines, and torn up newspaper. She was wearing a white diaphanous nightgown that hardly concealed the folds and furls of her mountainous flesh. She was a big woman. Junoesque. With heels on, she stood a couple of inches taller than Noman. She could bring a room to a halt by walking into it; but as a rule, she preferred to remain in bed. She had a huge mass of black hair, a large nose, and a wide mouth that could take on many shapes and fit many things. Her complexion was her claim to beauty, and like that other fearsome Punjabi Benazir Bhutto, her skin was almost cream-white and such wanton skin, pillows of it, soft and pliant as dough.

She was awake, of course. Like the wretched chowkidar at the gate, he had never managed to surprise her. She was smoking and the curls of drifting smoke were as yellow as the nicotine-stained canopy of the bed. She felt him examining her from the doorway, and raised her eyes to glare at him, the magazine in her lap sliding off the covers and onto the floor, a glimpse of a buff male torso on glossy paper. There was something about her fierce stare and the way she held the cigarette in her mouth that had always aroused him.

"You look awful," she said. Her voice was a master-class in contempt. "You really are a loathsome little Hindu."

Did she know about him drilling the boy's arse? Khan might have told her, but it seemed just as likely that she knew it from looking at him. She had dark powers, Noman was convinced of it. She was psychic, and she had the power to lay a curse. Once, after a fight with her, he had been shot at three times in twenty-four hours: once by a Tajik assassin sent from Kabul; once by a vengeful husband whose wife he'd given a bad case of crabs; and once by a nervous gate sentry who had taken him for a suicide bomber. It had been a warning from Mumayyaz, he was certain of that. He imagined her alone in bed, taking a break from pleasuring herself, waving her glistening fingers to spark the bullets in their chambers and send them spinning towards him.

"I saw bin Laden," he said.

"How is he?"

Noman shrugged. "Fine."

"He's a very attractive man. Don't you think so?" she said, partly to annoy him, but she believed it too. She was a sucker for any kind of celebrity. "Dignified and so accomplished. History is not going to forget him, is it? Did it make you jealous?"

"Why should it?"

"Come on, darling, I know you better than that. You're in a sulk. It must be bad, otherwise you wouldn't be here snivelling at my feet. You'd be off tupping one of your little girls." She smiled slyly. "Or is it a little boy this time?" She knew all about his wayward behaviour. There was nothing she liked better than to taunt him with his failings: the unruly temper so easily sparked to violence; the shameful upbringing that wrought the colossal chip on his shoulder; the bouts of mania and depression; the urgent promiscuity; the desperate need for power and recognition. She seemed to regard each weakness revealed with Machiavellian indulgence, as if they were tools to be used in the years ahead. And as for his taste for buggery, his near-philosophical obsession with mining the depths, it provoked near-gleeful torrents of abuse: "The cunt is too wide a berth and too deep a port for my anatomically challenged husband. Only the smallest and tightest of holes will fit his eager little soldier."

"No, you must be really in a funk to have shown up here," she said. "It's a shame you weren't here earlier. You could have seen Rifaz before she went to the airport." Rifaz was Mumayyaz's daughter, Noman's stepdaughter. Mumayyaz's first husband had been a Punjabi politician once tapped for high office. He'd died in a mysterious explosion after two years of marriage. Rifaz had been the product of that marriage. She was a clever, rebellious girl with a grievance against the world. She'd flown back to an English all-girls boarding school that afternoon. "You know what the last thing she said to me was?"

"No?"

"That I should stop pretending to love you."

"Maybe she was right."

"Please. Spare me your self-pity."

"I've had a hard day."

"Don't whine. I can't bear it. You're such a pathetic whiner. Sometimes, I lie marooned here and wonder how you ever became a hero."

"You're not marooned," he told her, "you're just too lazy to move."

She ignored that. "I suppose the Indians must have been even more scared than you, shivering and shuddering in the snow, you crying out for your mummy and them crying out for their mummies, and all of you wetting yourselves and you firing your little gun at them. It's really nothing to brag about."

"I don't brag about it."

"Except for when you're too drugged up to remember, of course. Then you shout about it from the rooftops."

"I didn't have a gun."

"Pardon me, I forgot. You did it with a tradesman's tool. You know, you really do look terrible, I mean, you look like some unwashed holy man from a shrine."

"I'm descended from holy men."

"You don't have to remind me," she said, "those terrible smelly fraudsters. No wonder you're such an accomplished liar."

"Watch your tongue," he snapped.

She looked at him coolly and blew smoke before saying, "You know what I've been reading? I've been reading about psychopaths."

"In *She* magazine? Don't be ridiculous!"

"I thought you were one. In fact, I was convinced of it. But it says they dream in black and white."

Noman did not care to dwell on his turbulent childhood and its after-effects. He did not like to speak of it. Not for the first time, he regretted telling her about his dreams. Looking at her, he felt murderous anger. He'd have happily strangled her without feeling an inch of remorse.

"Don't worry," she told him, suddenly playful. Nothing turned her on so much as making him angry. She shifted on the bed, and her nightgown gaped, offering him a view of her massive breasts and their maroon nipples. "Your secret is safe with me."

Who would she tell? The only time she left the house was on her monthly shopping spree to Dubai.

"Come here and kiss me."

"I'd rather not."

"You're fragile tonight, aren't you?" She looked sideways at him, her face almost gentle for a moment, before resuming its customary shrewdness. "Is it bin Laden? Or is it Papa? Papa says you're going looking for the House of War. You're only going up there because he doesn't want you to. You can be so childish sometimes."

"That was a private conversation."

"Silly." She nudged him with a painted toe, setting off a shiver of the bells on her ankle, the nightgown sliding back to reveal her thighs. "You know that Papa tells me everything."

Her toes described slow spirals around his groin. He felt himself stirring, despite himself. She knew exactly how to play him. She could coax an erection out of him in even the most trying circumstances.

"And do you tell him everything?" Noman managed.

"Everything, darling."

She hooked a heel behind his thigh and pulled him towards her, rising from the bed so that she was level with his groin, her busy henna-stained fingers unbuckling his belt and unbuttoning his jeans. She could move fast when the fancy took her.

"I tell him that you are a man of vast appetite and uncommon desires," she said, scooping out his cock and balls. "I tell him you are a lion who must have red meat. I tell him that you will let nothing stand in the way of getting what you want. You're not a psychopath, my love. You're so much more than that. You're an afreet. A demon!"

She tossed her head to throw her hair back and made her mouth into a humid jungle cave, and he went barrelling in. He groaned and extended his hands under her nightgown and down her broad pale back. She was a magnificent woman. If he was a lion, then she was easily a lioness. As she went up and down, she never lost eye contact; her flashing eyes a beacon of promise.

"Yes," he said, urging her on, "Yes! Fuckin' yes!"

Then he was gripping her hair, knotting the curls, while escalating spasms racked his pelvis and the backs of his legs, and his arse began to throb.

"Yes! Yes! Yes!"

She didn't let him come, though. With a popping noise, like a vacuum seal broken, she abruptly released him. He staggered backwards, wild-eyed and stiff as a tightly drawn bow, his arse vibrating and his face flushed with blood.

"What the fuck?" he yelled.

Mumayyaz smacked her lips and wiped them with the tips of her fingers.

"Your phone's ringing," she said.

"What?"

She shook her hair out.

"It's in your back pocket."

He grabbed the phone and held it to his ear.

"What?"

It was the duty officer in the watch room at ISI headquarters.

He sounded terrified. He told Noman that the Americans had crossed the border in helicopters and killed bin Laden.

"When?" Noman demanded.

"At least an hour ago."

"An hour! What the fuck? Why so long?" He should have been informed within minutes of any assault on the Abbotta-bad house. "What about the bloody surveillance team?"

Silence.

"Dammit man, tell me!"

9

The Abbottabad Raid

They began amongst the debris in the animal pen where the Black Hawk had come down. The Americans had destroyed it with thermite grenades before leaving, and the heat of the fire had warped the helicopter's rotors so that it resembled the charred husk of a mutilated spider.

"We have spoken to Haqqani's people who have watchers in Jalalabad," Noman explained in a steely monotone. "They say that just after eleven o'clock last night, two MH-60 Black Hawk helicopters lifted off from the airfield there. Shortly afterwards, they crossed into our airspace undetected."

"Why undetected?" Khan demanded.

"Because our principal air defences are pointing east, at India," Noman told him, "and the Americans have radar-dampening and noise-reduction technology. We were wide open. We always have been."

Noman had never seen Khan look so unsettled. The old man was standing with his mouth hanging slightly open and his shirt mis-buttoned, looking all of his seventy years. He'd rushed up here as soon as he'd heard the news, arriving not long

after Noman. It was clear that whatever outcome Khan had
expected from bin Laden's long confinement, it had not been
this—an American raid.

"Forty-five minutes after the Black Hawks, four Chinooks
took off from the same airfield in Jalalabad," Noman told him.
"We're not sure, but we believe that at least two of them crossed
the border into Pakistan."

"We think the Chinooks put down in the tribal areas," Raja
Mahfouz added. "We're talking to some of our sources in the
villages and trying to identify the exact location. We think the
Chinooks were kept in reserve with their engines running as
backup in case of complications."

Major Raja Mohammed Mahfouz, Chief of Staff of the SS
Directorate and Noman's deputy, was a shaven-headed giant
with a thick ridge of bone running across his brow and a black,
bushy beard that covered his chest. He was a gruff, melancholy
Pashtun from the North-West Frontier who had commanded
one of Noman's companies in the Seventh Commando Battalion, and Noman had brought him with him to the ISI. Like
Noman, he had been up all night.

"Meanwhile, the Black Hawks circled the city to the north
following the ridgeline there and came in from the east,"
Noman said, pointing at the Sarban Hills. He was standing
beside a detached helicopter wheel. "As you see, one of them
crashed here."

"Why?" Khan demanded.

"We don't know yet. I've requested an air-crash investigation team from Mushaf Air Force base. They're on their way. We
don't think that any of the Americans were injured in the crash,
and the setback doesn't appear to have slowed them down. They
used explosives to blow open the gate there."

He led them through the metal gates that were hanging
off their hinges and into the alley that ran alongside the main
building. A second locked gate had also been blown open. They

entered the small courtyard where the courier lived with his wife and four children. There were crimson bloodstains in the dirt and flies feasting on them.

"The courier Abu Ahmed al-Kuwaiti was shot dead here and his wife beside him. The discarded shell casings are NATO standard 5.56 mm."

"What about the neighbours?" Khan asked.

"They undoubtedly heard the noise," Noman replied.

"One of the locals posted on Twitter," Raja Mahfouz added, squinting at the Blackberry that was tiny in his hands. "*Helicopter hovering above Abbottabad at one a.m.* . . . then in brackets . . . *is a rare event.*"

"Did no one investigate?"

"Anyone curious enough to come outside was told by a Pashto speaker that a security operation was underway and that they should go back inside their houses and turn their lights off," Noman said. "It was dark. There was no moonlight. The Pashto speaker was dressed in a *shalwar kameez* and flak jacket and could easily have been mistaken for a plainclothes policeman."

"And our surveillance team?" Khan asked.

"Your surveillance team," Noman said, grimly.

Khan blinked myopically. "My team?"

"We'll come to that." Noman led them to the paved patio at the front entrance to the house, where the courier's brother, Abrar, and his wife had been shot, and together they went inside. There was a large, unfurnished room with unrendered walls and a crumpled gate that had once blocked the base of the staircase leading to the second floor. Near the top of the staircase there were more bloodstains and bullet holes in the concrete, marking the spot where Khalid, the Sheikh's twenty-three-year-old son, had been shot several times and died.

"They jumped over Khalid's body," Noman explained. "Blew open the cage leading to the third floor and advanced to the landing." He climbed to the next level, swivelled at the top of the stairs and pointed to the nearest bedroom. "The Sheikh was in there with two of his wives."

He pushed open the door. More bloodstains.

"The women resisted arrest," Raja Mahfouz said. "They attempted to shield him. The Americans shot one of them in the leg."

"Which one?" Khan asked.

"The Yemeni."

"Where is she?"

"In the military hospital," Raja Mahfouz told him.

"So?"

"The women were pushed aside. The Americans shot the Sheikh in the chest and in the head. He died there on the floor."

In silence, they contemplated the ransacked room. Nine years and seven months after the Sheikh's emissaries had brought down the Twin Towers and enraged a nation, the Americans had finally got their man. It wasn't much of a place for the founder of Al-Qaeda to die—a bare room with cheap nylon curtains and threadbare mattresses in a half-finished, shoddily constructed house.

"They put the corpse in a black body bag and cuffed the women and escorted them down the stairs," Noman continued. "For the next twenty minutes or so they searched the house, gathered the surviving women and children against an outside wall and questioned them in Arabic, and then they destroyed the crashed helicopter with explosive charges and thermite grenades. They were careful to ensure that nothing was recoverable from it. In that time, one of the rescue Chinooks arrived. The Americans were on the ground for less than forty minutes, and we know from our allies in Jalalabad that the helicopters returned there at three a.m. The Sheikh's body was sent from there to Bagram, and then at dawn it was flown to the US aircraft carrier *Carl Vinson* and buried at sea."

"You're a hundred percent sure about that?" Khan demanded.

Noman shrugged. "The Americans called our friends in Saudi Intelligence and warned them what they were about to do. The Saudis informed us immediately."

"And our response?"

"We have arrested five locals on suspicion of collaboration," Raja Mahfouz told them, "including a doctor who was running an immunisation drive in the town."

"And the surveillance team?" Khan said, repeating his earlier question. "Why didn't they report this?"

"You had better follow me," Noman said, grim faced.

A bundle of fur and a dark crimson smear on the concrete marked the spot where someone had clubbed the monkey to death. They stood in the hide by the window and stared back at the compound they had just vacated. Black soot scorched the wall of the pen and part of the Black Hawk's tail hung over it.

The tripod and telescope was on its side, as if tipped over in a struggle. Omar was lying beside it with a bruised and puffed-up face, the belt that had been used to strangle him still looped around his neck. Tariq was gone.

"Everything has been left the way it was found," Raja Mahfouz said.

"According to the logbook, Omar was on watch here and Tariq was sleeping over there." Noman explained, pointing at the bedroom. He could feel Khan watching him. *Yeah, I fucked him here*, he wanted to yell. *But he was your boy. A traitor.* "Gunfire. Explosions. Tariq must have woken up as soon as it kicked off."

"You're saying he wasn't expecting this?"

"I don't think so," Noman said. He squatted down beside the body and loosened the belt, revealing the dark lesion on the neck. The blood vessels in Omar's eyes had burst and were bright red. "Using a belt doesn't suggest premeditation. I think Tariq reacted to the situation. In my opinion, he woke up and as soon as he realised what was happening, he recognised that his cover was blown. Or at least it soon would be. He knew we'd be digging around trying to understand this thing for years to come. No cover would withstand that. And he must have realised that he had to stop Omar from reporting the events if he was to have a chance of escape. So he killed him and fled."

Khan was frowning. "And the Americans took him with them when they left?"

Noman shook his head. "We don't think so. A witness claims to have seen someone fitting Tariq's description leaving this house and approaching the Pashto speaker at the gate of bin Laden's house. There was a heated exchange. The man we think was Tariq was shouting, *'Zamaa num bulbul dai.'*"

I am Nightingale.

"He went on shouting until one of the Americans hit him with a rifle."

"You're sure about this?" Khan asked.

"The police arrested Tariq's wife and parents this morning in Lahore," Raja Mahfouz said. "The wife is denying all knowledge. She's insisting he was loyal. The parents are singing, though. They were promised relocation to England and an annual stipend for the rest of their lives."

"The boy was a British spy," Noman said, accusingly. "He must have been recruited when he was stationed in England. All the time he was working for you, he was working for them."

"The Americans didn't wait," Khan said, ignoring him. There was a hint of grudging admiration in his voice. "They didn't tell anyone, not even their allies. They went and did it, and to hell with the consequences." He glanced at Noman.

"Have you apprehended Tariq?"

"He's still missing," Raja Mahfouz said.

"We're hunting high and low," Noman growled. "Airports,

train stations, and bus terminals are all on high alert. There are checkpoints along the length of the Grand Trunk Road. We've closed the border crossing at Torkham Gate, and we've mobilised helicopter patrols in Mohmand and Bajaur."

Khan pursed his lips and stared down at the dead monkey at his feet.

"Did you suspect him?" Noman demanded. "Did you know Tariq was a spy?"

Khan looked at him. After a pause, he led him across the room and out of earshot of Raja Mahfouz. "Who knows you came up here?" he asked in a low voice.

Noman stiffened. "What?"

"Who knows you came up here the day before yesterday?" Khan repeated.

"What are you suggesting?"

"If Tariq is arrested, he will be questioned and undoubtedly he will reveal that you were here two days ago."

"And what if he does? I told you, I didn't trust either of them."

"Keep your voice down," Khan told him. "I'm trying to protect you. Who else, apart from Tariq, knows that you came here?"

10 ﭒ

Waiting for Nightingale

The Americans called it the "Valley at the Edge of the Known World." The soldiers joked that they were so close to it they might fall off at any moment.

They lived in narrow crawl spaces behind battle-scarred ramparts of sandbags and cedar logs, staring out at an implacably hostile and alien world through fire-ports as narrow as the arrow slits in Crusader castles. It was considered one of the most dangerous postings in Afghanistan and in some quarters, one of the most dangerous places on earth. It had a reputation for messing with your head. More than forty American servicemen had died defending the Forward Operating Base, and several times it had come close to being completely overrun. It was a haunted battleground built on the remnants of a long-abandoned Soviet hilltop fortification that had claimed as many Russian lives and come just as close to being overrun. It looked east down the valley, across a rock-strewn landscape where an elusive and ever-moving enemy lurked amongst the boulders and bushes—*dukhi*, or ghosts, was what the terrified Russian conscripts had called them—men in dusty turbans and blankets, wearing shoes without laces, possessing nothing of any significance but their guns.

At the end of the valley was the Durand line marking the eastern edge of Afghanistan, a border as incomprehensible as the Iron Curtain or any other arbitrary ceasefire line or swerve of a pen on a map. It is unlikely that the Emir of Afghanistan, who could read no English, knew what he was signing when he put his mark to the one-page document drawn up by Sir Henry Mortimer Durand of the colonial office of British India. It was winter 1893, and with his pen, the Emir divided the unruly Pashtun lands. It is equally unlikely that the British regarded the line as anything more than a temporary demarcation beyond which either side agreed not to interfere. But interfere they did, just as those who followed them also interfered, and went on interfering. From the Third Anglo-Afghan war, in which the Royal Air Force bombed Kabul and Jalalabad in 1919, through Operation Cyclone in the eighties, in which CIA and Saudi-funded Mujahideen groups crossed into Afghanistan to fight the Soviet occupation, and through to the present day, when Taliban fighters emerged from Pakistani tribal areas to do battle with the Americans.

"This is a really fucking dark place," said Winslow, the agency man, who had known many dark places in his life.

The remark was accepted in silence. No one took the trouble to even grunt. The long-limbed soldier kneeling in the dirt lifted a scratched metal tin from the gas stove and poured coffee into four chipped enamel mugs. He passed them to the four visitors, two Americans and two Brits, who were squatting in the dirt.

"*Mocha Harrar*," the soldier said with grim satisfaction. He was a sharp-featured and dark-skinned Ethiopian from Minneapolis. "Peaberry beans . . ."

Winslow and the two security guards drank the coffee without comment.

"It's delicious," Ed Malik said. "Thank you."

He stared out through the sandbags at the dirty ribbon of the river far below and across the valley at the dark face and snow-capped peak of Arghush Ghar, the Black Mountain. The enemy owned the Arghush Ghar. He was reminded of a line in *Heart of Darkness*, of a young Roman citizen in some inland outpost who felt "the savagery, the utter savagery, had closed all around him."

"We can't wait here much longer," Winslow said.

Ed said nothing. He was aware of both Winslow and Draper watching him closely, trying to gauge his reaction. Winslow, an ex-army ranger whose ruddy complexion made his face appear perpetually sunburned, was a CIA officer based out of FOB Chapman down in Khost. Draper was his security guard, a similarly weathered forty-five-year-old former Green Beret working for the private contractor XE Services, formerly known as Blackwater. He had an M4 carbine slung across his back.

"Your man is twenty-four hours late," Winslow said.

"You don't have to stay if you don't want to," Ed told him. Winslow had been wounded in the 2009 attack on Camp Chapman, when the Jordanian asset Humam al-Balawi had crossed over from Pakistan to meet with his handlers and blown himself up, killing seven CIA officers. It had been the most lethal attack on the CIA in twenty-five years. It was no wonder Winslow was jumpy.

"I'm staying," Ed told him.

Beside him, Dai nodded to indicate that he was steadfast, that he wouldn't argue with his boss in front of strangers.

"How long are you gonna wait?" Winslow asked.

"As long as it takes."

"You said he'd come across yesterday."

Ed suppressed his anger. "His cover's blown. He's on the run. Khan is hunting for him. Somewhere out there, he's terrified. If you'd told us what you were going to do, maybe we could have got him out earlier."

"And risk the integrity of our mission?" Winslow shook his head. "Only a handful of people outside the White House Situation Room knew we were going after bin Laden. We've been burned by you Brits before."

And so Tariq had been sacrificed in the interests of the greater good, and Ed's work had been written off. Four years of work, four years of burrowing Tariq into the ISI and the painstaking gathering of evidence linking the ISI to militant groups responsible for the death of coalition servicemen across Afghanistan and evidence linking the ISI to training camps providing bomb-making lessons to British-born South Asians—all of it burned in a single operation.

Ed went over to speak to the squad leader.

"It's a big risk letting an unknown in here," the squad leader said. The shadow cast by the attack at Camp Chapman was a long one.

"I appreciate what you're offering to do," Ed told him.

"No problem," the man said after a pause. "We're all on the same side."

"What are your rules for engaging the enemy?" Ed asked him.

"If we feel we're in danger, we can shoot. That's the rule. The tactical directive says that's fine but asks, 'Should we?' Then there's an interpretation that says we need to see a weapon no matter what the circumstances."

"What about on the other side?"

The whites of the squad leader's eyes shone in the fading afternoon light. "In Pakistan?"

"Yes."

He shrugged. "If they're firing at us, maybe."

"And if it's the Pakistan Army?"

The man shook his head. "Shit! I don't know."

*

Darkness came, and with it another attack. The enemy launched a salvo of RPGs from a nearby ridgeline and then raked the outpost with plunging fire from the Arghush Ghar.

They knew it was coming: *Prophet*, the American eavesdropping operation further up the valley, had warned the FOB minutes before that there was an uptick in enemy radio communications. They ran to the mortar pit, firing shells back at grid coordinates they'd long since memorised, and then darted back behind the sandbags for cover.

The squad leader called in fire support from company headquarters, and a few minutes later, 155-mm artillery shells began to explode on the ridgeline. An air strike took longer. By the time an Air Force jet roared by and dropped a five-hundred-pound bomb, the enemy fire had stopped.

Silence followed.

There were no casualties. It was the third such attack since Ed and Winslow had arrived at the outpost. Dusk and dawn seemed to be the most dangerous times. It was when the soldiers wore their body armour and hunkered down in their fire positions to wait.

Ed knelt against a sandbag wall.

You were too damn bold, Tariq, Ed thought. *You were too damn confident of yourself. You should have done what you promised and stayed well away from Abbottabad, and I should have made sure of it.* As he was thinking this, the soldier manning the tripod-mounted Long Range Acquisition System called out, and his colleagues eased into their fire positions.

"There's someone out there, on the far side. I can see him on the thermal imager. He's heading this way."

Ed stepped up to the observation platform and looked through the viewfinder.

A bright, white shape moving casually amongst the rocks, three thousand metres out. It was Tariq. *It had to be. He'll make it. He'll be here soon. And when he gets here, I'll give him a bloody great hug because he's the best damn agent we ever had, and I'll forgive him for every transgression, every lie and sly barb.*

The soldier began his commentary at two thousand metres, calling out each time the target advanced a hundred metres. When he was less than a kilometre out, Ed lifted his binoculars and gazed at the dark figure flitting amongst the boulders.

"Is this your man?" Winslow said.

"Hang on."

"Where is he?" Winslow demanded. "Can you see him?"

"I can see him," Ed confirmed.

Come on! Tariq was at the border. He was almost through it. He had nearly made it.

At that moment the figure stopped and crouched down.

Then Ed heard it: a helicopter approaching.

The helicopter's searchlight flicked on, a bright white spear in the darkness.

"Open fire!" Ed roared. "The chopper's crossed over to our side. Open fire!"

Then the figure was running. There came the sound of a voice shouting through a loudspeaker, the searchlight sweeping across the rocks.

"Open fire," Ed pleaded. "Please."

The soldiers stared through their night-sights and did not fire.

The helicopter banked suddenly, turning away from them, heading back into Pakistan. Tariq was still coming.

"Let him through," Ed shouted. "Let the guy through."

The man ran out into open ground and scrambled up the steep sides of the hilltop. He was barefoot, his legs covered in scratches and bruises. He scaled the sandbag walls and dropped like a sack into the centre of the outpost.

Ed was the first to reach him. It was Hakimullah, Tariq's elderly Hazara manservant. He was crouching in the dirt, wrapped in the remnants of his blanket. He looked like a beaten dog.

"Where's Tariq?" Ed demanded in Pashto, shaking him.

"It's not safe for him to cross," Hakimullah replied. "They are searching everywhere for him."

"Where did he go?"

"The safe house in Peshawar."

Winslow was standing at Ed's side. The two guards were hanging back, pointing their rifles at Hakimullah.

"This is the guy?" Winslow demanded. "This is your agent?"

"No," Ed replied. "This isn't him."

"Jesus Christ!" Winslow swore. "Are you crazy?"

"Fuck you," Ed snapped.

"I'll go," Hakimullah said. He reached into a pocket and retrieved a scrap of paper that he pressed into Ed's hand. "This is Tariq's number. You can call him."

"Where will you go?" Ed asked, after a pause.

"Back over. My granddaughter is there."

"They'll hunt you down."

Hakimullah shrugged. He climbed wearily to his feet, rearranged the blanket around his shoulders, and without a backward glace climbed back over the sandbag walls, slid down the hillside, and disappeared amongst the rocks and bushes.

Ed groaned in frustration. He wanted to punch a wall. After a few carefully controlled breaths, he regained his composure. Winslow was watching him.

"I have to make a call."

He squatted down in the shelter of a sandbag wall and punched the numbers written on the piece of paper into his sat-phone.

11

A Knock on the Door

For the third time that minute, Tariq glanced down at the phone in his hand and willed it to ring.

Please Ed, bloody well call me! Meri madat karo! *Help me!*

He was standing in darkness at the window's edge, shielded by the weathered carcass of a wooden shutter, shivering despite the heat. From his vantage point he could see the shadowy entrance to the courtyard several floors below. He had never felt more alone and afraid. It was only a matter of time before he was discovered. He listened to the hiss and drip of elderly air conditioning units lashed to boards on the surrounding walls and tried not to imagine that the rooftops and passageways sheltered men with guns. He had been standing here for hours, tracking the movement of the sun as it crossed the sky and sank beneath the jumble of roofs in the Khyber Bazaar. In the morning, he had watched as the pot-seller moved stacks of cooking pots from his shop out on the street to the storage unit on the ground floor and, in the far corner of the courtyard, the tailor at his sewing machine, running up American flags in preparation for a flag-burning protest planned that afternoon.

The safe house was close to the Street of Storytellers and he had listened to the chanting of the crowd and watched as groups of protestors had spilled into the courtyard several times for respite from the late afternoon heat. The whiff of tear gas made his eyes smart.

He had always known that revealing bin Laden's location might cause the Americans to react, but he had anticipated a drone strike, not a full-scale commando assault. And he had expected to receive some kind of prior warning. Even so, he had known exactly what it meant when he woke to the sound of the circling helicopters. Naked, pausing only to snatch his belt from the chair, he had gone straight to the hide and strangled Omar, who was in the act of tapping numbers into his phone, presumably to raise the alarm. He had looped the belt around Omar's neck and twisted savagely, pulling him down off the stool onto the floor, tightening his grip until eventually he'd stopped struggling.

Afterwards, he'd dressed quickly to the sound of gunfire and explosions, and then he had gone out into the street.

There was an armed man in *shalwar kameez* and a flak jacket standing outside bin Laden's house. He was yelling at the neighbours in Pashto to go back inside their houses and turn off their lights. Behind him, in the shadows by the gate, there was another larger man, the unmistakable outline of an American with a German Shepherd on a leash.

"I am Nightingale," he called out as he approached, first in Pashto and then Urdu, and then Punjabi, and finally in English. He felt certain they had been briefed to extract him along with bin Laden at the end of their operation.

"Get back!" the man in the *shalwar kameez* shouted at him, raising his rifle.

"It's me," he protested. "Tariq! Rule Britannia!"

"Get back!"

The dog lunged with its teeth bared, and the man in the

shalwar kameez swung the rifle around and slammed the butt into the side of Tariq's head. He fell to the ground.

He came around as the Americans were leaving. The crashed helicopter was burning, and the others were lifting off in a storm of dust. He picked himself up and staggered away from the house. He wasn't sure how long he kept moving, or in which direction, but at some stage he curled up and slept for several hours.

He woke up with a raging headache and the certainty that he was being hunted.

The Peshawar apartment was the remnant of a long-defunct intelligence operation run in the late eighties by a British Military Intelligence outfit known as the Afghan Guides. It had served its purpose as a safe location to debrief Afghan military defectors in the late eighties, and then after the Wall came down, it had somehow remained on the books as a final fallback position, only to be used in extremis. He'd collected the key from the blind vendor on the corner, who sold stripped and cubed bags of sugar cane, and warily climbed the stairwell of the crumbling concrete building to the apartment on the fourth floor. Inside, there was a thick layer of dust covering everything, and it looked as if it had been unoccupied for years. There was running water, though, and he was able to wash the blood out of his hair.

He settled in to wait, alternating between sleeping fitfully on the cot bed and standing at the window.

Hakimullah came on the afternoon of the second day. Tariq watched him scurry across the courtyard. He brought the news that there were roadblocks along the length of the Grand Trunk Road, the border was closed and army patrols were scouring the tribal areas for any sign of him. It wasn't safe to move. He'd sent the old man out for a second-hand phone and a pay-as-you-go

SIM card, and then scribbled the number on a piece of paper and entrusted it to him.

"Find Ed. He'll be waiting for me on the other side. Tell him to call me."

Hakimullah had accepted the task without complaint. That was more than thirty hours ago, and Tariq was getting increasingly desperate. What if Hakimullah had been arrested? He wouldn't last long under questioning. Perhaps the ISI already knew his location. Perhaps they were even surrounding the house now, Black Stork Commandos climbing the stairs and crawling across the roof. He knew that his wife and parents must already be in custody. He couldn't bear to think what must be happening to them.

The phone in his hand lit up and began to vibrate.

"Ed?"

"Yes."

He was flooded with relief. "Can you get me out of here?"

"It's not safe for you to cross the border."

"I can't stay here much longer. They're looking everywhere."

"I'll talk to the British embassy in Islamabad. Maybe they can offer you refuge until we sort something out."

"Maybe? *Maybe?* What do you mean maybe? I'm way out on a limb here, Ed!"

"I'll talk to them. I'll make a case. We can get a local contact to pick you up and drive you down there."

"Which local contact?"

"I don't know yet."

There was a knock on the door.

"*Maa chod!*"

"What is it?"

"Someone's at the door."

"Don't answer it."

But he was already moving. He paused for a few seconds with his ear to the door, and then he pressed his eye to the peephole. It was Khan, staring right back at him through the fisheye lens, an undersea predator emerging sinuously from its reef.

"I know you're in there."

Tariq swore under his breath. Khan had probably known where he would be before he got here. "It's Khan."

"Don't open the door," Ed told him.

"I've come alone," Khan said.

Tariq opened the door, and Khan stepped in and surveyed the room. Tariq carefully closed the door and turned to face him. Khan had produced a pistol and was pointing it at him. His dark eyes, wet and shiny behind glass, were utterly without warmth or compassion.

Tariq held out his hands in supplication. "Please, don't do this. Not here."

Khan pressed the trigger.

Ed flinched at the sound of the gunshot and then the clatter of the phone on the floorboards and the thump of the falling body.

"Tariq? Tariq?"

Silence. Then footsteps, followed by a scuffling sound, as the phone was picked up.

An unfamiliar voice: "Hello?"

Ed kept his mouth shut. Inside, he was yelling. *No! No! No!*

"Who's there?"

12

Kabul by Night

By night, Kabul was a city of monstrous shadows and fiery embers, of scurrying human shapes and hole-in-the-wall shops lit by fluorescent tubes that flickered and flared like insect exterminators, revealing skinned carcasses hanging from rafters, stacks of gnarled firewood, and piles of charred flatbread.

Ed sat in the passenger seat of the Land Cruiser and watched the brake lights of the battered Afghan Police pickup in front of them, bouncing in the potholes. He glimpsed rutted alleyways strewn with rubbish and festooned with overhead electrical cables; dirty, helot faces lit up by the sparks rising from street fires; and a woman's hand reaching out from a burqa, pleading.

Beside him, Dai steered the car through the melee of traffic with good-humoured vigilance. A Corolla cut in front of them, getting between the Land Cruiser and the police pickup in front, Hindi pop blaring from its open window.

"Easy now," Dai muttered.

Ed was furious, really furious. At Tariq, for ignoring a direct order. At himself, for not insisting they pull Tariq out as soon as they'd realised who was in the Abbottabad house. And most of all, angry at the Americans, for abandoning Tariq to his fate.

They slowed for a police checkpoint, one of the twenty-five that formed the so-called "ring of steel" around central Kabul, and crawled forward through the crumbling concrete chicane while Afghan policemen stared listlessly at them from the shelter of a sandbagged hut.

They turned into a narrow cul-de-sac hemmed in on all sides by pockmarked blast walls, and rolled to a halt.

"Want to take a condor moment, boss?"

"I don't think so," Ed replied through gritted teeth. He paused with his hand on the door handle. "I won't be long."

"We're not going anywhere," Dai told him.

Ed got out of the car and crossed in front of the vehicle, aware of the policemen in the chase vehicle watching him. He slipped through the gap between two blast walls and approached a battered metal door. He knocked twice, and a small hatch at eye height slid open. He was studied. Seconds later, he listened to the sound of bolts being drawn and the door opened. He stepped into a small and garishly lit vestibule. A large man in a leather coat pointed at a metal detector. Ed put his wallet and mobile phone in a plastic basket and stepped through the detector. On the far side there was another metal door. The man nodded, and Ed knocked.

It opened into a different world.

Uzbek waitresses in miniskirts carrying bottles of South African red wine weaved between tables. The restaurant was full of the usual crowd of foreign-educated Afghan businessmen and international diplomats. Ed spotted Bob Hagedorn, the CIA station chief, sitting in a corner of the windowless room. He was dining with an Afghan MP from the Panjshir

Valley who was reputed to be behind Kabul's largest kidnap and ransom racket.

If Hagedorn noticed Ed approaching, he did not openly acknowledge it. Instead, he fiddled with his cutlery. That was Bob, always fidgeting. Always interfering, his critics said. He was a small, round man in his fifties, with watery eyes behind thick-lens spectacles, reddish hair, and a beard flecked with grey.

Ed stood over the table. He hadn't washed since his return to Kabul and was dirty and smelly, sorely in need of a bath and a change of clothes.

"I know what you're gonna say, Ed," Bob told him in a quiet voice.

"Do you, now?"

Apart from a brief glance at Ed to gauge the measure of his anger, Bob didn't take his eyes off the cutlery. He was a moody and mysterious man. It was said that he was a jealous guardian of his patch and given to outbursts of violent temper behind closed doors, but in public he was a man of unassailable emotional control.

"We couldn't tell you for reasons of operational security," he explained.

Ed pressed his knuckles down on the table. "Tariq is dead."

"I'm sorry about that."

"No, you're not."

Eventually, reluctantly, Bob pushed back his chair and threw down his napkin. He murmured an apology to the impassive Afghan opposite him and stood up.

"It's understandable that you're angry," Bob said, finally making eye contact with him. "You formed an emotional attachment to the agent you were running. It happens."

"He was my friend."

"Grow up, Ed. None of us has friends. You have to cast that aside in order to do what demands to be done."

Ed looked away.

Even if Bob noticed the tightening of Ed's jaw, he surely didn't anticipate what was coming. At that stage, Ed was not known for impulsive or self-destructive behaviour.

"Go get some rest," Bob said. "We'll talk in the morning."

Ed swung around and head-butted him, smashing his forehead into Bob's face. Bob staggered backwards and fell into his chair.

The Afghan raised a hand, and within seconds Ed was being manhandled out of the restaurant. He was thrown onto the tarmac beyond the blast walls.

Dai stood over him.

"Let's get you on the first plane out of here, shall we, boss?"

13 ❖

Seducing the Widow

At first he'd thought he was crazy, that he was seeing treachery everywhere. But then a sneaky thread of suspicion had lodged itself in Noman's head. What if Khan was a traitor? The evidence was patchy and inconclusive—however, a pattern was emerging and Khan was at the centre of it.

Tariq was Khan's boy. Khan had recruited him, and it was his signature on the posting order that had sent Tariq to London in 2005 and brought him back in 2006. Since then, Tariq had been one of Khan's roving sets of eyes-and-ears in Afghanistan and the tribal areas, glad-handing informants and conveying messages. It had been Khan's decision to put Tariq in the surveillance house in Abbottabad two weeks before. And there had been something strange about Khan's response to the raid, as if he was surprised not to have received some kind of warning. On top of that, Noman was still seething at the decision by the Director General's office to issue a kill-on-sight order for Tariq. He couldn't prove it, but he was fairly sure that Khan was behind that as well.

Now that he was dead, Tariq couldn't implicate any collaborators.

Noman spent the days following the raid talking to his usual contacts in darkened doorways or hunched at his desk trawling through intelligence summaries from across the various ISI directorates. Not long after dawn on May 6, he read a short paragraph that made reference to an altercation in Kabul. A British advisor to the Afghan Ministry of Finance by the name of Ed Malik had attacked the CIA station chief in a crowded restaurant. The informant had overheard the outraged Brit say: "Tariq is dead."

Noman furiously rubbed his temples. He red-flagged Ed Malik and made a bid to the Counter-Intelligence Bureau, which handled ISI assets abroad, for a fuller personal profile. He was fairly sure that the Ministry of Finance job was a cover story, and Ed Malik would prove to be an MI6 officer. If so, it was likely he was Tariq's handler. If he could find out how Tariq was recruited and what information he had passed on, he might be able to establish whether Tariq was a lone wolf or, as he was beginning to suspect, under the protection of a senior figure in the ISI, namely his father-in-law. If Khan was a traitor, Noman had decided he would be the one to unmask him.

There was a knock on the door.

"Come in."

It was Raja Mohammed Mahfouz, his massive frame filling the doorway. In the midst of everything, Noman was glad to have such a reliable deputy. Mahfouz was a stubborn and loyal man, slow to offer counsel but indomitable when set in motion.

"What is it?" Noman asked.

"The coroner has released Tariq's body to the family. They are planning to bury him today."

"They've got a nerve." Noman looked at his watch. If they left now, the Range Rover could be in Lahore by early afternoon.

"Let's go," he said.

*

Less than four hours later, Noman strode into the house at the vanguard of a police raid. Inside, they were preparing to carry Tariq's corpse out, wrapped in a white cloth.

"Stop that!" Noman yelled. "Put the body down."

The crowd of mourners outside had fled as soon as the patrol cars swooped in, so all that now remained were the reluctant pallbearers, Tariq's elderly mother, and his young widow. They knew who he was, of course. And they knew the risk they were taking in being seen in the traitor's house: a gaggle of lawyers, doctors, and other self-righteous scum shitting themselves. All except the widow. Noman could feel his radar pinging as she lifted her chin in defiance.

"Let us pass," she said.

"Rip the place apart," Noman said. Beside him, Mahfouz barked an order, and policemen wielding crowbars spread out across the building. They charged up the stairs and down the corridors. "Leave no stone unturned."

"I said, let us pass!"

You had to admire the widow's pluck. Her whole world had been turned upside down. Her husband and her in-laws had betrayed her. They hadn't told her what they were up to. Now the family was disgraced, with no one to protect them. She faced the prospect of losing her home.

Noman looked her up and down. She was a *chikni* beauty, curvaceous with lustrous black hair peeping out from beneath her headscarf. She'd been chewing her lips and they were puffed up, but it only served to accentuate her beauty. It stirred his unruly cock just to look at her. She wouldn't last long on her own on the streets of Lahore.

Behind her, her mother-in-law looked half-crazed with grief. She snarled, "You devil!"

The old woman had only just been let out of Kot Lakhpat jail. Her husband, Tariq's retired-barrister father, was still locked up and probably wouldn't survive the experience. The last time Noman had seen the old woman was in a basement cell a couple of days ago. He'd almost felt sorry for her. Recent years had not been prosperous ones for the middle-class in Pakistan. They faced a growing inability to purchase what they once could. All they had left, apart from their large houses and dwindling pensions, was their sense of entitlement, their disdain, and envy. How quickly he had demolished that. He'd ripped her *shalwar kameez* open, scooped her meaty sixty-year-old breasts out of her bra and weighed them in his hands. "These teats have fed and nurtured a traitor," he'd told her. "You would have done better to have dashed his brains against a wall than given him your milk, witch."

Now, two days later, he was standing in the hallway of their house in Gulberg, one of Lahore's most prestigious addresses, with his chest puffed out and his cowboy boots spreading dirt all over their heirloom carpets.

"Put him down, or I will kill each and every one of you," he said.

"This is unacceptable harassment," a pallbearer protested. He was a small quaking man with shiny shoes.

Noman sneered. "Are you taking the piss, *panchod*?"

"Why are you trembling?" the widow asked the pallbearer. "Are you scared? Of course you are. I don't blame you." She returned her attention to Noman. "Get out of here, you filthy blue-eyed devil, and take your corrupt policemen with you. You could do what you like to him when he was alive. He's dead now and beyond your reach."

"Put the body down!" Noman yelled.

They put the body down on the floor.

"Now get out." The pallbearers fled. He jabbed a finger at the widow. "Not you."

The mother-in-law was more difficult to dislodge. He had to raise his hand to strike her. She scuttled away into the depths of the house, where the police could be heard breaking up the furniture and knocking holes through the interior walls.

"That will be all, Mahfouz."

His deputy nodded and followed the old woman. Finally, they were alone in the hallway.

"I didn't kill Tariq," Noman said. He softened his voice. "I did not kill your husband."

"Then he's not dead," she hissed.

He licked his lips. He hadn't come here with any kind of plan other than to vent his anger and break the place up, but now that he was here, a kind of improvisational faith had taken over. It was like going into battle. He was over the start line and it was time to wing it.

"Khan killed him."

"You're lying," she said. "Khan was our friend."

There was a hint of uncertainty in her voice. He saw that the cuffs of her shirt were shaking, and he knew it was costing her to be this brave. No wonder. She was in a fix. How could she be certain of anything any more? Suddenly, he felt giddy with promise.

"Khan was not your friend," he said, circling her. "This is what he said, word for word, on my honour: 'Hunt down the traitor like a dog and leave his bloody corpse to fester by the roadside. Kill his parents, his wife, and his servants. Demolish his family home.' It's only because of me that you're still alive and in this house. You wouldn't even have a body to bury if it wasn't for me. But, Inshallah, he is in a better place now."

"He's in Paradise, where you can't touch him," she retorted.

He grabbed her trembling arm and with his other hand pulled away the scarf so her hair tumbled free. It was thick as molasses. He leant in to whisper. "I loved him. He was beautiful. So beautiful. Such soft, smooth skin. Such a magnificent arse." Her doe eyes widened. He saw fear, but also recognition in them—she knew about her husband's tastes. Tariq was not such a great deceiver after all. "But he was not as beautiful as you are. If he was alive, I'd kill him again, here and now, for his betrayal of you, for his unfaithfulness and promiscuity, for his unnatural behaviour, but most of all, to keep your beauty for myself."

"I'd throw acid in my face to stop you."

He snatched her hands. "I wouldn't let you."

He pressed his lips to her fingertips. She flinched, appalled.

She spoke softly, her voice barely above a whisper. "I'd kill you if I could."

"What is wrong with you? I am offering to protect you. Do you have any idea how vulnerable you are?"

"You killed my husband."

"I killed a traitor, and besides, I have helped you to find someone better."

"There is no one better."

"Oh yes, there is! Me!"

She spat in his face. He let go of her. Obviously, he wasn't going to marry her, but it had occurred to him that he did need a new operational base if he was going to launch an investigation into how the British had managed to penetrate the ISI, if Tariq had acted alone, and whether he had help from on high. Headquarters was impossible at the moment, with recriminations flying and the threat of a full-scale witch hunt in the air. Hanging around there increased his chances of being scapegoated. And he wasn't going back to the house he shared with Khan and Mumayyaz in Rawalpindi. He didn't want Khan anywhere near his investigation. This seemed as good a place as any. The house was situated in an easily secured cul-de-sac at the heart of Gulberg. There were high walls protected with broken glass. With a bit of work, it could be made readily defensible. There was the potential for a mutually beneficial relationship. He'd need a regular fuck if he stayed on, of course. He ran his hand across his cheek gathering her spittle and licked it off his fingers.

"Why did you do that?" he asked, cultivating a wounded expression. He was really enjoying himself now.

"I wish it was poison."

He seized her again and twisted her arms behind her back. She turned her head away from him. "I can't bear it. Such scorn on lips that were made for kissing." He let go of her abruptly. He reached into the back of his jeans and took out his Glock. "If you can't forgive me then you must kill me. Take this gun and shoot me right in the chest." He put the gun in her hands and ripped open his kurta. "I killed Tariq!"

Her whole body was wracked with sobs. He felt exultant.

"Kill me or have me," he yelled. "Go on! Do it!"

He pressed the cold hard O-ring of the muzzle against his chest, and then it dropped. Her legs buckled, and she slumped against him as if he was the only person preventing her from falling apart. He buried his face in her hair and breathed in her musky scent.

"I can't do it," she whispered.

"Your husband was a traitor," he whispered softly in her ear. "He betrayed you in the bedroom. And he betrayed his country for money. Killing me would kill the one person who can protect you. I can keep you safe. Do you hear me? Safe. You could go on living in this house."

"I don't know what to do."

"You have to trust me," he said. He kissed the soft flesh of her neck. He lifted her chin and brushed her hair away from her face. He lifted the tears from under her eyes with his thumbs. "It's going to be all right."

He kissed her on the lips, and after a few moments she surrendered. A fresh thought occurred to him. Why was Khan so keen for him not to go looking for the House of War? And fresh on its heels, another thought: if he discredited Khan and took his place, he would become one of the most powerful men in Pakistan.

14

No Motto Please, We're British

From the window of the plane, Ed watched the meandering Thames beneath him, the U-bend of the Isle of Dogs and the red flashing pin-light on One Canada Square, the brash "loads-a-money" landmarks on the river's crowded banks—the tent-pole Dome, the unfinished Shard, the big-dick Gherkin, the fairground Eye . . .

He was a failure, grand and total.

British by birth, Asian and Muslim by descent, and agnostic by conviction, Edward Henry Malik found it difficult to explain why he felt such a strong allegiance to Britain, perhaps because he found it difficult to define what it meant to be British. Not just what it meant to him, but what it meant to anybody born in this beautiful, damp, varied country that was thankfully free of poisonous spiders. The British rarely seemed to have spent any time defining themselves. It was a mark of self-confidence, he believed—Britain was a trading nation whose instinct was to absorb influences and peoples—Jews, Poles, Afro-Caribbeans, Bangladeshis, Pakistanis, and Russians—rather than peevishly trumpet its superiority. He liked to belong to a country that was suspicious of cheerleading claptrap, where the goosestep had never caught on and satire refused to hold its tongue for long.

He loved the countryside with an unsentimental passion. His earliest memories were of school trips there, particularly a visit to Winston Churchill's family home at Chartwell. It was said of its views across the Weald of Kent that, in the dark days of May 1940, it inspired Churchill to promise nothing but "blood, toil, tears, and sweat" because it was better to die fighting than live with the shame of slavery. Like Churchill, Ed would suffer bouts of both belligerence and black-dog depression. But unlike Winston, who never saw the value of silence, Ed often disguised his true feelings behind bloody-minded indifference. And in that, he was more like that other Winston, the reluctant hero of George Orwell's nightmare parable *1984*. Like Winston Smith, he yearned, without much hope, for the ordinary pleasures of humanity—a walk in the countryside or the act of lovemaking.

He remembered the kindness and fairness of his teachers in Tower Hamlets, their colour-blind humanity. He remembered his mother helping him with his homework and afterwards reading to him from Dickens's *Great Expectations* and Kipling's *Kim*. Looking back further, he remembered building a snowman in Weaver's Fields and being taken to meet Santa Claus every year. He ate Marmite on toast and Wotsits. He hid behind the sofa during *Doctor Who*.

Ed's father was born in British India and his mother in Birmingham. His father was an emigrant from one country and a newcomer in two. He moved against his will from India to Pakistan, and from there to England by choice. He was a former Merchant Navy officer who arrived in England in 1963 and set himself up as restaurateur on Brick Lane. He was a stern man, of flinty and adamant Tory views, who gave his sons the names of Plantagenet kings. Father and sons were never close, nor were Edward and his younger brother, Geoffrey. The first love of Edward's life was his mother, and she was fiercely ambitious for him. She was a shopkeeper's daughter with aspirations. She was the one who demanded he apply to Oxford because "if there are going to be Muslims in the upper class, then Edward is going to be one of them." She didn't like her firstborn to be called Ed "as if he was a taxi-driver or a road sweeper." She was a bookkeeper by training, and she worked with his father at the restaurant.

The focus of Ed's early life was home and junior school. His days were filled with reading, writing practise, drawing, mathematics, and physical exercise. Family life was close-knit. His parents were not particularly wealthy, but neither were they poor. They lived in a narrow Georgian terrace in Whitechapel and avidly listened to Radio 4. They took care to ensure that Ed did not fall in with the Brick Lane Mafia or the Cannon Street Posse.

A teacher organised boxing lessons three nights a week and thanks to his father's steely insistence, Ed learned the mechanics of jump rope, speed bag, and heavy bag. He went from junior school to secondary school and did well. He grew in confidence and was quick to put his hand up in class.

His confidence was short-lived. At school, the other boys soon tired of his eagerness to please. They shouted "big head" at him and drew stick pictures of him with a bloated head. In response, he became withdrawn and introverted. He talked quietly to himself. The ringleader of those tormenting him was a new arrival from Bangladesh who lived in a council flat in Stepney Green. One winter afternoon, Ed followed his tormentor home and cornered him in a dark alley, where he proceeded to use his fists to pummel him into submission. They left him alone after that, but the damage was done. He became wary and suspicious. He had trouble making friends.

Nevertheless, he continued to do well at school, and in

accordance with his mother's wishes he applied—and was accepted—to read history and English at Balliol College, Oxford. At Balliol, he led a curiously dualistic life. By day, "Ed" marched in solidarity with the oppressed peoples of Bosnia and Palestine and addressed fellow students with a bullhorn from an upturned milk crate. By night, "Edward" wore a dinner jacket to dine with the warden of the college. He wrote his dissertation on "Modernism and Post Colonial Enchantment." He continued to box and continued to win in the ring. He told a friend, "The rich don't know how to fight." It was at Balliol that he was approached in the usual way and offered a career in the Intelligence Services. He refused. If anything, it caused him to pay greater attention to his Muslim heritage.

On coming down from Oxford and securing a job at HSBC Bank in the city of London, he registered for part-time Saturday morning classes in Arabic at the School of Oriental and African Studies so he could read the Koran in its original language. He joined the Islamic Society of Britain. The ISB was a home for middle-class Muslims who aligned themselves to the Egyptian Muslim Brotherhood and Palestinian Hamas and wanted to make Britain more of an Islamic country.

His flirtation with Islam was short-lived, however. Two experiences turned him away from it. They occurred during a placement with a bank in Jeddah, Saudi Arabia. It was there that he observed African women in black abayas scavenging amongst the rubbish bins outside wealthy Saudi residences, and in the slum known as Karatina, a perversion of "quarantine," that he first saw naked poverty: thousands of fellow Muslims who had been living in Saudi Arabia for decades were deemed illegal and abandoned to cardboard shanties under a flyover. It was then that it dawned on him that Britain, his home, had given refuge to thousands of black Africans from Somalia and Sudan. He had seen them in their droves in Whitechapel. They had their own mosques and were given council housing. Many Muslims enjoyed a better lifestyle in non-Muslim Britain than they did in Muslim Saudi Arabia.

The second event was the cataclysm of September 11, 2001. It was late afternoon on a Tuesday in Riyadh, and the bank was due to close. Ed got a call from a friend who worked at the military hospital who told him that one of the twin towers had been hit by a plane. He rushed into the manager's office and switched on CNN. Soon the small office was filled with Saudis, some in Western business suits, but most in long white *thobes* and red-checked headscarves. On the screen there was a vast dark cloud rising from lower Manhattan, and all around him his colleagues were wide-eyed and silent. Awestruck. Then the second plane struck, and one of the men said, "Wow! Hit it!"

Then they were all smiling.

Ed walked out of the bank and did not go back. Later that night, he would watch a member of the Saudi royal family describe the attacks as a Jewish-American conspiracy. The prince said that not a single Jew had been killed in the attacks because they had been warned to stay away. As for the American assertion that seventeen of the nineteen hijackers were from Saudi Arabia, he dismissed it as ridiculous and said they were regular passengers, tourists, and students.

What Ed did next he would always find difficult to explain, as if his actions were questions instead of answers. He caught a flight back to the UK and walked into a Royal Navy recruitment centre. Anger and restlessness both played a part, along with a sense that he had to do something in response to the attacks. His father had also been a seaman. All reasons, but none of them sufficient to explain his actions—maybe sometimes, he told himself, we do a thing in order to find out the real reason for it.

In the navy, Ed learned something of the arts of navigation and seamanship during a couple of months on a minesweeper in the Irish Sea. But the British state had other plans for him. After completing the officer's training course at the Royal Naval College, he was immediately selected for the Joint Services Intelligence Organisation in Chicksands. He spent no time on ships after that, working entirely with land forces on campaigns far from the sea. After his initial training at Ashford, which included learning Pashto, he worked briefly on "special duties" in Afghanistan. Then, in 2003, he was plucked out of Afghanistan and sent to Iraq. He spent the next few months alongside MI6 officers on a fruitless and frustrating hunt for weapons of mass destruction, followed by many more months of hunting down former Baathists, while around him Iraq descended into chaos.

He gave up for a while and went back to banking, but it wasn't long before he bowed to the inevitable. In early 2005, he joined "The Firm"—MI6—and once he'd completed his training, became a full-fledged spy. He was assigned to the AF-PAK Controllerate and tasked with developing relationships with potential informants within the ISI. MI6 wanted an asset inside the ISI for the simple reason that the ISI had so many assets spread across the range of terrorist networks that operated under the "umbrella" of the Taliban, and the requirement to know what was going on in the mind of the enemy had been given extra importance because of the 7/7 bombings and the upcoming deployment of British armed forces to Helmand.

A month after his arrival in Afghanistan, a covert MI5 operation uncovered a Pakistani intelligence cell operating out of Manchester University, where a young student in Oldham died of an asthma attack brought on by smoking heroin, and in Islamabad, Javid Aslam Khan answered the phone to a panicked cell member on his first overseas assignment, a young Punjabi named Tariq Mahoon who was ripe for turning.

Once turned, Ed was made his handler—a twenty-four hour assignment with all other activities on hold. For the next five years, Tariq Mahoon had been Six's eyes and ears inside the ISI, passing information on the links between Pakistani intelligence and insurgent groups operating in Afghanistan and the adjacent tribal areas, and the comings and goings of British-born Asians to the terrorist training camps there.

But now Tariq was dead, shot by Khan, and Ed was unsure what that meant for him.

15 ❖

Going Underground

When feasible, Ed preferred to travel above ground, so he took a bus from Paddington, travelling south down Park Lane past the Animals In War Memorial and, at the edge of Green Park, the half-built Bomber Command Memorial. Sometimes it felt like the whole city was a mausoleum, its open spaces punctuated by monuments to public sacrifice. The bus went around the back of Buckingham Palace and down Vauxhall Bridge Road towards Vauxhall Cross, the Inca-pyramid-on-the-Thames that was home to MI6.

He was allowed through the first airlock but stopped at reception and informed his pass had been revoked. He was given a piece of card with a handwritten Whitehall address on it and told to report there immediately. Slinging his rucksack over his shoulder, he set off east along Albert Embankment and crossed the river again at Westminster Bridge.

Craig's Court was at the north end of Whitehall, situated an equal distance between the horseback statue of Charles II and the Banqueting House, the site of Charles I's execution. It was a cul-de-sac so unremarkable that Ed had never noticed its existence before. He stood at attention before a set of wooden double doors in a stone portico with "Telephone Exchange" written on them and smiled up at a camera. The doors clicked open.

Roland Totty from Human Resources was waiting for him inside.

"Bloody bad news about Tariq," Totty told him, leading him down an unremarkable corridor with tiled walls. "Queen Bee is furious."

"With me?"

"Best if I leave it to her to deliver the news."

Ed didn't like Totty. He was a Home Counties boy who wore red socks and imagined it made him interesting. He lived in Putney or Chiswick, somewhere like that on the District line, and he struggled to pay school fees. Ed thought him a buffoon.

"Where are we going?" Ed asked.

"We're going underground," Totty replied, light-heartedly, "like the song."

Ed could imagine what Paul Weller would make of that. He remembered what Weller had said when the Prime Minister, a former Eton pupil and member of the cadet corps, had described Eton Rifles as his favourite song: "It wasn't intended as a fucking jolly drinking song."

They went through a fire door, down a spiral staircase and the length of an underground corridor, opening a series of internal doors with mesh-lined windows, and down a further set of concrete steps to an older, mustier tunnel that opened out into a suite of mothballed basement offices.

Totty stopped in front of a scuffed steel door.

"Far as I go old chap," he said. "She's in there waiting for you."

*

It was said of Samantha Burns (Queen Bee to her underlings) that she was not even a household name in her own household and the only time her name appeared in newsprint was when she shimmied over to the palace to upgrade her gong. She was a woman of secrets who had come up via Hutcheson's Grammar School, Glasgow University, Treasury, Six, and then the call to attend the newly formed National Security Council in the Cabinet Office. The remarkable thing about Burns was that she was so lively and twinkly-eyed, and always ready to kick off her heels and bustle about in stockinged feet. It was as if her anonymity was not a product of the usual institutional greyness but rather of an essential slipperiness, an ability to bend light around her and thereby render herself invisible. She delivered bad news with an emollient smile and expressed friendly concern when people had done wrong. Crisis never disturbed her bonhomie.

She was sitting on a plastic chair in one of the basement rooms with a tall skinny cappuccino in one hand. The object of her attention was plastered across several walls: a mishmash of satellite photos, mug shots, maps, receipts, waybills, freight certificates, Post-it notes, bills of lading, company accounts, bank records, transcripts of phone intercepts, letters, and newspaper cuttings. Things were crossed out and new bits superimposed and glued on. Strings of red thread made connections as complex as any spider's web.

"It's known as the Khyber Collage," Burns explained.

Ed had heard of the Khyber Collage. He'd even seen it mentioned in footnotes in classified reports in Kabul. It was said to chart the growth of the broad and diverse movement that was radical Islamic militancy, going back decades to its roots in the Jihad against the Soviets and progressing to the current day. Depending on who you believed, it was either a testament to diligent decades-long research or a metaphor for rampant paranoia. Ed struggled to remember what he'd heard of those responsible for its creation, not much more than gossip really, some kind of black ops outfit born of military intelligence known only as "The Department." It had evolved from an even older outfit, the Afghan Guides, which had set up shop in Peshawar in the eighties and provided military assistance to the collection of Mujahideen groups known as the Peshawar Seven that were based there. The Department had limped on through the nineties when no one gave much of a shit about Afghanistan, before enjoying a renaissance post-9/11. It was shut down after a controversy in 2005. Bodies had turned up in unexpected places: a bomb factory in Glasgow, a park bench in St. James Park, a seaside town on the Kent coast.

At the centre of the board where the red string met, there was a photograph cut from a newspaper clipping of a slim, donnish looking man with a high forehead and bifocals perched on his nose. It was Major-General Javid Aslam Khan, colloquially known as the Hidden Hand. Khan was the former head of the ISI, the Directorate of Inter-Services Intelligence, and generally regarded as one of the key members of Pakistan's Invisible Government, a cabal of "retired" military officers that formed a much more powerful counterpart to Pakistan's democratically elected one.

If you believed the collage, it was Khan who was responsible for channelling Saudi and American funds to the most unsavoury and extremist elements of the Mujahideen during the Soviet occupation. It was Khan who was directly responsible for the brutal civil war that followed the Soviet withdrawal from Afghanistan, when the Mujahideen groups turned on each other and fought over the rubble. It was Khan who created and nurtured the Taliban as a bulwark against foreign intervention. And when that failed spectacularly, it was Khan who fed and watered the terrorist networks, many of them former

Mujahideen, like Hekmatyar and Haqqani, who were now killing British and American servicemen. Ed realised that somebody had been keeping the collage up-to-date. There were links from Khan to recently formed groups including the *Lashkar-e-Jhangvi*, whose specialty was assassinating Shi'a; the Zarqawis, a bloodthirsty band of Pakistanis who operated in Kandahar; and the White Taliban, a motley collection of Europeans and Uzbeks who operated in Zabul province.

"Quite something, isn't it?" Burns rolled her eyes in the direction of the back of the room, and with a start, Ed realised they were not alone. There was a large, brooding presence in the shadows: a black man straddling a plastic chair.

"This is Jonah," Burns explained, "official custodian of the collage. I won't bother with his surname. He used to run the only other significant asset we had inside the ISI, and he's the only serving officer we have who's actually met Khan. Got on like a house on fire, isn't that right? What did you make of him, Jonah?"

"He's an unscrupulous bastard," Jonah replied. His verging-on-posh accent, with its gliding vowels, was at odds with his appearance, much more so than Ed's. "He's always happy to play both ends against the middle."

Burns looked pointedly at Ed.

"You're tired, aren't you? I expect you're angry as well."

"My agent was killed."

"There's no point getting all riled up because the Americans didn't give us fair warning. We all knew it would be that way."

"With respect, ma'am, nobody told me that it would be that way."

"It's Khan you should be angry at. Khan killed Tariq."

"I listened to it happen," Ed replied.

"Of course you did. And now you want revenge. Isn't that right?"

Ed opened his mouth and abruptly closed it again. Revenge

wasn't supposed to be a motivation for action, not out loud at least. But Queen Bee was right. He'd lost an agent, and he wanted someone to pay.

"If it's feasible," he said, "yes, of course."

"And there's the nub. Did Totty tell you the facts of life? The PM wants us out of Afghanistan double quick, all shoulders to the wheel to ensure a smooth exit. Did he tell you that the PM is proposing to hold a joint Anglo-Pakistan peace initiative for Afghanistan?"

"No, he didn't tell me that."

Where was she going with this? Everybody knew that the last thing the Pakistanis wanted was peace in Afghanistan. They preferred the place in turmoil.

"The status quo cannot hold," Burns explained. "We need new choice architecture."

"Choice architecture?"

"The PM's calling for a nudge."

"A nudge?"

"We've got to get out with a modicum of dignity intact. This isn't going to be another Basra."

"I'm sorry, but what does this have to do with me?"

"Nothing. That's my point."

"I'm sorry?"

She smiled her meaningless smile. "This gives me no pleasure, but you've left me no choice. Your agent's dead, and the Americans have made it plain you're not welcome back in Kabul, or anywhere else for that matter. We need a new approach to intelligence, and I'm sorry to say, you've ruled yourself out of it."

"You brought me here to tell me that?"

"No, I brought you here to tell you that you're suspended, pending a disciplinary inquiry."

16

The List

Lurking had become almost second nature to him. Ed stood in the shadow of a doorway with his hands in his pockets and a bag at his feet. London was blurred by autumn condensation, softened somehow. Maybe it was him. Was he becoming sentimental? He wasn't meeting an agent this time. There was nothing covert or clandestine here.

The object of his attention was a small Brick Lane curry house on the corner of Heneage Street. It was well after midnight, and the restaurant was closed for the night, but there was still movement inside. People were clearing up, stacking chairs on tables, and sweeping the floor. Eventually, the front door opened again, and the staff emerged. The last one out pulled down the bottom of the metal shutter from the shop awning and padlocked it. Terse goodbyes were said.

A stooped elderly man in the white shirt and black trousers of a waiter zipped up his windbreaker, walked a few feet, and then paused on the pavement to light a cigarette, the flame of the lighter briefly illuminating his face before he set off again.

Ed followed. He fell into step alongside him as he approached the southern end of Brick Lane.

The man gave him a sidelong glance.

"I didn't expect to see you," he said.

"Hello, Dad."

There had been a period in his twenties when Ed had been angry with his father, but as he approached his middle years he had achieved a kind of accommodation.

The old man looked at the black bag in his hand. "You need somewhere to stay?"

"Just for a few weeks."

"Come on, then."

They crossed behind the East London mosque on Fieldgate Street and turned down one of the narrow one-way streets. People had put their pink recycling bags out and they spilled across the pavement, resembling an obstacle course.

They stopped in front of a green door with three different locks.

Inside, the hallway was narrow and smelled damp. There were chauffeur cards and pizza flyers spread across the floor.

"You know how to find your room."

He lay on his bed and stared upwards at the triangular prism on the ceiling, bending light's path: *The Dark Side of the Moon*. A poster for an album released four years before he was born, an album about things that make people mad.

It was like travelling back in time. Nothing had changed. A bed as narrow as a coffin and posters on the ceiling because the walls were floor-to-ceiling bookcases, arranged with a librarian's care. His father called it the submariner's cabin. The last time he lay here was in the immediate aftermath of the breakup of a relationship. Then, as now, his life had seemed in ruins.

He rolled over and looked under the bed. His 2000 AD collection remained there in cardboard boxes, each individual comic stored in a clear plastic sleeve. Once upon a time, he had imagined himself as Johnny Alpha, the mutant bounty hunter who tracked down his own kind across an apocalyptic landscape. It was funny really, when you thought about it. He rolled back. Above him there was a ledge and wedged between Milan Kundera and Hanif Kureishi, a bundle of letters, communications from his mother during his first year at Oxford.

And the List: the archaeology of a failed romance.

As he was leaving, after she'd told him their relationship was over, his doctor fiancée had handed him a piece of paper. He remembered going out to the car and sitting and reading the contents. It was a list of who he was. It was more than just a parting shot; she'd clearly been working on it for weeks, if not months. It was a compilation of difficult truths in ink, pencil, and fluorescent marker. As badly written as her prescriptions. It had been folded and unfolded. It had clearly been scrunched up and then flattened out at some stage. There was a translucent smudge of olive oil and several burgundy wine-rings.

It said:

Who are YOU?
Alien
mask-wearing/stealth-loving
Angry idealist
~~good in bed~~
Autistic spectrum
Mama's boy
warmonger
JANISSARY
thief
SPY

His first act had been to neatly fold back the bottom line before tearing it off, carefully removing the word SPY. *Never advertise the fact of what you are. Always clear up after yourself.* He imagined how much that would have annoyed her. He hadn't been angry with her. The List was difficult to argue with. He took it as a measure of her frustration and despair. It was a variant of the questions that she had asked him throughout their short engagement: Who are you? What are you? Why do you do what you do?

He remembered one stolen afternoon together in the Print and Drawings Room of the Victoria & Albert Museum, and in response to an innocent question, he'd explained to her that the Janissaries were Christian boys captured by the Ottoman Turks in the fourteenth century, forcibly converted to Islam and trained to be soldiers in the Sultan's army, at that time the greatest army in the world. They were neither freemen nor ordinary slaves. They were supervised twenty-four hours a day, indoctrinated, and subjected to severe discipline. They were prohibited from taking up any skill other than war. As a consequence, they were ferocious and utterly loyal.

"They had no choice about it," he told her. "They had fought to erase their own civilisation. They had nowhere else to turn to."

She had waited until that evening before ambushing him. "Is that how you see yourself, as a Janissary?"

"I am what I am by choice," he'd replied.

"You wish!"

She hadn't mentioned it again, though she'd clearly saved it up for the List.

On the subject of the Iraq war, she had always been forthright: "You're an apologist for Blair."

He wasn't that. After all, he'd been there—he'd flown into Baghdad in April 2003 expecting it to be an Aladdin's cave of documents with evidence of WMDs and links between

Saddam and Al-Qaeda. In the days following, he'd sat in living rooms with agents who confessed they had no idea where the stuff was. These were the same sources that, before the war, had been telling anyone who cared to listen that a WMD could be launched inside forty-five minutes. They'd have said anything to be rid of Saddam. He felt that the endless to-and-fro over whether the public had been lied to about the threat in the build-up to the Iraq war served as a kind of smokescreen for a wider and more fundamental failing, the sheer incompetence of the endeavour.

"I don't mind that we did it," Ed had told her. "I mind that we did it so badly. Nobody gave a thought to how the country would stand up to invasion or what would come after. They didn't understand Iraq's tribal and social structures or its religious divide. I don't think Blair even knew the difference between a Shi'ite and a Sunni when we went in. He was the guy that put the New into New Labour. It was all about the future. Nobody was interested in history or past mistakes. They didn't read history books. They really thought that things could only get better. We charged into Basra with no thought for the consequences and to make our lives easy, we handed control of the city over to a bunch of Iranian-backed death-squads who went to work on the populace with electric cables and power drills."

"So why didn't you do something about it?" she yelled.

"What could I do?"

She sneered. "You're pathetic."

It would be the same in Helmand in 2006. Another failure. A too-eager government and the usual gaggle of over-ambitious generals had convinced themselves that a British contingent could deploy down there in soft-skinned vehicles on an operation in which not a shot would be fired. No one gave any thought to the skill with which the Mujahideen had used roadside bombs to disrupt Soviet armoured convoys down there in the eighties. No one imagined a repeat of that. No one gave a thought to what happened the last time a British army went down there. A thousand British and Indian troops slaughtered at the Battle of Maiwand in 1880. Nobody outside of a university in Britain remembered that. But they did in Helmand. They might not have the Internet or TV or much schooling, but they did have oral history. Tales they told themselves. Mostly about how they beat the invaders or died trying. Resistance was in their psyche and their folklore. They even had their own Joan of Arc: at Maiwand, a young woman named Malalai had ripped off her veil and used it as a standard to lead the Pashtuns to victory, shouting out: "If you do not fall in the battle of Maiwand, by God someone is saving you as a token of shame."

You couldn't beat people who believed that kind of hokum.

He remembered sitting in the car outside the house that he was no longer welcome in. He'd folded the List up and driven the car east, back to his roots in Whitechapel, the immigrant enclave that had first propelled him out into the world. He remembered thinking that he was ashamed of spying, of how little good it had done. It was a kind of drug, similar to heroin in its effects, a fetish that attracted violence and criminality. The realisation had come to him suddenly, here on this bed, as if it had been waiting for the chance to find him alone. He'd suppressed it and got on with his job. But now there was nothing to hold it at bay.

It wasn't just that his life felt like a succession of lies, it was that he felt like he was lost in a maze, a hall of mirrors, and the faces that stared back at him were distorted beyond all recognition.

17

On Tenterhooks

The Gulberg cellar reeked of blood, with a sly background whiff of piss and shit. The hanging man's veins were pumping out blood faster than a halal chicken, as if they were in a hurry to be rid of it.

Noman took a long and unsatisfying drag on his cigarette and tried to remember the first time he realised that blood had a smell. There had been so much of it over the years, buckets full of it, bathtubs even. It was difficult to remember. He felt sure that it would have been in a space much like this one, either a cell or a basement, or in the "fingernail factory," the ISI's purpose-built interrogation facility in Islamabad. Khan would have been there, of course, shepherding him through the first weeks of his induction in the methods of intelligence gathering. Khan had been so keen to show him the ropes. Somebody else would have been inflicting the damage, of course. Khan didn't like to get his hands dirty. Noman did remember Khan telling him to pay attention to the particulars of anatomy and painting: "You must find within yourself the knowledge, assurance, and dexterity of a surgeon but also the boldness, imagination, and daring of a baroque painter." Eager to please, he had learned the names of muscles, organs, bones, and veins. He had surfed the Internet for paintings. He had learned to wield the blade and the baton with both care and abandon.

Badchodiyaan! It was all bullshit. Torture wasn't an art or a science. Just because there were swags of blood on the wall it didn't make him Caravaggio. He was a mechanic salvaging scraps in a wrecker's yard.

As ever in the aftermath of an interrogation, Noman felt a wearying sense of disappointment. Every torture victim was initially fascinating and unique. It was a ritual as febrile as courtship. You ingested a life. It filled you with information, some of it useful. But the violence wore through the uniqueness so quickly. Soon the victim's will was gone, and all that was left was finite flesh with its dumb obedience to physics—cut deeply enough and this comes off, whack hard enough and that ruptures.

It was always a let down.

Noman stubbed out the Flake on the victim's skin. There was barely a response, just a soft and plaintive sigh. The man had resigned himself to death.

"Don't be afraid," Noman told him, whispering in his ear. "I love you, and I will shortly send you to Paradise."

This much Noman knew. The victim's name was Ghazan. He was a battlefield medic trained by the infidel Americans in the eighties, back when they were doing their utmost to turf the Soviets out of Afghanistan. Heady times. Back then, anybody could set themselves up as freedom fighter, and Mujahideen groups sprouted like mushrooms. They'd put a Kalashnikov in your hands and point you at the border. The Russians had gunned them down in droves, of course; hence the need for medics.

For the last few years, Ghazan had made his living puttering around the tribal areas on a motorbike, providing first aid to sick and wounded Taliban fighters in their mountain hideouts. In return, he'd been offered food and lodging and occasionally a few rupees. In 2008, he had come to the attention of Baitullah Mehsud, the black-bearded head of the feared and powerful Mehsud clan and leader of the newly formed Tehrik-i-Taliban, the Pakistani Taliban. Ghazan's training as a medic held great personal appeal to Baitullah, who was afflicted with diabetes and peripheral arterial disease in his legs. Deemed trustworthy, Ghazan had become his personal physician and remained so until just before Baitullah's death in a drone strike in August 2009. The recent rapid increase in the tempo of drone strikes and several close shaves with Hellfire missiles had forced Ghazan to park-up his bike and curtail his activities. For the last two months, he'd been holed up in the South Waziristan market town of Wana. It was there that he had come to Noman's attention. Noman arranged to have Ghazan watched and followed, and when he next made an attempt to leave the town, Noman had him detained at a police checkpoint and brought here, in the trunk of a car, to the basement of Tariq's parents' house in Lahore.

On the subject of the House of War and its elusive, shadowy leader Abu Dukhan, Ghazan had little to reveal. He claimed that he had no direct experience with the man or the organization. He had never treated any of its fighters and had no knowledge of the group's whereabouts. Like others in Baitullah's circle, he had heard whispers of an *itami* device being prepared in the mountains, but he had not been privy to any secret conversations. Under interrogation, he had revealed one interesting piece of information, though. It was said that a mullah, who had fought and lost his leg at the Battle of Jalalabad, had officiated at the wedding *nikah* of Abu Dukhan's youngest son to a local girl in Bajaur Agency.

Noman felt the first flicker of excitement at the news, a stirring of the loins. After weeks of fruitless searching, he had finally uncovered a clue. It wasn't much, he knew that. More than ten thousand fighters had been involved in the disastrous assault on Jalalabad and one-legged mullahs were ten-a-penny in the tribal areas, but it was a start. It demonstrated that Abu Dukhan wasn't infallible. He hadn't entirely erased his tracks.

He realised that while he had been standing there thinking, Ghazan had bled out. The man was dead, and there was no point lingering. He banged on the door to be let out.

"Clear up the mess," he told Raja Mahfouz, once the door was opened. "Dump the body in a ditch."

He climbed the stairs to the waiting widow.

Throughout the arid parts of the earth, almost everyone sees Paradise as an oasis. Was that what Ghazan had been thinking of there at the end, a lush garden in the desert? For most of Noman's army colleagues, the image of Paradise was the military cantonment with its clean, neatly signposted streets gleaming with antique artillery pieces. But when Noman dreamt of Paradise, he dreamt of a world rid of people. Everything engulfed in brilliant, cleansing fire.

He had slept, woken, fucked, and now lay limbs akimbo, spread-eagled like a starfish beside the widow. He'd forgotten that sex could do this, cause total dissolution, cast him into the void of his dreams and then reel him back out again, scourged.

The widow was so gloriously unhinged, a study in Stockholm syndrome. He'd shared with her his belief that Ghazan would lead him to the House of War, and then he'd described the act of torture in all its colourful detail. What he'd mistaken at first for horror and agitation had turned out to be feverish arousal—during the telling she had developed the glazed, hilarious expression of an Abu Ghraib guard. A little girl caught in a dirty act. He'd winked like an over-friendly uncle and told her what he was going to do to Khan once he proved that he had betrayed his country.

He felt like he'd died and been reborn. He felt as bliss-fully content as an alley cat. Nothing would now stop him from finding the House of War. But then, as abrupt as a dawn raid, a question came needling into his brain: what if he found them? What then? He doubted that he'd be satisfied with break-ing up the group, killing its members, and confiscating their bomb-making materials. Stripping Abu Dukhan of his ano-nymity in a basement cell didn't hold any particular appeal. So what was it that he wanted from the House of War?

If he was honest with himself, part of him wanted them to have a bomb, realistically a dirty bomb (the army wasn't miss-ing any of its hundred-and-ten A-bombs). He imagined it as a thick coat of chopped-up radioactive waste packed around an explosive core, like a sweet *laddoo* ball rolled in coconut flakes. He tried to picture them using it. Where? America and Europe were too risky. Afghanistan, maybe. He could see an explosion on the Shomali Plain, a cloud of deadly particles sweeping towards the massive American base at Bagram, eviscerating filthy, Indian-sympathising Tajik villages along the way. But what if they decided to use it in Pakistan? It made his imagi-nation soar. A mighty upheaval that swept aside the networks of corruption and patronage that were throttling his country, a baptism of fire that would see a stronger and more determined Pakistan reborn. People would have to die, of course, but there were already far too many Pakistanis, too many for the land they found themselves in, and more all the time. What would it be like to wake up and find the world as it was in his dreams?

His phone beeped, a text message. He picked it up from the bedside table and peered at the screen. It was from his wife, Mumayyaz.

You're a cold-hearted bastard.

She was right. He was. But he was also a man of vision and daring, a man who had chosen to live by his dreams.

18

Tell Me How This Ends

Afghanistan was as dismal a failure as Iraq, and no one wanted someone like Ed hanging around as a visible reminder of that failure.

They didn't want to be reminded that he'd spent Election Day in 2009 on an Afghan Army base, and while he kicked his heels waiting for Tariq to show up for a meet, he watched as the Colonel commanding the base set up an unregistered polling booth and stuffed the ballot boxes with several thousand votes for President Hamid Karzai.

They didn't want to be reminded that he'd spent a night on the border near Spin Boldak in Kandahar Province, also waiting for Tariq, and watched as trucks full of opium were escorted over the border into Pakistan by men working for the Afghan border police.

Most of all, they didn't want to be reminded that the only reason the British Army was in Helmand Province was because they were already in Helmand Province. We were there because we were there. And because we were there, we were there some more.

The Afghan government was a criminal syndicate made up of warlords, drug-runners, and thieves. British soldiers weren't combating terrorists but instead were fighting and dying in local political disputes. The Taliban was just a catch-all phrase for people who didn't like foreigners.

The reasons behind the war were long forgotten. It was no longer a war of retribution for 9/11, no longer a war of democratic nation-building or educating girls. It was merely a place where soldiers were sent by politicians to pretend to win, even as they died. It was now just an unending treadmill of pride, money, heroism, and national prestige.

Blah, blah, blah . . . yadda, yadda, yadda . . . give it a rest, Ed! Who do you think you are, Cassandra? It was all right to hear this stuff from whining liberals in the media, but from a serving officer? It wasn't acceptable.

He'd done good work; everyone knew that. He'd certainly worked hard, in both Iraq and Afghanistan—it was just that with every log he turned in and every upbeat assessment he shot down, the more misguided Britain's overseas adventures came to seem.

Nobody liked that, least of all top floor at Vauxhall Cross. After all, they had almost completed the transition from an intelligence-gathering organisation to a sexed-up, dossier-producing propaganda arm of the government of the day.

Consequently, there was no one to speak up for him at the disciplinary hearing. The prosecuting officer described his regrettable transformation from a poster boy for diversity in intelligence (the go-to guy on Pakistan, South Asia, the Third World, multiculturalism, whatever seemed alien and incomprehensible) to a resentful thug who took no care of his appearance and even less of his surroundings. Called as a witness, Totty described how he'd railed against Upper Caucasia—the double-barrelled boys and girls who populated the upper floors at Vauxhall Cross—and raged obsessively against the Americans and their intelligence agencies and their oh-so-special forces. According to Totty, he seemed to hate them more than the ISI.

No extenuating circumstances were offered. Ed made no defence. He admitted assaulting the CIA head of station in Kabul, and he was summarily dismissed.

Jonah, the taciturn keeper of the Khyber Collage, whom Ed had last seen in a basement under Whitehall, was waiting for him in the corridor outside.

"I'm sorry," he said. "It's a bloody mess."

Ed shrugged. There was nothing to say.

Jonah scribbled a mobile number on a piece of blank card and handed it to him. "I've got a job for you if you're interested. It's not much. A courier run. The usual guy has ducked out on me, and I need a replacement. You'd be doing me a favour."

Ed took the card and two days later, in the absence of anything else to do, he agreed to the job.

On the last Thursday of that month, he collected a briefcase full of dollars from a man in a hotel room within shuttle distance of Heathrow and boarded an Emirates flight to Dubai. On arrival, he was driven to a city-centre hotel by his old friend, Dai Llewellyn. He lay on the bed in the air-conditioned chill of a hotel room with the case beside him. An hour or so later, he received a call from a Somali in one of the suites on the upper floors. He rode up in the elevator. He knocked on the door. The Somali escorted him into the suite where a woman, entirely disguised by a black burqa, was waiting. After he had handed over the briefcase and the money was counted to everyone's satisfaction, the woman left, and he left soon after. He went straight down to the car park and was driven back to the airport.

In the days following, Ed walked and ran across the city. He ranged along the Thames Path from the Barrier to Richmond. He followed the network of canals. In the gothic undergrowth of Tower Hamlets Cemetery, he watched a fox and her cubs emerge warily from behind a gravestone.

After a week, Jonah contacted him to tell him that the usual guy was back and his services were no longer required.

"Thanks for helping me out," Jonah told him. "I'll let you know if anything else comes up."

"Don't bother," Ed told him.

To all appearances, his career as a spy was over.

19 ❖

Comprehensive Logistic Solutions

On a crisp Monday morning, Ed walked like a gift into the life of Sameenah Kassar, the exasperated proprietor of J&K Cargo and Travel Limited.

Ed strode past the grim Victorian portal of the job centre on Settle Street, past the crowd of lost souls (Poles, Estonians, Somalis, Bangladeshis, and Pakistanis like himself, but with lousy English) who hung around outside, towards the impatient blare of car horns. The traffic was backed up to Commercial Street.

He crossed the road, easing between bumpers, and went past the Somali corner shop and nodded to the butcher in his bloody apron outside Hazara Meat Trading and the Sylheti barber standing beside his revolving candy cane. Then he stepped, deft as a boxer, between the sacks and suitcases freshly arrived from Lahore by way of Heathrow, which were spilled haphazardly across the tarmac behind the abandoned J&K van that was blocking the road.

Ignoring the scowl of Nasir, Sameenah's dolt of a nephew

who was on crutches with his leg in plaster, Ed went right up to her and said in his politest English, "Can I help?"

Sameenah Kassar was a small, round woman in her midfifties with a sonorous voice and a piercing eye. She was wearing a crimson-red *dupatta* and a similarly red mackintosh, and as she looked around, with her hands on her hips, Ed thought she resembled the put-a-brave-face-on-it ringmaster of an out of control circus. The clowns were in the ascendancy. In the last week, she had been struck a triple blow. On Tuesday, she had been disqualified from driving her beloved BMW X5 for eight weeks and fined £200. On Wednesday night, Nasir had been struck down by a hit-and-run driver on Whitechapel High Street. And now, to cap it all, her most reliable driver, Mohammed Akram, had flung his keys on the pavement, accused her of being a slave driver, and marched off in the direction of Wapping, leaving half a van full of luggage spread across the street.

"I won't hear of it," Sameenah was saying to her nephew when Ed intervened. "I'm not hiring one of your good-fornothing Bengali friends again, and I'm most certainly not hiring another bloody relative. I want someone with more than two brain cells to rub together."

It seemed like she didn't hear him the first time so Ed repeated the question, "Madam, can I help?"

Sameenah looked him slowly up and down, taking in his polished shoes, his pressed trousers, his calloused and capable hands, and the spark of desperation in his eyes.

"Do I know you?"

Ed nodded. "I'm Rifaz Malik's son."

Sameenah frowned, seemingly oblivious to the increasingly angry shouts and staccato car horns. "The one that went to Oxford?"

"That's right."

"I thought you worked at the Bank of England?"

There didn't seem to be any point in correcting her.

"You want me to move the van?" he asked.

Her mind made up, Sameenah grasped Ed by the sleeve and pressed the truck's keys into his palm. "I expect the best of you, and I expect it now."

"You won't be disappointed."

Quickly and without fuss, pausing only to placate the grid-locked traffic with a cheery wave, he cleared the road of baggage, emptied the van of its last bags, and moved it out of the way. Next, he found a space in the crowded lanes to park it without taking off anyone's wing mirrors. Then he returned to sort the luggage into local deliveries by minivan and a larger consignment for onward transfer to the Bradford office. He did all this under the suspicious and resentful eye of the spurned would-be heir, Nasir. *I'm going to have to watch him*, Ed thought.

At the end of the day, as expected, Sameenah offered Ed a job.

J&K Cargo and Travel offered comprehensive logistic solutions ranging from a courier and cargo booking service specialising in fast deliveries to Pakistan and worldwide, to secure and reliable same-day/next-day money transfer, to the provision of tailored packages for the minor and major pilgrimages to Mecca, the Umrah, and the Hajj, all of it overseen by its larger-than-life founder, Sameenah Kassar.

She was an observant widow with a prodigious appetite; every lunchtime and afternoon prayer, a feast of lamb chops, dry meat, and naan bread was hand-delivered to her office by Tayyabs Restaurant, and every other afternoon before prayers she spent an energetic hour in the company of a local widower who served as an Independent on the local council. Most mornings she performed callisthenics in a garish shell-suit with matching headscarf, and most evenings at sunset she put in an appearance at the East London Mosque before returning to an empty house. She indulged herself by owning a top-of-the-range blue BMW that was as big as she was small, and she was not averse to the occasional glass of finest Speyside single malt.

If there was a blot on the landscape, a cloud that darkened the horizon, it was that she had only produced one child. But what a child! Ed had heard it said of Pakistan that its women were more impressive than its men, and he quickly decided that Leyla Kassar was the living proof.

Ed first set eyes on Leyla, Sameenah's dangerously attractive only daughter, on a Wednesday afternoon. It was no different from any other day. Sameenah was enjoying the widower and Ed was in the shop, seated across a desk from an elderly pilgrim intent on completing the Hajj, who was counting out tens and fives and the occasional twenty-pound note from an ancient-looking red Rover biscuit tin. First he heard the chime of the door opening and then felt Nasir bristling beside him. He looked up and felt the world lurch sideways.

Standing a full six inches taller than her mother, with a bare midriff and black skinny jeans, she scowled as she stalked across the room. She tugged out her white ear-buds, emptied her vintage carpetbag on the desk, and collapsed into the out-of-bounds Aeron chair in front of the iMac that was hers and hers alone. She spent an hour updating the website and answering feedback forms while Ed snuck glimpses of her slender wrists and long tapering fingers adorned with chunky silver rings and bangles and multicoloured wristbands proclaiming "Make Poverty History, Occupy" and "Ban Cluster Bombs."

And Ed found a new mission. He became an instant and surreptitious student of her. He committed her parts to memory: her spiky black hair, glossy and exotic as a sea urchin on a tropical reef; smooth sugarcane-coloured skin; high, sculpted cheekbones; and her angry and smouldering green eyes ("Those bloody Greeks!" Sameenah would exclaim). Then abruptly, just as Ed was summoning up the courage to introduce himself, she shovelled all her stuff back into the voluminous bag, slung it over her shoulder, and stalked out again, without even throwing a glance in his direction.

She was beautiful. It didn't matter how much effort she went to disguise it by cutting her hair short and slouching around in army-surplus boots and jeans holed at the knee, none of it worked. Her face was luminous, and the more she stooped, the more sensual she seemed. The grace of her movement was criminal. And everywhere she went, the jungle drums followed.

Sameenah hurried in five minutes after she'd left, red-faced and hoarse. "Did I miss her?" she gasped.

Nasir nodded.

Sameenah was crestfallen. "Did she say anything?"

Nasir shook his head.

Sameenah strode back and forth with her brow furrowed and her hands on her hips.

"Not a word?" she demanded. "You're sure?"

"Not a bloody word," Nasir confirmed, grimfaced.

Sameenah stopped in front of Ed's desk. "She's a bloody genius, that girl," she told him. "She's studied art, she's studied politics, she's studied philosophy, she has degrees coming out of her ears, she has read just about every book ever printed. Has it done her any good? Not a bit of it. She's a wild cat. What am I going to do with her? I'm telling you, it's driving me crazy."

She retired to the reinforced glass cage in the corner of the room to count her cash.

It was her sullen nephew Nasir who filled in the gaps. On the subject of Leyla, he wouldn't shut up. As soon as Sameenah stepped out of the office he'd start ranting on about her, a torrent of pent-up frustration.

She lived, against her mother's wishes, in a mixed house

in Dalston with anarchist girls and infidel boys. She smoked cigarettes and left lipstick smears on the butts. She drank pints of beer. She popped pills. She steered clear of Friday prayers, and although she understood Punjabi, the language her mother spoke at home, she obstinately refused to speak a word of it herself. There had been a string of unsuitable boyfriends in London and Lahore, including the latter city's most notorious bootlegger. Word had leaked out, and she would never find a husband.

It wasn't hard to imagine how word had leaked out—Nasir's obsession with her was the enemy of discretion.

Ed thought her perfect. When he wasn't working, he was scouring the Internet for the impassioned blogs that had caused so much ire back in Pakistan, her equal condemnation of the state for its out-of-control intelligence services and illicit arms industry, and the Tehrik-i-Taliban for their bloodthirsty sectarianism and medieval attitudes to women. But she didn't just have Pakistan in her sights. She wrote about the plight of women in London who had been trafficked for sex from Eastern Europe and the Horn of Africa. She condemned the use of Soviet-era cluster munitions by the Syrian government against its own populace. She was without doubt a dervish.

He lay awake at night imagining her long limbs and the fire in her eyes. He lived for the rare occasions that she graced the office with her presence.

In return, she ignored him completely.

As the days shortened, Ed immersed himself in learning the workings of every nut and bolt in the company. And just as intended, the zeal of her new employee delighted Sameenah. She warmed to him with each new skill he revealed, and in return, Ed worked extremely hard. No job was beneath him, from untangling snarl-ups caused by wrongly delivered baggage to meeting the latest plane from Lahore when all the drivers were committed elsewhere. He proved to be an enthusiastic salesman, extolling the exclusive features of J&K's Hajj packages, and when word got out that he spoke both Farsi and Pashto, the Afghans started coming over from Stratford to buy them. Ed's proudest moment came when he introduced Sameenah to a former colleague at HSBC who was able to offer her a bespoke exchange rate that widened her margins even further.

In Sameenah's mind, Ed's name became equated with profit.

But Ed's reticence on personal matters gave Sameenah pause. What was he doing back in Whitechapel after so many years away and with so little to show for it? At first she decided that Ed must have returned to care for an ailing relative, but a few discreet enquiries on Brick Lane established that Ed's father Rifaz was hale and hearty and as truculent as ever. A call to the treasury in search of a reference was met with polite refusal, and a gentle probing conversation with Ed's former colleague from HSBC revealed that the bank was mystified and not a little hurt by his departure.

Eventually, Sameenah decided that Ed was nothing less than an enigma, which was not normally a good thing, but as long as he continued to contribute to the wealth of the company, it was to be tolerated. The only time that Ed gave Sameenah cause for concern was one afternoon, about a month into his employment, when one of the bushy-bearded Wahhabis from the local sweetshop appeared at the door of the shop and started asking questions about what Ed had been doing in Afghanistan.

"I don't know anything about that," Sameenah told him, shooing him away from the doorstep. "Don't you go making trouble . . ."

*

In November, Ed was sent to spend a month at the suboffice in Bradford, and when he came back he was greeted with the news that Leyla was making regular appearances in the office and, most surprising of all, she'd moved back into the parental home.

Sure enough, the next day Leyla slipped into the office and set to work at her computer and Ed struggled to concentrate.

This new version of Leyla made his head reel. It felt like the countdown to a clandestine meeting with an informant, the same giddy feeling of weightlessness, of time stretching like elastic, of events rushing towards collision.

20 ❖

Knight in Shining Armour

It was late. Leyla had been attending a seminar at the School of Oriental and African Studies on live-blogging titled *Citizen Reports from the Middle East*. She was riding home on the District Line, the carriage rocking loudly in the darkness.

Three youths in hoodies with low-slung jeans slunk on at Tower Hill and sprawled on the bench seat opposite her with their legs spread wide. The one directly opposite leered at her and made an obscene gesture with his pierced tongue. He had a narrow rat-like face with a pointy nose and shiny black eyes. The mixed-race one sitting to his right was overweight and muffin-topped, with a bad case of acne. He tugged ostentatiously at his balls. The third was short and skinny, malnourished, deprived of a mother's love. He was carrying a sharpened screwdriver up his sleeve. Panicked, she glanced each way. The two other passengers were at the far ends of the carriage and studiously ignoring the situation.

Thank you Londoners, Leyla thought.

She jumped out of her seat as the train approached Aldgate East. She stepped out onto the platform the moment the doors opened and hurried towards the nearest exit. With a start she remembered that the Whitechapel Art Gallery exit was closed at this hour. She was walking in the wrong direction. She turned around. Damn! They were standing there in a loose picket, between her and the other end of the platform.

Rat-face, Skinny, and Acne.

She took a deep breath, hefted her carpetbag on her shoulder and walked towards them, with her chin raised and a defiant expression on her face. As she approached they seemed to shrink back, parting before her. She was past them, with the stairs just ahead of her, when one them called out after her, "Paki cunt!"

She hurried up the stairs and out through the barrier, emerging at the bottom of Commercial Street. It had started raining. She headed east, cutting across Altab Ali Park, which at least had cameras, and into the darkened streets beyond.

She heard footsteps behind her, quickening in pace. She snatched a glance over her shoulder, glimpsed a hooded figure darting between two parked vans. She started running. She turned a corner next to an industrial unit and ran straight into Acne. She stumbled backwards, dropped her bag, and tried to run back the way she'd come. Rat-face was there, darting out from the shadows. He grabbed her by the sleeve and pulled. She twisted away and the fabric ripped. She ran a few more steps. Then she was grabbed from behind, lifted up, and carried into a darkened doorway. She was slammed against a door and it took her breath away. A hand was pressed over her mouth. Her head was ringing. Then she felt something sharp against her neck, the screwdriver. Skinny's breath in her face, whispering what he was going to do to her. Rat-face pawing at her breasts, Acne tugging her jeans down.

It had started to snow. But it couldn't be snow. From the collar to the waist, her down jacket had been cut open, the down tearing loose and swirling around her.

They pulled a plastic bag over her head. Suddenly she was fighting for breath, the crackling plastic stretched taut across her mouth, the reedy whistle of her breath filling her ears. Her legs buckled. Her skull felt like it was going to explode.

Then she could hear screaming. But she wasn't the one screaming. She fell to the ground. Someone fell over her and was dragged away. There was more screaming. The distinctive crack of a bone snapping. Then the bag was being torn apart, and she was taking great, gasping breaths.

Someone took her gently by the shoulders. A familiar face looking down at her. It was the new guy from the shop, Edward, the tall melancholy one who averted his eyes whenever she looked his way.

"It's okay, you're safe now," he said in a reassuring tone. Her attackers were on the ground behind him, two of them curled up like insects; only Rat-face was moving, crabbing sideways and cradling a broken arm. "Everything is going to be okay."

He picked her up, effortlessly it seemed. She was being carried down the street, with her head lolling on his shoulder. The next thing she knew, she was sitting in the kitchen of a house, and he was planting a mug of hot, sweet tea in her hands.

"Drink that."

Dutifully, she blew and sipped. From over the lip of the mug she watched him range across the kitchen, opening cupboards and drawers. He was lean and loose-limbed, a picture of unthinking health and strength. Good looking, too. She was surprised she hadn't noticed it before.

"Bingo," he said. From a drawer, he took a bottle of antiseptic and a ball of cotton wool. He pulled up a chair alongside her.

"Turn your head this way," he said in a matter-of-fact way. The antiseptic stung. "It's just a graze. I'm afraid your jacket was less fortunate."

"Where am I?" she asked, looking around her. She noticed a pair of boxing gloves, once bright red and now faded from use, hanging from a hook on the wall. There was a punching bag leaning against a wall in the corner.

"This is my father's house," he told her. "Come on, let's get you home."

The following morning, Sameenah ushered him into the back office and ordered him to sit, which she preferred given that she was a good six inches shorter than him. She opened her hands.

"I cannot begin to thank you for what you did."

He shook his head. "It was nothing."

"It was most definitely not nothing. You saved her life."

"You're exaggerating."

"As far as I'm concerned, you're part of the family now," she announced. "You tell me what you want, anything at all."

He shrugged. "Give me a proper job with real responsibility."

Sameenah immediately looked suspicious. Her shoulders hunched together and her brow furrowed. "What do you mean?"

"Put me in charge of the Lahore office."

Her lips condensed into a thin line. Lahore might be underperforming and in need of his talents, but it was where the bribes were paid and the books were cooked. Only a truly trustworthy soul could be put in charge of that end of the operation, a member of the family.

"I'll think about it," she said and then her voice softened. "I'll give it serious consideration. I promise."

On the outside he maintained a facade of composure, but inside, he was cheering.

21

Tikka and Naan

That evening after work, Leyla rang the doorbell. She stood in the street with a pile of books in her arms and a laptop bag hanging over her shoulder. *Go now*, a compassionate part of him thought. *Before it's too late.*

"Were you following me?"

"I was walking across the park," he explained. "I saw you up ahead of me. Then those thugs ran past me. I realised the danger you were in."

She looked away while chewing her lip, trying to make up her mind. Then she looked at him again, and the knot in his stomach tightened with sexual urgency.

"I need somewhere to work," she said. "My mother's creeping me out."

"Of course." He stepped back to let her in.

"You like it here, do you?" she asked as she brushed past him in the hallway. "Living with your dad?"

He followed her down the stairs. "It's okay for now."

"What do you do when you're not working?"

"Read. Walk. Hit a punching bag."

Behave like an out-of-control vigilante.

She was examining the stack of books on the kitchen table. She picked up *Milestones* by Sayyid Qutb and made a face, a flicker of suspicion. "You're a jihadi?"

"No. I'm just trying to understand," he said.

"I won't have any truck with that kind of stuff," she said. "Qutb was a middle-aged virgin, a bigot, and a misogynist. He went to New York and all he could do was moan about the pigeons." She put her books down on the table beside his and unpacked her laptop. "He didn't lift his eyes from the ground. He didn't see the Statue of Liberty. I'll sit here." She sat and switched on the laptop. "You think I'm defending America now, don't you? Maybe I am. The Declaration of Independence is a thing of rare beauty."

"Do you want to be left alone?" he asked, after a pause.

"No."

"I'll sit there, then," he responded, pointing to the armchair in the corner.

"It's your house," she said, rolling her eyes.

He made tea. He sat down and opened his book, stared without seeing at the words swimming on the page. It felt like an interview. She was studying, transcribing notes or writing a blog, he wasn't sure which, but she was watching him too.

At nine, he went out for tikka and naan. They ate amongst their books. For dessert, they had two outrageously sweet *gulab jamuns*.

"Why did you come back here to Whitechapel?" she asked.

"I didn't know where else to go."

"Where were you before?"

"In Afghanistan."

The same flicker of suspicion. She wasn't sure yet whether to trust him. "What were you doing there?"

"It's not as interesting as it sounds." By now, lying about his job was second nature to him, as easy as putting on his clothes in the morning, but even so, he felt a stab of regret. He did not want to lie to Leyla. "I was on loan from the treasury as an advisor at the Ministry of Finance. I was supposed to be advising them on how to collect taxes."

"How did that go?"

"Not very well."

"Do you have anything to drink?" she asked.

Without answering, he went to the kitchen cupboard and took out a bottle of Lagavulin. He poured them two generous measures. Where his choice of reading material had unsettled her, his choice of alcohol was evidently reassuring.

"Are you going to stay?" she asked, after she'd taken a sip.

"Here? In Whitechapel? I'm going to leave as soon as I can."

There was a pause.

"Something happened to your mother, didn't it?" she asked.

"You've been listening to local gossip."

"People talk," she said. "Information comes to me."

"She's dead," he told her.

"I gathered that."

"She committed suicide."

Typically, once the basic facts were laid bare, people couldn't get away fast enough and made some expression of sympathy that made him feel embarrassed and uncomfortable but also excused him from explaining any further. But not Leyla; she was different. She wanted to understand. "Why?"

"It was some kind of death pact," he explained. "She had a lover, a teacher at a local school. It had been going on for years, apparently. Things came to a head when my brother and I left for college. I guess she thought there was no further reason to stay. She asked my father for a divorce, but he refused. So they killed themselves in a hotel room in Tunbridge Wells. They were found in each other's arms."

"Did it make you angry?"

"It made me sad. I thought I knew my mother, but it turned out I didn't know her at all."

Leyla finished her whisky and announced that it was time to leave. She packed up her things and popped an extra-strong mint in her mouth. He walked her to the door. He regretted that he had not changed the subject or said something to lighten the mood.

The next night, she told him a joke. It was a commentary on the state of a criminal investigation in the Punjab. The joke was told to her by a labour activist who'd been fitted up by the police.

"Once upon a time, a king lost a prized and extremely valuable deer," Leyla told him. "All sorts of investigation teams were called in from all over the world, but none were successful in tracing the deer. Eventually, a wise man suggested that the Punjab Police might be called in to assist with the seemingly impossible task. The king took the wise man's advice. Within twenty-four hours, a crack squad of extremely efficient police investigators appeared with a wailing elephant between them. 'What is this?' the king demanded. One of the policemen struck the elephant with a *chittar,* a leather shoe, and the elephant screamed, 'I'm the king's lost deer! I'm the king's lost deer!'"

Ed despised torture as much as she did.

He didn't tell her that he'd once spent four days at a black site in Damascus listening to a cowering man in a cell repeating, "I'm the Sheikh's engineer! I'm the Sheikh's engineer!"

They settled into a kind of routine. He read and she worked, and then over dinner, they bartered parcels of information. He told her about his childhood and his job at the bank. He described his anger at the fate of non-Arab Muslims in Saudi Arabia. He explained away his years in the navy as a series of cold and uneventful tours in the North Atlantic. He told her about his brother, who was a dentist and part-owned a dental practise in Henley-on-Thames. They were not close. He told her about his short-lived engagement. He did not mention the List. He explained how his father had failed as a restaurateur and ended up as a waiter in the restaurant that he had once owned. He laid the facts out where he could, lied where he had to, and hardly embellished at all.

She in turn described a ping-pong childhood, shuttling back and forth between London and Lahore, never quite feeling that she belonged in either. She shared her feelings of antipathy towards her mother for what she saw as her exploitation of elderly fellow Muslims, who used up their savings on her overpriced Hajj tours. She regarded money changing with a distaste that seemed to originate more from a general anti-capitalist urge than from any argument that it contravened the prohibition rules of Islamic law.

She explained how she had come to activism via a dynamic aunt in Lahore who had inspired her and encouraged her. She told him that she was in the second year of a two-year masters programme at the School of Oriental and African Studies, that she wrote a blog that was gaining followers, and that she earned money by conducting research for campaigning organisations. Their priorities inevitably became hers.

The interviews with on-street and off-street prostitutes in the boroughs of East London were commissioned as part of a joint charitable/police project operating out of Toynbee Hall. Her focus was on trafficking. It was the most depressing and least fulfilling of her disparate tasks.

Home, by which she meant Pakistan, was by far the most exasperating. She threw her arms up at its incompetent police, whose methods could best be described as "brutality tempered by torpor," its corrupted courts that conducted their glacial business in incomprehensible English, its kleptocratic politicians, its death-trap factories, and its mendacious anti-Hindu press. She railed against the state's failure to provide modern services.

"Why can't you drink the water out of the tap? Where are the medicines and the buses? Why can't we educate our daughters? The problem is that our democrats have tried to be dictators, and our dictators have tried to be democrats. So the democrats have not developed democracy and the dictators have not developed the country." But she was not without Nationalist urge. She insisted that it was not a failed state. "It works," she said, "just on its own twisted terms. It will still be here in a hundred years, with its nuclear weapons and its bloated army, its runaway population, and its massive diaspora."

The passion came off her in waves.

22

Combustible City

Noman dreamt of a wall of water twenty storeys high bull-dozing the length of the Indus Valley and when he awoke, he was lying on the beach by the ocean.

He got out from under a thorn bush into the blazing sunlight and stumbled, cursing, over the sand, like someone walking on hot coals, to the cool, wet strip at the water's edge. Sparkly junk littered the shore: condom wrappers, empty cans, broken glass. He waded into the surf and plunged his head into the water.

He was standing in the shallows, squinting at the shifting horizon while smoking a Flake, when his iPhone rang. It was Raja Mahfouz.

"Good morning, boss."

There was nothing good about it. His mouth felt like a monkey had taken a shit in it.

"Where are you, boss?"

He grunted. "Clifton beach."

"On my way."

Noman flung away his cigarette and struggled back to the

road. He was sitting on the curb amongst the usual gaggle of rickshaw drivers when Raja Mahfouz pulled alongside him in the Range Rover about half an hour later. He climbed in the passenger seat, rooted around in the glove compartment until he found a strip of paracetamol, and dry-swallowed four.

Noman blamed the entire bloody Pashtun race for his hang-over, for their overabundance of pride and their pigheaded refusal to see sense. You couldn't spend a day listening to their endless complaining without wanting to spend the night smeared in lube, rolling around in bed with a couple of Napier Road's fin-est. He couldn't, anyway. How he'd got from the city's red light district to its beach was the usual mystery, but he still had all his stuff: gun, money, phone, drugs, watch, and sunglasses.

Now they were driving up University Road, heading for the Karachi Institute of Nuclear Medicine.

"Whose idea was this?"

"Yours," Raja Mahfouz replied, cheerily.

The big man was right. This had been his idea for trying to salvage something from a wasted trip. The ostensible reason they had come down to Karachi was to mediate in a territorial dispute between the Afghan Taliban and the Pakistani Taliban. For some time, the Afghans had been using the seaside metrop-olis as a kind of rear base, to lie low or seek medical treatment for injured fighters. Mullah Omar, their reclusive one-eyed leader, spent several months a year down here and in the past, Noman had sat in on a couple of meetings of the *Quetta Shura*, the Afghan Taliban's leadership council, as an observer for the ISI. It was an arrangement that all sides were happy with. Thus far, the Afghan Taliban had limited their armed activities to kidnapping and bank robbery, which was considered an accept-able price to pay. But now there was a new gang in town. The Pakistani Taliban, namely the Mehsud clan from Waziristan, had arrived and launched a series of attacks on police stations that had left scores of police officers dead. They were in danger of upsetting the city's delicate balance of competing criminal, ethnic, and political groups that fought over money, turf, and votes. The Afghan Taliban, which could do without the bad publicity, was particularly incensed.

Noman had spent yesterday with a succession of grizzled Afghan fighters who aired their grievances, from the poor quality of weapons available on the market and the rising cost of ammunition to the venality of border guards and the difficulty of making a reasonable living from smuggling, but always returning to the subject of the Mehsud clan and their heavy-handed tactics in the city. By nightfall, he was sloshing with tea. The problem was he had nothing to offer. The ISI had no leverage. The Mehsud clan was refusing point-blank to talk to him or any representative of government. They'd even issued a death threat against him, which was ironic, given that he was on their side. It was the usual bloody fuck-up.

So he'd decided to go looking for the ingredients of a dirty bomb. He wasn't getting anywhere fast trying to locate the one-legged mullah, and it seemed the only remaining approach was to identify the sources of medical and industrial waste that might constitute the radioactive elements of a dirty bomb. If the House of War really had built an *itami*, an atomic device, then they must have got the waste somewhere. Raja Mahfouz had produced a list of Atomic Energy Commission–registered labs and facilities across Pakistan.

Karachi seemed like a good enough place to start.

They arrived unannounced at the Institute and demanded to speak to the Radioactive Safety Officer. He turned out to be a thin, nervous-looking man with a prominent Adam's apple. He talked them through the protocols for the delivery and safe custody of received isotopes, their application on the isolation wards, and the disposal of the radioactive waste generated. He showed them the storage procedures for unused capsules and the sealed sharps boxes for used syringes. Raja Mahfouz had a go with a Geiger counter while Noman flicked through the written records submitted to the Ministry of Health.

"Let me get this straight: you inject people with radioactive isotopes?"

The safety officer nodded, enthusiastically. "Exactly so, it is extremely effective in the treatment of cancer."

"It's not dangerous?"

"Ha, ha! Only to the area of tissue that is affected by the cancer. You see, we use very small quantities."

Noman frowned. "What happens to it after you've injected it?"

"Over a typical patient's five-day stay, eighty-five percent of the administered isotope has left the body."

"Left the body?"

"In the natural manner."

"They shit it out?"

"Yes. Indeed, the outlets for the toilets of patients undergoing diagnostic procedures are connected to a delay tank designed for the collection of radioactive isotopes. The tanks are emptied by certified members of the National Union of Sanitary Workers. They transfer the excrement into lockable waste-storage trolleys that are secured on site."

Noman and Raja Mahfouz exchanged glances.

"Show us," Noman said.

"Shit!" Noman lifted his sunglasses and peered through crusty eyelashes at the rows of locked metal trolleys stretching away into the shadows.

"Shit," Raja Mahfouz agreed.

They were standing in a cavernous hangar hidden away at

the back of the institute. Noman's head was pounding, and he was experiencing a scatological epiphany.

"Holy fucking shit . . ."

It was mind-boggling, enough to make your brain boil, a whole hangar full of radioactive shit.

"We keep it here until radioactive decay renders it safe," the safety officer explained. "It might only be a matter of days. Then the waste is buried. The isotopes with the shortest half-life, like Iodine-131, are here at the front, and the isotopes with a longer half-life, including Caesium-137, are located at the back of the facility."

"What's the half-life of Caesium-137?" Noman growled.

"Thirty years," the safety officer replied. He led them about halfway into the hangar. "From here on in, it is all Caesium."

"Open them up," Noman said, kicking the nearest trolley.

"I'm sorry?"

"Open every damn one of them," Noman growled.

An hour later, they were standing at the back of the hangar surrounded by empty trolleys.

"They stole the shit," Noman said.

"They stole the shit," Raja Mahfouz agreed.

It took Noman only a few minutes of delving about in the data and factoids on the web to come up with a theory. They must have shovelled the shit into a smelter with molten iron for the bomb casing.

When Noman found him later that day, Gul Rassoul was standing at the edge of a pond with a bucket beside him, and every few minutes he flung a lump of raw meat from the bucket over the railing to the crocodiles in the pond.

"Pilgrims used to feed them," Gul Rassoul explained, "but not so much now. The Taliban have banned it. If it wasn't for my members, they might starve."

The pond was located next to a Sufi shrine in Manghopir, an impoverished neighbourhood of cinderblock houses clustered around marble quarries on the northern edge of the city. As General Secretary of the Sanitary Workers Union, Gul Rassoul controlled a huge workforce spread across the city, many of whom lived in the illegal housing settlements that spilled into the surrounding desert.

"I'm looking for some missing shit," Noman told him.

Gul Rassoul nodded as if the question was not unexpected. "The men responsible are no longer employed by the union."

One of Rassoul's bodyguards brought a fresh bucket of meat and set it down beside him. There must have been at least a hundred crocodiles writhing and snapping in the pond.

"Who were these men?" Noman asked.

"Nomadic people from the mountains in the north. Hardworking, resilient fellows who came here five years ago, I think. They stayed on, giving me no complaint. And then one day, eighteen months or so ago, they left. "

"Three and a half years! They were systematically stealing radioactive waste for three and a half years?"

Gul Rassoul shrugged and flung another lump of meat. "Perhaps. Who can say?"

"Where did they take it?"

"Back to wherever they came from, a land of stones."

"What tribe? What clan?" Noman demanded.

"It is said of nomads with no livestock that they have no right to a name, let alone a clan or tribe. But I can tell you what I told your colleague, that they lived under a *bamiyat*—an oath of allegiance—to one known only as the Father of Smoke."

"My colleague?"

"I think Khan was his name."

Noman swore under his breath. So Khan knew. Khan, who maintained that the House of War was a tall tale, a bugbear to frighten the Americans, knew that, in reality, the House of War had in its possession enough radioactive waste to manufacture the dirtiest kind of bomb imaginable. Why had he kept it secret? Why was he so adamant that Noman should stay away?

It was as he was striding back to the Range Rover that Noman first caught sight of the boy, a skinny, rat-faced beggar in a ragged black overcoat that made him resemble a bat. He was staring at Noman with an impudent expression on his face. Noman might have dismissed him as wholly unremarkable, but there was something about him that made Noman think of himself at that age, the same barely-suppressed orphan anger.

Noman scowled in return and slammed the door behind him as he climbed in the car beside Raja Mahfouz.

"Let's get out of here."

23

Nadifa's Story

The doorbell woke him. Ed looked groggily around. He'd dozed off in front of the television with his father in the chair beside him. The old man was still snoring. He looked at his watch. Two a.m.

When he opened the door, Leyla was standing there with her mother's X5 blocking the street behind her. She was wearing a black woollen hat and the tip of her nose was pink with cold.

"Is everything all right?" he asked.

"Can you do me a favour?"

He nodded without thinking. "Sure."

"I need to go to Newham. Do you think you could come along?"

"Sure."

She seemed surprised. "Just because you work for my mother doesn't mean you have to jump to it. You can make your own mind up."

"I'll get my coat."

He got in the car, and she turned the music down. It was Asian Dub Foundation, "Where's All the Money Gone?"

"I'm sorry," she said. "I'm kind of a dick sometimes."

"That's all right."

She accelerated down the street and turned onto New Road. "You're a boxer, right?"

"Yes."

"How come?"

"It's a family tradition. My father boxed in the navy. I boxed at college."

"Did you win much?"

"I won more than I lost, put it that way. Now tell me what's going on."

"It's something I've been working on for a while. A woman has agreed to be interviewed. She works in Forest Gate, off the Romford Road."

"She's working at this hour? What does she do?"

"She runs a brothel."

He laughed. "You're serious?"

"Absolutely." She was an impatient driver but wary too, short bursts of rapid acceleration with her eyes roaming the road ahead. "The police have launched a crackdown. They're closing down brothels across the East End and putting ASBOs on the women barring them from the area. They're putting their pictures up in shops and pushing them through letter-boxes. It makes it dangerous for the prostitutes because they can't phone the police to protect themselves. It's pushing them further underground. If I don't do this interview now, I'm worried I won't get the chance again."

"Does your mother know you've got her car?"

"No. Are you going to tell her?"

He was enjoying himself now. "No."

"Look, I just need you to be there with me as a precaution. Don't say anything, and don't start any fights. Is that clear?"

"Crystal."

She parked underneath a railway bridge beside an ominous sign encouraging anyone witnessing a collision with the bridge to call an emergency hotline. They walked along the side of the railway arches and cut down an alleyway between two brick walls, emerging onto an expanse of waste ground and a long, low-rise sixties housing block. They stood at the entrance to the block, and she pressed a buzzer. Soon after, the intercom crackled into life.

"Name?"

"It's Leyla for Nadifa."

The door clicked, and they were in. They climbed two flights of concrete stairs and walked along a corridor past a man zipping his fly. Leyla knocked on a door. A large man with bloodshot eyes opened the door.

"I'm here to see Nadifa," Leyla said.

The large man stepped back and allowed her to enter, but when Ed made to follow, he stopped him with one hand. "Not you."

Ed locked eyes with him and, stifling the urge to break the man's arm, he carefully removed the hand from his chest.

"She doesn't go in there without me."

"It's okay," Leyla said. "You can wait out there. I'll be fine."

"It's not okay," he said, continuing to stare at the man. "You don't go in there without me."

From inside the flat a woman's voice called out. "Let him in if he's so keen."

The man stepped aside. Ed brushed past him and followed Leyla down a carpeted hallway, past two closed doors, and into a room lit by candles on a low table.

Sprawling on a long sofa was a young black woman with a moon face, long braided hair, and painted-on eyebrows that gave her a startled, mask-like expression. She was wearing a white robe with the hood thrown back and the longest nail extensions Ed had ever seen. They were crimson and sharp as blades.

She pointed one of them at Ed. "I know you."

"No," he said, emphatically.

The woman chuckled, "Of course not. It was your father."

"We're not that alike."

"Are you sure about that?"

"I'm sure."

"You have a pretty face," the woman said, switching her attention to Leyla, flashing a sly grin, "but you're too skinny. My clients prefer their bones with flesh on."

"I eat like a horse," Leyla told her.

The woman raised her eyebrows. "I'm sorry, but I don't think I can offer you any work."

There was a pause.

Leyla smiled, grimly. "You agreed to drink tea with me, Nadifa."

"How silly of me, of course I did." She clapped her hands. It was an ungainly gesture, with her talons spread and only the heels of her palms making contact. "Please sit down."

They sat opposite her. An unnervingly young girl in a child's pink pyjamas brought in a tray with tea things.

"What can I do for you?" Nadifa asked.

"Tell me your story," Leyla said, placing her iPhone on the coffee table with its recorder app on.

Nadifa laughed. "Are you going to make me into a celebrity?"

"No real names will be used."

"It's not a fairytale. Though I was a beautiful girl once, full of promise like Amal here," she pointed at the child pouring them tea, "but more innocent."

"What happened to you, Nadifa?"

"My parents were very poor and couldn't afford to feed me, so they sold me to a man in Mogadishu. I was sent there in a suitcase. When I got to the house, I was raped. First by the man, and then by his sons."

Leyla closed her eyes.

Nadifa chuckled. "Why so sad? It is the way of these things."

"Then what happened?"

"The man told me that he could not afford to keep me and I could never return to my village, because I had shamed my family. He said that my father or my brothers would kill me. Of course, I was terrified. He said the only hope for me was to go to Europe to be adopted. How could I say no? A mixed Italian-Somali couple that had children of their own flew with me to Rome. They did it all the time, passing children off as their own. You see, you didn't need a photograph of children under the age of ten on a passport in those days. When I got to Rome, I was told that the best chance for me was in England with a man from Bosaso, and I travelled here in the back of the truck. But when I arrived in Newham, the man told me I was too old for adoption and I would have to pay back the cost of my transport. I was made to have sex with men to pay my debt. I did it for ten years. I was fortunate that the man from Bosaso was fastidious in certain matters. He insisted on the use of condoms."

Ed looked at Leyla, but she didn't acknowledge him. The two women were staring at each other.

"Go on."

"The man from Bosaso became sick in his liver. It is a common sickness with people from my country. He could not work, and someone had to run his business. He could not trust his family. It was natural that he put me in charge. I soon discovered that I have a talent for this work. The girls respect me, and so do the clients. And here I am."

"And the man from Bosaso?"

She chuckled. "He died, of course, although not before he married me. He died in the bed beside me. Some people say I smothered him with a pillow."

Ed sat in silence while the interview continued. Nadifa was explaining to Leyla how many girls she had working for her, in this flat and in others locally. Ed looked through the curtain of beads at the bouncer standing just the other side. It was clear from the sounds coming through the walls that business was being conducted as usual. Once a man emerged from one of the other rooms and was shown to the door. After a short interval the intercom buzzed and the bouncer answered it. "Name?"

"It's Hussein for Nadifa."

"Let him in," Nadifa called out. A few minutes later, a man knocked on the door and was admitted. She smiled at Ed. "I prefer to deal with established clients . . . or their relatives."

When the interview was over, Nadifa clapped her hands again and the child collected the tea things. Nadifa's eyes met Ed's for a moment, and she said, "Do you want her?"

"No."

"What about your father?"

"No."

"I haven't decided on the price yet, but I can tell you she is going to be very expensive the first time."

The girl carried the tray back into the kitchen and closed the door behind her.

Neither Leyla nor Ed said anything until they were on the Romford Road heading west. She was driving too fast, shifting up through the gears and overtaking slower traffic. He almost told her to slow down but mastered the urge.

"Thanks for coming," she said. "I wasn't sure how safe it would be."

Soon they were back in Banglatown, near his house. He wanted to say something about the young girl in pyjamas but nothing he could say seemed adequate.

She pulled up in front of his father's house. They stayed like that for a moment, without moving. But then a car turned into the narrow one-way street behind them and flashed its lights. He had to get out. He was reaching for the door handle when she gave him a quick, darting kiss on the cheek. She looked away immediately afterwards. He got out of the car. They didn't say goodbye.

He watched the taillights of her car flash red at the end of the street, and then she turned out of sight. He was standing still but it felt like he was falling.

24 ❖

An Impulsive Act

"It's Rifaz for Nadifa."

The door clicked open. Ed steered his father up the stairs and along the corridor with the crowbar hanging loosely at his side. He crossed in front of the door to Nadifa's flat at a crouch and pressed himself against the wall on the far side. He raised the crowbar and nodded to his father.

Rifaz stepped up to the door and knocked. He stepped back a pace and stood there, trembling.

Ed was counting, a snake of sweat sliding across his temple. *One, two, three* . . .

The door opened. Ed pivoted and swung the crowbar down like an axe on the bouncer's forehead. He crashed to the ground.

"Police!" Ed shouted.

He jumped over the body and advanced down the hall, banging the crowbar against the walls and shouting. He pushed through the bead curtain and crossed the living room without pausing to look at Nadifa. He kicked open the door to the kitchen.

The girl, Amal, was curled up in a dog crate. She was awake and watching him.

"Don't worry," he told her. He jimmied the door open and helped her out. "This way."

He led her back into the living room.

"You're right, you're not like your father," Nadifa said. She hadn't moved since earlier.

He pointed the crowbar at her. "The girl is mine."

She stared impassively back at him. "You think you can just walk in here, damage my property, and then steal my property?"

"Yes."

"I think you are foolhardy and stupid."

"No."

He turned his back on her and guided the girl through the bead curtain and along the hall past the bouncer. Ed's father was still standing in the corridor outside.

"It's done," Ed told him.

He felt strangely liberated. They were sitting on a bench outside the entrance to Accident and Emergency at the Royal London Hospital. Amal was wrapped in a blanket and curled up beside him. His father was standing some way off smoking a cigarette.

A police car parked at the end of a rank of ambulances in the forecourt, as far from the entrance as possible. Two men got out of the back and moved as swiftly as possible away from the vehicle, as if embarrassed by it. Ed recognised them both. One was Jonah, and the other was Rat-face, one of Leyla's attackers. He was wearing a plaster cast on his arm, and it was Ed who had broken it.

Jonah crossed over to the bench.

"May I?"

Ed nodded. Jonah sat on the bench. He looked down at the sleeping girl, then around the forecourt. It was relatively quiet.

"I hate hospitals," he said, eventually. "Too many cameras."

He seemed at a loss for anything else to say, and then he

noticed Rat-face hanging back, with a sullen expression on his face.

"That's Carl," Jonah told him, "one of the lost boys. Carl thinks you're a sociopath."

Ed met the young man's gaze and saw there a mixture of fear and defiance.

"It's just injured pride," Jonah said. "You were supposed to hurt him. After all, it was part of the plan. You remember the plan, right? Burrow you into J&K Cargo and Travel, make yourself an invaluable member of their team, and get yourself sent to Pakistan."

Ed nodded. "I remember the plan."

"So what is this? What the hell is going on?"

"I need you to take this girl into care."

"Who is she?"

"Her name is Amal. She's Somali. I rescued her from a brothel in Newham."

"You did what?"

"You heard me. Get her adopted."

"Just like that?"

"Pull some fucking strings."

Jonah shook his head. "You're out of control."

"Yes, I am. And that's what you wanted. 'Parade your impulsive side' were your exact words."

"What kind of mess have you left behind in Newham?"

"A fractured skull, a concussion, and maybe a broken bone or two. Nothing that hasn't already been done in the name of this operation."

"You're a piece of work," Jonah said.

"That's what people say about you. If you want me to do this thing for you, you'd better get this girl taken care of. You can tell Queen Bee that's my condition."

"You're pushing your luck."

"There's something else," Ed told him. "If you don't want a war with me at the centre of it, you better explain to the brothel keeper the futility of any kind of response. Her name is Nadifa. I'd make it very clear to her if I was you."

25

Rolling with the Punches

Leyla didn't show up for work the next day. She came at night though, this time without her laptop. She was wearing track pants and running shoes and a white v-neck T-shirt under her coat.

"I want you teach me how to punch someone." The expression on her face left him in no doubt that she was serious.

"Sure." He hung up her coat and asked her to sit at the kitchen table. "Show me your hands." He turned them over, hesitant when he touched her, because he didn't want it to seem like a caress.

"I got a call from my contact in the Met," she said, her tone of voice giving nothing away. "Apparently someone went in and broke up the brothel in the early hours of this morning. The bouncer is in hospital with a fractured skull, and Nadifa has disappeared. An eleven-year-old girl has been taken into care."

"I'll wrap your hands," he told her, not sure if she was looking at him or not, because he was staring into the corner of the room.

He got up and went to the counter. He took a rolled-up

hand-wrap from a drawer and returned to kneel in front of her, head down, concentrating on her hands, trying not to look at the slice of exposed cinnamon-coloured skin between her track pants and her T-shirt. He slipped a loop over her thumb, and wrapped her left hand, covering her knuckles and binding her fingers together before tying off the ends. Next, he did the right hand. Then he reached for his gloves and put them on her.

"Stand up."

He folded away the table and hung his old heavy bag on a hook attached to one of the roof beams.

"I've worked out what you are," she said.

He turned around. He kept his voice as level as hers. "Spread your legs slightly, and bend your knees."

"I've been investigating you."

"Get up on the balls of your feet," he told her. She glared at him, but complied. "That's right. Now raise your hands higher." She squared her shoulders and raised the gloves. He tapped her left glove. "That's your lead hand." He tapped her right glove. "That's your rear hand. You're going to use your lead hand to punch the bag and your rear hand to guard your jaw. You swivel and punch, bringing your fist into the horizontal."

She stepped up to the bag. She hit it hard.

"That's good."

She hit it again.

"Next, you're going to hit with your rear hand. You roll your hips and throw it from your chin in a straight line."

She hit the bag like she wanted to punch right through it. As well as the jab and the cross, he showed her the hook and the uppercut. She was a quick learner. Her movements were deft and assured. She focussed on him when he was explaining and on her body when she was punching. She settled into a measured pace, twisting her body to throw her shoulder into the punches. Soon, the bag was swinging. She looked fierce as an Amazon, like she really meant it, and his surprise at her strength gave way to admiration for her endurance.

Eventually she stopped, shut her eyes, and wiped the sweat from her brow with her forearm. She turned and stood with her back to the bag. She was watching him, breathing steadily, her face and chest shiny with perspiration, her nipples sharp points.

"You're a lie, Edward Malik."

He was half-expecting it, but when the blow came it knocked him back a step. He raised his hand to his nose, and when it came away, there was a smear of blood on it.

"I have a blogger friend in Kabul. I faxed him your photo, and he showed it to his cousin who works in the Human Resource Directorate at the Ministry of Finance. Nobody there remembers you."

"It's a large ministry," he said, "and staff turnover is high."

She punched him again, harder this time, driving him back against the counter. He made no attempt to resist.

"My friend's cousin has access to the personnel files for foreign consultants. Sure, there's a file for you. There's a whole stack of them for people no one's ever seen. They call them ghosts. You're a spook, Edward Malik."

He looked away. "Stop it," he said.

"I'm not the only one who thinks so. You're out there on the web, Ed. And I'm not talking about stuff picked up by search engines. I'm talking about the deep web, the encrypted and the unlinked; jihadi's in chat rooms know your name. You need to have the right keywords in the right language, but you're not that difficult to find. You really burrowed your way into my family, didn't you?"

His voice softened. "What do you want me to tell you, Leyla?"

She narrowed her eyes, up on the balls of her feet, ready for the next punch. "The truth."

"I love you."

He hadn't meant to say it. Under the circumstances, it was the most irresponsible thing to say. But it was the truth.

"You bastard."

She threw herself at him. He grabbed her by the wrists. She started to struggle, and he held her close so that she couldn't break free. His face next to hers, his mouth against the shell-like curve of her ear.

"I'm sorry."

She started to sob. He wrapped his arms around her. She reached up with her mouth and they were kissing, gently at first, and then more urgently. She clung to him fiercely, pressing herself against him. His hands roved down her back, following the cord of her spine. She broke away and gasped. He pulled off the boxing gloves and flung them across the room. Then he was kissing her again, his hands on her shoulder blades, her wrapped hands cupping the back of his neck, her leg hooked around his calf.

They broke away again, and he led her to the stairs. In his bedroom, he unwrapped her hands. He lifted her T-shirt over her head and she kicked off her track pants. Next he removed his own clothing. Naked, they stood before each other. He was overwhelmed by the sight of her bare limbs, the dark aureoles of her nipples, and her glossy black pubic hair.

She drew him to her again and down onto the narrow bed.

Making love to her, with her head on the pillow and his hands knuckling down into the mattress, he stared at her and she stared back, her mouth opened slightly, her eyes boring into him.

"You," she said.

Afterwards, she slept and he lay beside her, while the moonlight falling through the open window dappled her skin with silver, and he listened to the rise and fall of her breath. He had never before felt this mixture of awe and promise, the expectation that life had something to offer, which few people knew anything about, the promise of happiness with another person who felt the same way.

Around eleven, he went downstairs and made two cups of tea. When he returned, he found her cross-legged on the bed with the List.

"Isn't it just another way of saying you're a prick or a pathological narcissist? I mean, at least twice a week I get told some man or other is on the autism spectrum. It's like bad shorthand."

"Sometimes people say things they don't mean or that they later regret," he told her, gently. "The end of any relationship is messy."

"She called you a thief."

"She said I stole her heart."

"Is that what you do?" She shuddered and drew the sheet around her. "I always knew there was something not right about you. You've torn something off. What did it say?"

"Spy."

"You better tell me your story."

Over the next hour, he told her what had happened since his deployment to Afghanistan, how he had recruited and run Tariq as an agent in the ISI and how the information provided had saved the lives of soldiers and civilians alike. He explained that Tariq had revealed the location of Osama bin Laden, and he described Tariq's lonely death at the hands of Khan. He shared with her his sense of anger and betrayal. He described the assault on the CIA head of station that had led to his disgrace. And because she had seen him angry and violent, she had no difficulty in believing any of it.

He did not tell her that after he came back to London from Kabul, when Burns had finished telling him his career was over in the basement under the old War Office, she had offered him another job, an off-the-books operation with the politicians kept out of the loop. She'd graced him with her sunniest smile and said, "I want you to help me destroy Khan."

And because he hated Khan more than anything, he had said yes.

26 ❖

Hugging a Hoodie on Petticoat Lane

It was close to midnight. Ed was walking down Wentworth Street, past closed shops and the metal brackets that would be market stalls in the morning, when a large man in a hoodie fell into step alongside him.

"You were supposed to make yourself invaluable; nobody said anything about you screwing her daughter."

"Fuck off," Ed growled.

Jonah gave him a sideways glance. "You really like her, don't you?"

Ed stopped and turned on him. They stood facing each other for a few moments, weighing each other up with their hands loose but ready, each one waiting for the other to make the first move. Jonah was bigger, his fists like axe-heads, but Ed was younger by ten years and fast on his feet.

"I went to see the Somali girl," Jonah told him, his face impassive. "She's now with a foster family down in Brighton."

The fight went out of Ed. "How is she?"

"She's fine. She's got good people looking after her. They're confident she can be placed with an adoptive family soon."

"Thank you," Ed told him.

"You ruffled a lot of feathers with that particular stunt," Jonah told him. "Now come on, Queen Bee wants to talk you."

They hurried down rain-slicked back streets. Jonah led him through an unmarked door beside a commercial waste bin and up a narrow set of carpeted stairs past signs for an actuary's office on the first landing and an immigration lawyer on the second. The flat was on the top floor, behind a scuffed white door. Jonah produced a set of keys.

Inside, the flat smelled of curry, empty beer bottles, and stale cigarette smoke. There was a dimly lit corridor with a threadbare carpet and at the end of it, a kitchen with two large windows that were big for the room and looked out on Whitechapel High Street. Burns was sitting there, in a linen suit and leopard-print heels, with a skinny cappuccino on the table in front of her and an open briefcase at her feet.

"Sit down."

Ed sat, and Jonah pulled up a chair alongside him. From the briefcase beside her, Burns took out a sealed envelope and placed it on the table.

"You've always suspected that there was someone behind Tariq, that someone else was writing his script. Isn't that right?"

"That's right," Ed conceded, staring at the envelope.

"We think its time the Pakistanis thought the same thing." She glanced at Jonah. "Open it."

Jonah tore the envelope open and shook out the photos inside. He spread them out like a dealer at a table. Three mug shots: two men and a woman. Ed recognised Javid Aslam Khan but not the other two.

"That is Noman Butt," Jonah said, pointing. In the photo, the man resembled a boxer at a photo call. He radiated brute hunger. He looked as if he was about to bite. "He is head of the ISI's SS Directorate, which monitors terrorist groups that operate in Pakistan and is responsible for covert political action and paramilitary special operations. We believe that he had operational control of the surveillance operation that was overseeing bin Laden's confinement in Abbottabad. We know that you know the name. Tariq mentioned him in his last face-to-face meeting with you."

"Give us the known-knowns, Jonah," Burns said. "Tell us about the humble beginnings and the rise to power, the Janissary zeal. Give us a feel for the man."

"This is what we have learned," Jonah replied. "Noman Butt was born in a village of low-caste Hindus that has since been destroyed."

"You wouldn't want to be a Hindu in Pakistan," Burns said. "They fall into the category of Graham Greene's 'torturable class.'"

"Hindus in Pakistan are outside the system altogether," Jonah continued. "They have no access to protection, patronage, or charity. Add to that both his parents died while he was still a baby. He was taken into an orphanage, and we assume that it was there that he converted to Islam. We have no idea whether he was coerced or chose to convert voluntarily. As soon as he was old enough, he joined the army. It can't have been easy. Twenty years ago, a convert officer in the infantry would have seemed as likely as a girl flying a fighter jet. But now they have three girls flying fighter jets. Noman was one of the first. The army is the only Pakistani institution that works as it is meant to, and in the Pakistani military nothing is impossible, even for one such as Noman. He was an exceptional soldier and recognised for it. He graduated from the Kakul Academy as one of the top students. He served with the elite Baloch regiment and the Special Services Group before joining the ISI. It was there that he came to the attention of Javid Aslam Khan, who was then head of the ISI's Afghan bureau and chief architect of the rise of the Taliban. Noman became Khan's factotum and enforcer, a man he could turn to if secrets needed burying or fingernails needed pulling. And to bind him close and to ensure that Noman would stick by him whatever happened, Khan married him to his daughter and brought him to live in the family home."

Burns leant forward in the chair, her eyes shining with excitement. "Noman is the loyal acolyte. The son Khan never had."

It was obvious where they were going with this. "You want the acolyte to stab his master in the back," Ed said.

"Exactly so," Burns said. "Well done, you."

"He's the only one who is a match for Khan," Jonah said. "We think he's in a vulnerable position following bin Laden's death. After all, he was supposed to be keeping the bogeyman safely in the basement. It didn't work out, and now he's in danger of being scapegoated. He's become suspicious, paranoid even, seeing enemies under the beds everywhere, even close at hand. His loyalty to his father-in-law, and the ISI, is on a knife's edge."

He glanced at Burns, who nodded in unspoken agreement.

"We believe that the situation is ripe for exploitation," Jonah explained. "Which is where you come in."

"We want you to be the weapon that Noman uses against Khan," Burns said.

"How?" Ed asked.

"The delivery job you did for us in Dubai. Tell him, Jonah."

Jonah tapped the remaining photo. "This is Mumayyaz Khan, the beloved only daughter of Javid Aslam Khan and wife to Noman Butt. Once a month, she visits Dubai. The deliveries that you and others made correspond with the dates that she was there."

So that's why they had him flying to Dubai, Ed thought. It was an entrapment operation. Their plan was to trick Noman into thinking Khan was a British spy and his daughter a willing accomplice.

"You've been planning this all along," he said.

"We have," Burns agreed.

From the briefcase, she retrieved a bound document with yellow tabs to indicate where a signature was required and a black rollerball pen, and put them on the table in front of him.

"I have here a disclaimer for you to sign," she said. "Jonah is going to witness it."

"What does it say?" Ed asked.

"Nothing out of the ordinary. We didn't coerce you. You'll never sue us. Whatever happens to you, it's your own fault."

"And if I refuse?"

"We close down the operation. Khan goes unpunished. You go back to work at J&K, and it's as if none of this had happened."

"You're the only one who can do this," Jonah said.

It was an impossible decision. He should throw it back in their faces, their outrageous plan and their stupid bloody disclaimer. He should run right back to Leyla and have nothing more to do with it. They were in love. He was done with secrets. Nothing trumped that. Nothing, that, is except unfinished business.

Khan.

He couldn't help himself. He owed it to Tariq.

With a sense of foreboding, he took up the pen and signed where indicated. Jonah signed after him.

"All done," Burns said, brightly. She slipped the document into the briefcase and walked with Ed to the door.

"See you on the other side," she told him.

They shook hands. It would have been bad form for her to wish him luck.

Jonah waited until after Ed had left before lodging his protest.

"We should have told him."

"Told him what exactly?" Burns replied. "That Khan really is one of ours, that we've paid him good money for more than five years with almost nothing to show for it, and now we've decided to discard him? That political expediency has trumped loyalty? That we're prepared to roll the dice for Noman Butt instead? You think that someone in Ed's situation would find that reassuring?"

"He'll work it out, eventually."

"So let him. Better still, let Noman force it out of him."

27

Bomb-boy

At first it was just a feeling, a hint of constancy, a sense that something was different: Noman checked out the pedestrians—the usual melee of hawkers and beggars and eunuchs and fakirs that always seemed to swirl around him—and over the course of a couple of days, he gradually became aware that he was being watched. He was in a crowded market place in Dera Ghazi Khan, eight hundred and fifty kilometres from Karachi, when he realised who it was that was watching him. He was walking away from a meeting with an informant, taking the usual precautions, when he felt the hairs bristle on the back of his neck, swung round, and caught the briefest glimpse of the boy's pinched face between market stalls, his black eyes shining like jet—the boy from the Manghopir shrine.

The next time he saw him, the boy was sitting in the shadow of a tree opposite the widow's house in Lahore, five hundred kilometres further north. It was not long after dawn, and Noman was standing scratching his balls at an upstairs window when he spotted him. He ran stark naked out into the

street—the terrorised neighbours knew better than to com-
plain—but by the time he got there, the boy was gone.

He reappeared that night, just after the bootlegger had
made his weekly delivery of drink and drugs. This time the boy
showed no inclination to flee. Noman dashed down the stairs,
pulling on a dressing gown as he went.

He was within a few yards of the boy when he simultane-
ously realised two things: that he should have grabbed a weapon,
any kind of cudgel; and, more importantly, that even if he had
brought a weapon it wouldn't make a blind bit of difference.

The boy was a bomb: a living, breathing bomb.

Noman stopped in his tracks. His mouth hung slack. *What
the fuck?* In front of him, the boy had parted his coat and
revealed the rows of shiny ball bearings glued to his chest like
chain mail, and the length of cable disappearing into his sleeve,
his grubby thumb on a fire-extinguisher-red trigger switch.

"Are you here to kill me?" Noman managed, in a tremulous
voice. His mind was racing. Who'd sent this boy to kill him?
He'd done so many people wrong there was no point in trying
to draw up a short list. He'd tortured a dozen people in the last
six months alone. It could be anyone. *Fuck!*

He felt his bowels loosen. *Not that. Please don't let me shit
myself!*

"Why?" he pleaded. He thought about dropping to his knees
and pressing his forehead into the dirt. It was pathetic. He was
within a hair's breadth of death, and he was blubbing like a girl.
Not like this! Where was a fucking sniper when you needed one?

The boy shook his head.

No? What did that mean? Noman felt a surge of fury. He
wasn't going to kill him, or he wasn't going to give him a reason? Why wasn't the boy being clear? Was he mute?

"Take me to Loyesam," the boy said.

He obviously wasn't mute. Did he mean Loyesam in Bajaur

Tribal Agency, on the Afghan border? It would take at least fifteen hours to drive up there.

"You want me to take you to Loyesam?"

The boy nodded.

"Now?"

The boy nodded.

"Like this?"

He pointed to his bare feet and bathrobe.

The boy nodded.

Fuck!

"We'll need money for fuel," Noman said.

"I've got money," the boy said. Then he used the Arabic phrase all good Muslims are supposed to utter before setting out: "I hope Allah has written a safe journey for us."

And then he smiled, his teeth a row of blackened stubs—it was terrifying.

Sometimes at night, driving fast on the highway, Noman had seen two headlights rushing towards him and felt a sudden impulse to spin the wheel, floor the accelerator, and charge head-on at the oncoming car. He could imagine the collision, the shattering glass and tearing metal, the slow-motion somersault and the car's bodywork unravelling. In the aftermath, a few moments, stillness amongst the noise and smell and smoke, and then the creeping flood of gasoline.

A spark.

Whoosh!

At times in the last decade he'd given himself a taste of it, veered into the oncoming lane and held his nerve for a few seconds before veering away again, usually in a blare of flashing lights and horns. But he'd always turned down the option of suicide. He couldn't do it. No fucking way! How could he leave?

The truth was that he felt an uncontrollable tenderness for his own shit-filled life. Everything he despised was here: family, colleagues, and victims. And besides, his appetites were intact; he had not yet filled himself up. He wanted more drinks and drugs, more deceit and violence, more cunt and God willing . . . more arse.

He really didn't want to die.

He was thinking these things as he drove his Range Rover up the Grand Trunk Road, and beside him, Bomb-boy sat rubbing the trigger switch.

Noman had spent some time studying suicide bombings, mostly in crowded areas. It was part of his job. He had the statistics memorised. He knew that the worst crowd formation was a semicircular one—like a concert audience—with a 51 percent death rate and a 42 percent injury rate. And vertical rows, such as those in a mosque, were the best for reducing the effectiveness of an attack, with a 20 percent death rate and a 43 percent injury rate. Secular targets yielded a higher death rate. Some took it as proof of God's existence.

He knew that 80 percent of the ammonium nitrate used in IEDs in Afghanistan and Pakistan came from just two fertiliser manufacturers in the south of the Punjab province: one was PalmTree and the other was the Chuppa Group, which was owned by the Khan family. He knew that a young suicide bomber could be bought for as little as four thousand dollars and much of the training was done in the tribal areas.

He knew that in most cases when the explosion occurred, the bomber's head was severed from his body and found intact afterwards at the scene. He fervently hoped that if the boy detonated himself, he wasn't smiling when he did it. He didn't want them to find the head with that smile on it.

He wanted to be buried properly and intact. He wanted his

body washed and covered in a white shroud. He didn't want to be scraped off the pavement. He particularly didn't want to die as a result of a bomb manufactured from fertiliser produced by his wife's family.

If he was going to get out of this, he needed a plan, but he couldn't think of one. All he had was this giddy feeling, as if events had taken over. He was in, whatever *in* meant.

They stopped for fuel. Nobody seemed to find it remarkable that a man in a grubby bathrobe and a feral, dirty-faced boy in what looked like a batsuit were travelling on the road at night. The boy's money was good. He produced fistfuls of it from the pocket of his voluminous coat. The tank filled, they set off again. Soon they turned off the highway and headed into the shadow lands of rock that marked the edge of the tribal areas. The boy seemed to have an unerring ability to anticipate and avoid police and army checkpoints. He told Noman to switch off the headlights, and they drove that way for several hours, not knowing what lay more than a few seconds overhead. At one point, lightning exploded overhead and illuminated the blasted landscape with a wash of cold blue light.

The next time they stopped was for predawn prayers. Noman couldn't remember the last time he'd risen for *Fajr*, though it was a sin to miss it and he was often awake at that time. And he never bothered with the compensatory *qaza* prayer. In fact, he couldn't remember the last time he'd prayed at any time of day or night. For a moment, he wondered if he'd forgotten how and what kind of wrath that might provoke in the boy. But he found Raja Mahfouz's prayer mat rolled up in the back of the car, and under the boy's watchful eye he performed a barely adequate *rak'ah*, a cycle of prayer in remembrance of God.

The boy did not pray. Perhaps he thought he was already dead.

"They said you were a Hindu," the boy told him when he'd finished.

"I'm an officer in the army of the Islamic Republic of Pakistan."

"Get in the car."

They set off again. A fan of light came from the sky as the
sun rose.

Later that day, they found the one-legged mullah waiting
for them in the *hujra*, or meeting room, of a malik's fortified
compound on the outskirts of Loyesam. The compound had
twelve-foot-high stone walls and a scattering of dun-coloured
buildings, with the house on one side of an open dusty space as
large as a parade ground and the *hujra* on the other. The distance
between the two buildings suggested that the landowner didn't
like to spend much time in his *hujra* talking to his tenants.

Inside the *hujra*, the walls were painted a dark institutional
green to waist height and then a dirty white all the way up to
the cheap and shiny tin plates on the ceiling, each decorated
with a crude impression of a fleur-de-lys. It was several degrees
cooler than the outside and filled with a sweet, pungent scent of
opium. At the centre of the room, a stoned *bacha*-boy in a sari
was slowly turning like the ballerina on a music box, his eyes
glazed and unseeing.

The mullah was sprawled on a pile of cushions with his plastic leg lying beside him. Noman entered just as he was sucking
on a long-stemmed pipe, his face shrouded by smoke. The mullah closed his eyes and drifted away for several moments. Then
he jolted awake. He was looking beyond Noman, at Bomb-boy
standing in the doorway, and the expression on his face suggested a curious mixture of horror and resignation.

"While you were gone, I dreamt that you were never coming back," he said.

Without answering, Bomb-boy knelt beside him and

crossed his legs, drawing his ragged coat around him. He looked up at Noman, expectantly.

"You've been looking for me," the mullah said.

"Actually, I am looking for Abu Dukhan," Noman corrected him.

The mullah nodded as if it was the answer he was expecting. "He is looking forward to meeting you."

"He is?"

"Sit down."

Noman sat. The mullah leant forward and offered Noman the pipe. Accepting it, Noman raised the stem to his mouth and pulled smoke into his lungs. He exhaled and returned the pipe.

"Tomorrow I will take you into the mountains," the mullah said. "The next day or the day after that we will meet with Abu Dukhan. God willing, he will let you live long enough to hear his story. If he is happy, I think he will help you."

"How will he help me?"

The mullah smiled, his eyes as flat as a snake's. "You want to know the truth about Khan, don't you?"

28

The Father of Smoke

Fighters of the House of War came down through the narrow wooded ravine with their guns on their shoulders, moving silently like wraiths in the early morning mist. The mullah stood up from the embers of the campfire and waited for their arrival. Taking his cue from him, Noman climbed self-consciously to his feet. As well as the filthy dressing gown, he was now wearing rubber sandals and a pair of blue jogging pants with holes at the knees. It was cold, and he was shivering. He rubbed his arms and tried to tell himself it was all going to be okay. It didn't help that the mullah was clearly nervous. Only Bombboy was unaffected—he was squatting some way off, scratching at the dirt with a stick like a hen pecking in a farmyard.

The fighters stopped short of them, forming an attentive perimeter. They were pointing their guns now, sawn-off shotguns and Kalashnikovs with the bluing rubbed off, as if they spent a lot of time poking things with the muzzles. They were in a terrible state, with starved lupine faces, and several of them had what looked suspiciously like radiation burns and hair coming out in clumps. They were wearing a motley collection of rags, blankets, and animal pelts festooned with leather bandoliers of ammunition. It occurred to Noman that he was probably going to be shot and dumped here at the bottom of the ravine for the jackals and the buzzards to fight over. He'd seen large animal prints down by the river when he went to wash his face at dawn, and he'd sensed something watching him from the undergrowth. He'd never been so far into the tribal areas, so far beyond the writ of the Pakistani army, let alone the state, and it was terrifying to think of what kind of beasts must carve out a living here, alongside these remnants of humans.

By rights, he should have something snappy to say, a final exclamation, but he couldn't think of anything. He really didn't want to die.

The tallest and most cadaverous of the fighters stepped up to Noman. He had a grey-streaked beard to his waist, and his eyes were sunk in cups of grime, as if he were an animal looking out through the eyeholes of a skull. He wore a rolled wool *pakol* hat, and there was a filthy homespun pattu blanket wrapped around his scrawny shoulders. He searched Noman thoroughly, rummaging in his pockets and running his fingers along the seams of his clothes, and then he did the same to the mullah. He made him remove his artificial leg, and holding it by the foot, shook it as if expecting something to fall out. Satisfied, he flung it into the bushes. He nodded to the boy but made no effort to search him.

Noman was appalled. What was wrong with these people? He wanted to shout, *You dolt! Search him! He's a bomb!*

The man nodded to one of his comrades, who walked some way off and spoke quietly into a handheld VHF radio. After a short wait, there was further movement in the ravine. Some kind of large and swaying contraption was coming down through the trees towards them. It took Noman a few moments to realise what it was: four men holding a palanquin, the carrying poles resting on their shoulders and a covered litter suspended beneath.

They moved slowly, treading carefully amongst the rocky outcrops, the litter's ragged curtains dragging along the ground like
unravelling bandages. When they reached the campfire, they
stopped and put down the litter.

The boy was the first to move. He scurried over and knelt
beside the curtain with his head bowed like a supplicant. Noman
saw that he was whispering to someone inside. He realised then
that the boy and his bomb did not belong to the mullah, but
rather they belonged to whoever occupied the litter. The curtain
parted briefly, and a scarred and scabrous hand reached out and
pressed a livid thumb to the boy's forehead. The boy backed up
a little and then turned and motioned for Noman to approach.

The first thing he noticed was the awful smell: the sweet,
gagging stink of necrotic flesh. It gave him a fleeting sense of
some long-forgotten, long-suppressed experience. Was this what
it smelled like, crawling across the dirt floor of his parents shack
with his mother's corpse blocking the doorway? He swallowed,
fighting a wave of nausea, and pulled the lapel of his dressing
gown over his nose as he knelt down alongside the litter.

The boy drew aside the layers of ragged curtain, and Noman
looked upon the charred body of Abu Dukhan, the Father of
Smoke, in a heap on the canvas bed, like an insect, crushed and
lying in its own juices. Here and there, fragments of shrapnel
glimmered like fragments of glass. Whatever dreadful thing
had happened to him, it had clearly happened a while back,
and that he was still alive was clearly a testament to his force of
will rather than any medical assistance subsequently rendered.

When he spoke, his voice was low and rasping and almost
completely unintelligible. "He says that you have the evil eye,"
the boy translated for him. "He wants to know why you are
looking for him."

"I came looking for you because I was told not to," Noman
told the ruined man.

"Who told you not to?" the boy demanded.

"Khan."

At the mention of the old man's name, Abu Dukhan raised his hand, his thumb tipped awkwardly in the direction of mullah. Noman glanced back at the mullah who was pushing himself along the ground in the direction of his leg. Realising that he was being watched, the mullah stopped. He clasped his hands together as if pleading.

"Khan betrayed us," the boy said.

"He has betrayed us all," Noman replied.

"He sent us his emissary, this weak and pathetic creature, this snake in the grass," the boy told him, pointing at the mullah. "The message that he brought from Khan was that, although we were discovered, we could continue to live in the cave under his protection and that we could continue to build our mighty weapon, provided that when we came to strike a blow, it was at a time and place of Khan's choosing. He gave reassurance that, when the time was ripe, using the device would strike a mighty blow for God. He even offered us help in transporting the device to its target. We knew Khan's reputation and the extent of his reach. We decided to believe him and place our trust in his emissary. When the mullah offered to officiate at the wedding of his son, Abu Dukhan gladly accepted. And that is when Khan chose to strike. The mullah snuck away from the wedding party and sent a message to Khan, giving him our location, and soon the drones came and the missiles rained down. Many died: men, women, and children. The cave was buried and the device destroyed. Khan is a traitor."

"You're sure?" Noman asked.

The boy shrugged. "The snake has admitted it."

Noman wasn't sure which one was the most disappointing conclusion: that Khan was a lackey of the Americans or that there would be no dirty bomb.

"What are you going to do?" he asked.

The boy leant forward and listened. When Abu Dukhan

was done he looked up at Noman. "It is not enough to kill Khan. Abu Dukhan says we could have done that long ago. I could have done it." The boy tapped his chest. "I have been as close to Khan as you are to me. Abu Dukhan is very clear. Khan must be discredited. He must be exposed as a traitor and stripped of his rank and his wealth and his lands and his children must be disinherited and only then should he be put to death. Only then can Abu Dukhan die in peace. Do you understand?"

"Sure." Abu Dukhan was completely fucking insane, Noman understood that much.

"You are married to his daughter?"

Noman swallowed. "Yes."

"You are his son?"

"No!"

"You live in his house."

"I hate him as much as you do! That's why I'm here."

The boy leaned in close to Abu Dukhan again and listened and nodded. Then he gestured for one of the fighters to come close, and he whispered in his ear. The fighter stepped behind Noman.

"We can work together on this," he pleaded. "I can help you!"

Something was happening. Silence thickened in the ravine around him, a vacuum in which the tension grew towards the intolerable and with it, the cold realisation that his earlier fears had been correct, that he was about to die. Eyes sliding towards him, then sliding away. Noman felt the colour rising in his cheeks, a snake of sweat running down his temple.

He heard the distinctive *click-clack* of a Kalashnikov being made ready. He swallowed. There was movement behind him. He closed his eyes. The crack of the bullet was ear splitting.

Noman screamed.

He crabbed around sideways, astonished to find that he was unhurt. Behind him the mullah was writhing in the dirt, leg and stump flapping, blood from the artery in his neck squirting twenty feet across the clearing. The tallest of the fighters stepped up to the mullah and shot him again, in the head this time. His dead jaw gaped.

Noman glanced back at the boy.

"I have passed from him to you," the boy said, as if he was making some kind of solemn commitment: a *bamiyat*—an oath of fealty. But Noman understood that he was the one that had made the oath. He had committed either to bring about Khan's downfall or to die together with the boy in a shrapnel tsunami.

29

The Grapes

They were sitting beside each other on a small wooden balcony above the Thames at the back of The Grapes pub in Limehouse, and their fingertips were touching. The winter sun was low, a dull red orb without heat in a pale immensity. It was just past high tide, and the current was beginning to ebb, a great roiling mass of brown water rushing beneath their feet and curving away past the crowded shimmer of Canary Wharf. As in Afghanistan, Ed was reminded of Conrad:

> *What greatness had not floated on the ebb of that river into the mystery of an unknown earth! [. . .] The dreams of men, the seed of commonwealths, the germs of empires.*

He had started out from here, like so many others had done before him, with the belief that he could make the world a safer place, not as a conqueror like those others, but rather as liberator—or so he had told himself. It had carried him to Iraq and Afghanistan, as far as a distant valley at the end of the world. He had been wrong to imagine that he could make any difference, foolish to imagine that the result would be any different than Conrad's French destroyer hurling shells blindly into the jungle.

He had thought when Tariq died that he would not go back, that that period of his life was over. But now he was preparing to return. And this time, he faced a much greater challenge.

"Your mother's asked me to go to Lahore to manage the office there," he said, breaking the silence.

Sameenah had called him into her office that morning and made the offer that would trigger the next part of the plan.

He could tell that Leyla wanted him to tell her that he would not go. When he didn't, she did that thing with her lips—when they went in two different directions at once.

"Is it safe for you?"

She'd noticed the change in him, of course. He had become withdrawn and uncommunicative. It sometimes felt like he was two people, the one here now, touching fingers in the balcony, falling ever further in love, and the other, ready to do Burns' bidding—for the sake of what, exactly? Revenge? It was about more than just Tariq, he told himself, and more than just doing his job, more than any sense of patriotism fed to him at Oxford or in the navy. It was about trying to secure a better future for Afghanistan and Pakistan. Getting rid of Khan would be like felling a massive old tree in a forest. It would allow light to reach the forest floor and encourage new shoots to grow. Of course it was fraught with danger, of course you couldn't entirely control what came after, but for the sake of the people of those countries, it was worth taking the risk. Or was it? Was that what Conrad had meant when he talked about the "dreams of men?" Was he about to make the same foolish mistake again?

"How long are you going to stay?" she asked.

He withdrew his hand. "I'm not sure."

Sometimes it was better not to think about it, to just get

on with it. He had a sequence of actions that had been mapped out for him.

"Will you come back?"

"That's up to your mother," he said.

"You don't have to do what she says," she said.

"Of course I do," he said, cruelly. "I'm not like you. I need this job."

"Why are you being like this?"

"Like what?"

"You're so bloody angry. You're the angriest man I know."

They ran back down cobbled streets between converted warehouses. He caught her by the arm and pushed her into a darkened loading dock, his hands roving under her coat, reckless with lust. She was right, he was angry. At himself and at Burns, who had made a liar of him. He couldn't bear the thought that this might be their last night together. She broke away, and he ran after her, her smile bright white in the gloaming, her mocking laughter echoing around the high walls. They crossed the Highway and Cable Street, and under a railway arch he pulled her to him and they kissed hungrily. He pressed himself against the upward curve of her thigh. She pushed him off and ran. They had crossed the line back into Whitechapel.

They reached the house just as his father was leaving. A moment's awkwardness as they passed each other in the hallway, followed by a helter-skelter rush to the bedroom, discarding clothing on the way. He made love to her with the urgency of a soldier on the eve of departure for battle.

Afterwards, Leyla arched her back and stretched like a cat in the narrow confines of his bed. He told himself that he was not going to do this.

Who was he kidding? The spy in him was already preparing for the dangerous journey towards Javid Aslam Khan.

30

Non-compliant Subject Removal

Ed flew out of Terminal 4 on a sunny June evening on the return leg of a Pakistan International Airways flight, the cabin's stale air saturated with the sour smell of ghee. He was wedged between two large, ill-tempered women and one row behind a hysterical infant. He didn't sleep.

After eight hours, the plane landed in Lahore, and as soon as the roar of deceleration had ended, the aisles were full of pushing and shoving families, pulling down suitcases and bundles of gifts, as they taxied to the terminal. Ed was dragged along in a rush to the covered walkway at the front of the plane. He passed through immigration without incident. Standing by the carousel, waiting for his bag, he could hear the hubbub of an over-excited crowd.

There was an eager young man with stiff toothbrush hair waiting for him in the arrivals hall. He was carrying a cardboard sign with the name *Edward Henry Malik* handwritten on it. He introduced himself as Faisal and assured him that his uncle, general manager of J&K Cargo and Travel Lahore branch, was waiting with much anticipation to greet him at the office. After a brief tour of the premises, Faisal would escort him to his residence and give him the opportunity to rest before assuming his new responsibilities bright and early the next morning. He took Ed's bag by the handle and wielded it like a riot shield through the press of people while Ed followed.

The terminal was a chapel of calm in comparison with the chaos of the morning rush hour: so many auto-rickshaws, cars, buses, and minibuses, all jostling for position in a moraine tide of eddies and blockages and moments of sudden acceleration.

"How is my Auntie Sameenah?" Faisal asked. "It's been ages since she has been to visit us. How is my very beautiful cousin Leyla?"

"They know you're coming," Jonah had told him, just before they parted. "We've made sure of that. They'll come to you. My guess is they'll do it quickly. Noman will want to have hold of you before Khan finds out."

He didn't even make it to the office. They dragged him out of the car while it was boxed in at a roundabout. The first indication of what was happening was when he caught a fleeting glimpse of someone dodging between cars in the offside wing mirror. Then, the unmistakable pop and hiss of smoke grenades. He turned in his seat in time to see several black canisters with contrails of yellow smoke, arcing over the top of the traffic and tumbling down around the car. Within moments the view was obscured by shifting smoke.

Faisal was trembling, looking left and right. "What's going on?"

"Stay calm," Ed told him, gently but firmly. "Keep your hands on the wheel."

"Just let it happen," Jonah had advised him. "Don't try and resist."

Four masked men carrying batons stepped out of the

smoke and surrounded the car. They were wearing sandbags over their heads, with ragged eyeholes cut in them that gave them a nightmarish aspect. They were shouting in Pashtu. They methodically smashed the windows and stove in the bonnet, and while one of them held a gun to Faisal's head, another, a mountain of a man, opened Ed's door and pulled him out onto the tarmac. His arms were pulled behind his back and his wrists bound with Plasticuffs.

He was lifted onto his feet and guided out through the smoke, across the chaos of the roundabout and into a side street, where a black Range Rover was parked. They bundled him in and jumped in after. He was wedged between two of his kidnappers, bent over to release the pressure on his arms, with his head on his knees. When they pulled off the sandbags, he struggled to contain his alarm. They looked sick, maybe even terminally so, with red eyes, sores on their cheeks, and bald patches in their beards. The only one who didn't look like he was on the brink of death was the largest, a bushy-bearded Pashtun who drove the car.

"I am Raja Mahfouz."

"I think you've got the wrong person," Ed told him. "Whatever this is, I'm sure you've made a mistake."

"I don't think so," said Raja Mahfouz.

He flicked a switch that lit up the dashboard with a flashing red and blue light. They eased out into the traffic.

"They're going to take you somewhere private where they can question you," Jonah had said. "They may threaten you, but we don't think they're going to hurt you. After all, you have no reason not to cooperate with them."

Ed knew Lahore reasonably well, and despite being folded over, he soon had a sense of where they were going. They entered a quieter district of large, high-walled compounds and mature banyan trees set back from the road. Gulberg. Eventually the car turned off the asphalt road onto a sandy track, hemmed in by high walls topped with broken glass that formed a cul-de-sac. At the end of the track the car pulled up in front of a twelve-foot steel gate, and the driver beeped his horn.

Two bearded men with Kalashnikovs and Salafists' short trousers opened the gate, and one of them checked underneath the car with a mirror on a pole while the other watched the road behind. They were in the same appalling physical condition as his kidnappers. Satisfied, the man with the pole waved them in before retreating behind a sandbagged emplacement.

The car pulled up in front of a large three-storey flat-roofed concrete house that looked like it had been built in the fifties or sixties. It stood in the midst of a waste of parched brown lawn bordered by dead shrubs. They pulled Ed out. He stared up at the house. Its darkened windows were secured by bar grilles with scorch marks on the surrounding walls that suggested they had been hurriedly put in place, and he could see two more guards silhouetted on the roof.

An old, wild-eyed woman rushed forward and hissed at him.

"Foul shame on you," she said.

Raja Mahfouz shooed her away.

"Go on," he said.

As Ed climbed the steps towards the front of the house, a man pushed through the steel-bar gate that covered the doorway. He was a bull of a man, with a fighter's stance and fathomless blue eyes that gave nothing away.

"I am Noman."

31 ﺑ

Janissaries

Ed followed Noman through the ransacked house, past smashed-up furniture and graffitied walls. This close, Ed realised how short the ISI man was. Only his musculature made him seem tall.

"I thought you might like to see your room." Noman led down a narrow stairwell to the basement and along a corridor with mould-stained walls to a bolted metal door. "It's Spartan, but functional. Guests rest here between innings." He drew the bolts and gave the door a nudge. It opened on an impenetrable black rectangle. "The light is controlled from outside." He flicked the trip-switch on the corridor wall and the underground cell was flooded with light. It was just large enough for a mattress, and beside it, a cheap plastic bucket without a handle. There was an orange overall neatly folded on the mattress. Noman grinned, all teeth and gums. "We've provided you with a change of clothes, Gitmo style." He closed the door and bolted it again. He turned off the light. "Now let me show you where we'll do our work." Midway up the corridor, Noman opened another door and stepped into a larger windowless space, a cellar with a concrete floor. "I've made do with the equipment available." At some stage it had been used as a gym, and various anti-quated pieces of equipment, including leather medicine balls and a suede-topped vaulting horse, were scattered about the place. At the centre of the room was an improvised rack. Two inclined wooden benches had been arranged in a V-shape, with the open ends of the V raised on a third perpendicular bench and the apex above a drain in the floor.

"I prefer to raise the feet when waterboarding," Noman explained, cheerily. "And I find it to be more efficient and less wasteful of water to follow the Spanish method and force the cloth into the recipient's mouth rather than cover the whole face, though if you prefer a different method I'm open to suggestion."

"Look, I'm not in a position to tell you anything that you don't already know," Ed replied. "We both know how this works. I spent five years deliberately cut off from my colleagues, running a single high-profile agent inside your organisation. He's now dead, and any information that he provided has outlived its usefulness."

"That's for me to decide."

"You think that my former employers would have let me leave the country if they thought I knew anything valuable?"

Noman shrugged. "Then there's no reason not to tell me everything you know. Come on. Let's go for a walk. Who knows when you'll get a chance to see daylight again."

Ed followed him back up the stairs and through the house to the front door.

They were walking on dead grass, alongside the perimeter wall, with two of the guards following. A coat of red dust covered everything.

Noman stopped beside a bench beneath a bower of

Bougainvillea that had shed all its leaves. Behind them, the guards also stopped.

"Sit."

They sat beside each other. Noman offered him a cigarette.

"No thanks."

Noman shrugged and lit one. "I wish it would rain." He reached into his pocket and took out a digital voice recorder. "Tell me about when you went to work for the British State. First state your name." He leant back with his legs outstretched and the air of someone expecting to be entertained, "Give me the whole nine yards, don't leave anything out."

"Edward Henry Malik." Jonah had told him to tell the unalloyed truth, and Ed saw no reason not to. He didn't want to find himself back in the basement. "In October 2001, I returned to the UK from Saudi Arabia and joined the Royal Naval Reserve."

Noman seemed surprised. "You're a boating man?"

"I didn't spend much time at sea. Because of my background and my skill with languages, I was selected for the Joint Services Intelligence Organisation. I received training at the Defence and Intelligence Security Centre in Chicksands. I studied several HUMINT modules. I learned Pashto in the language-training wing, and I completed a resistance to interrogation course."

"What did they do to you there?"

"The usual pride-and-ego-down stuff."

Noman whistled. "I can see we're going to have to throw the manual out when dealing with you, bypass the early stages, and go straight to the sexy stuff."

Ed paused. "You want me to go on?"

"I would, if I was you." Noman looked in the direction of the two guards. "You don't want to give them any reason to think you're withholding information. They'll go to work on you."

"Who are they?" Ed asked. "They aren't exactly regular troops, are they? They look like you scraped them out of a hole. Does Khan know I'm here?"

Noman flicked the stub of his cigarette on the ground and crushed it beneath his heel.

"I'm the one that asks the questions."

"If I'm involved in some kind of off-the-books operation because you can't trust your own people, I think I deserve to know."

"You're not in a position to make demands." Even sitting, there was something explosive about Noman that seemed barely contained, as if he might burn a hole in the ground. "Tell me your story. Make me believe in you."

"Once I'd completed my training, I was sent to Afghanistan. For three months, I served in the ISAF Security Mission Headquarters in Kabul."

"What were you doing there?"

"I was part of an American-funded intelligence cell tasked with buying back surface-to-air missiles."

Let out all that anger and bitterness at the mess we made, Jonah had told him. *Remember, you were dismissed. You don't owe us any loyalty.*

"We were negotiating with former Northern Alliance commanders to buy back the missiles we'd given them during the fight against the Soviets. These were warlords, most of them now in government and nominally on our side. They weren't going to just hand the stuff back, though. They wanted money for their toys, and we gave it to them by the pallet-load. They then spent the money on kick-starting opium production, which had pretty much dried up under the Taliban."

"Who was running the operation?"

"Bob Hagedorn from Langley; it was a CIA operation. That was the first time I met him. I came across him again later in Iraq and then again when he was made head of station in Kabul. We didn't get on."

"You head-butted him in Kabul."

"I'm not proud of what I did."

"We'll come back to him."

"I didn't stay that long in Afghanistan."

"Why not?"

"Because I knew Arabic, they wanted me in Iraq."

"So you went to Iraq?"

"I flew into Baghdad Airport in April 2003 with a mixed party of soldiers and civilians led by Director of Special Forces. US armour had just reached the airport, but it wasn't secured yet. Baghdad was a mess. Disbanded Republican Guards, Fed-ayeen irregulars, and criminals let out of the jails were tearing the city apart."

"What task were you given?"

"Our first job was to make contact with agents that had supplied information prior to the fall of Saddam. The Prime Minister had put so much emphasis on weapons of mass destruction that the pressure was on us to find some."

"But you didn't," Noman said.

"No. Not a goddamn thing. We were deep in the shit."

"But you stayed on?"

"Yes. I was attached to a British intelligence unit tasked with identifying the location of High-Value Targets—HVTs— elements of the old Baathist regime, on the American's deck of cards. We were to stick close to the Americans and help them in any way we could. Several HVTs were taken down as a result of intelligence we supplied, but it soon became clear to those of us on the ground that the real threat was not from former-regime elements, but from the jihadists who had put out a call across the Middle East for Mujahideen to come and fight in Iraq. Iraqi society was collapsing and we were doing the

jihadists a favour, removing local leadership and creating a vacuum they could step into. Things got better when McChrystal
took over Joint Special Operations Command. He went after
the jihadists. But we still had problems."

"What kind of problems?"

"The jihadists were much tougher customers than the
Baathists. Being locked up and interrogated was an unpleasant
experience for the Iraqi elite who'd enjoyed an easy life under
Saddam, but many of the religious extremists already had experience of torture at the hands of secret police across the Arab
world—they weren't intimidated by us. We also had problems
back in the UK, where the Ministry of Defence understood
why British forces were in Basra, but they couldn't see why we
had to be in Baghdad. They started interfering. We lost operational independence. The Americans accused us of being semi-
detached. At the same time, everything the Americans were
doing was going wrong. The body bags were building up. The
Provisional Authority was wasting billions. Iraq wasn't going to
be some kind of model for democracy in the Middle East. It
was a fucking disaster. I got fed up with it and resigned from
the navy. In late 2004, I returned to the UK and went back to
work for the bank."

Noman lit another cigarette. "How did that go?"

"How do you think? I tried to stick it out at the bank, but
I couldn't settle. I couldn't talk to anyone about what I'd been
doing. I fell out with my line manager. Then out of the blue I
got a letter from MI6, would I like to join?"

"So you joined MI6?"

"Yes. First, I had to take the Civil Service Selection Board.
Then I was sent to Fort Monckton in Hampshire for operational training."

"But you'd already been in the field for several years," Noman observed.

"Sure. I knew as much as the instructors did. But I bit my

lip and got on with it. The end of my training coincided with
the 7/7 attacks, and because I had experience of running agents,
I was temporarily attached to MI5, who were scrambling to
set up a network of informants in Muslim communities in
England to prevent anything like that happening again. After
a few months of lurking around mosques, I returned to MI6
and a desk at Vauxhall Cross in the Af-Pak Controllerate. In
February 2006, I was sent to Afghanistan."

"Why?"

"I was supposed to be processing intelligence reports, making assessments of the capacity of insurgent networks, tracing
individual commanders and their modus operandi. Because of
the proposed deployment to Helmand, it was now a priority.
But then Tariq came along, and everything changed."

"When was Tariq turned?"

"A month after I arrived. March 2006. Because of his
importance, I was instructed to drop everything and run him
myself."

"Now he's dead."

"Yes. Khan killed him. He should never have taken the
assignment in Abbottabad. I warned him not to."

"We'll return to Tariq in due course. After he died and you
made yourself persona non grata in Kabul, you flew back to
London?"

"Yes that's right."

"And you were dismissed from MI6?"

"That's right. I was initially suspended, and then after a few
weeks, I was dismissed at a board of inquiry. Burns threw me
to the wolves."

"And that was it for your association with MI6?"

"Yes, officially that is. I did a one-off courier job after I left,
mostly because I didn't know what else to do. Then I got the
job at J&K."

"What courier job?"

"I delivered a suitcase full of cash to a woman in a hotel room in Dubai."

"That's it?"

"That's it."

"That will do for now," Noman said. He held up his hand, and the guards approached. "Take him down to his room."

32

Schedule 7 Detention

Leyla was in the departures lounge, with her MacBook open on her knees. A large black man with a mournful expression on his face sat down beside her and said something.

She removed her ear-buds and said, "Excuse me?"

"Where do you think you're going?"

"What do you mean?"

"Look over there," he said. There were two armed police officers pointing their submachine guns at the floor in front of Hugo Boss. "And over there." She looked in the opposite direction. Two more armed officers hovering by Sunglasses Hut, also intent on the floor. "They're going to throw you on the ground and shout at you if you don't do as I say."

"What do you want?"

"See the door over there." He tipped his head in the direction of a nondescript grey door between Costa and Travelex.

"Yes."

"It's Mr. Ben time."

"I'm sorry?"

"Don't worry. You're too young. Just go through the door."
She did.

"I'm not signing these," she told the woman, pushing the forms
back across the Formica table. "Do you seriously think I'm
going to waive my rights?"

"Why are you going to Pakistan?" the woman asked her.
She was black, in a navy blue uniform with Border Agency
epaulettes. There was another standing, blocking the door, a
Bengali by the look of her.

"What horrible irony means that the border agency is the
most ethnically diverse arm of government?" Leyla wondered
aloud.

"Just answer the question."

"My mother wants me to marry a nice boy from Lahore."
She turned to Jonah. "What is this?"

There were four of them in the interview room: Leyla, the
border agency women, and Jonah, but there was a mirrored
glass wall that suggested others were watching.

Jonah grimaced. "We'd like to understand *why* you have
decided to travel to Pakistan."

"I don't believe this. Under what authority am I being held
here?"

"Under Schedule 7 of the Terrorism Act 2000."

"You think I'm a terrorist?"

He shrugged. "Are you?"

"Fuck you," she said. She stretched out in her chair with her
arms crossed. "You have nine hours."

Jonah sighed. He glanced at the Border Agency officers.
"That's all, thanks." He waited until they had left before pro-
ducing a cigarette packet from his pocket. "Do you mind if I
smoke?"

"I mind that you won't let me see a lawyer."

"The usual rules don't apply." He shook out a cigarette. "Do you think you're going to find him?"

"Find who?"

"Ed."

"Why do you care?"

"We'd like to find him, too."

"I bet you would."

He lit the cigarette, inhaled and exhaled. "What do you think happened?"

"What do you mean?"

"What happened to him? Was he abducted, or did he decide to disappear?"

"Why would he decide to disappear?"

Jonah shook his head. "Perhaps he's gone over to the other side."

"Why would he do that?" she sneered. "After all, you've treated him so well."

Leyla's next visitor was a woman wearing a dark red Jaeger jacket and matching pencil skirt. She entered carrying a coffee in a cardboard cup and perched on the edge of the seat beside Jonah.

"I've become a fan of your blog," she said, without introducing herself. "You're beginning to cause quite a stir."

"Ed was abducted in broad daylight. Of course I'm going to write about it."

The name Tracy was written on the woman's cup. Leyla didn't suppose it was the woman's real name; a random, slightly manic thought struck her: maybe a spook computer spat out a list of names every week for use with over-eager baristas. And then another even more random thought: maybe the woman's father was a fan of *High Society*.

"Are you planning to post anything further on the matter?" the woman asked.

"Like the fact that he used to be an MI6 officer involved in spying on Pakistan?"

"Yes."

"I'm waiting for the right moment."

The woman sighed. "Edward Malik was one of our best. Nobody was more cut up than I was when we had to let him go. He had such a bright future and then to have it all snatched away, it must have been a bitter pill."

"Spare me."

"Am I correct in saying that you're going out to Pakistan to search for him?"

"Why am I being held here?"

She took a thoughtful sip of her coffee. "I have a problem. There are eight Taliban moderates in prison in Rawalpindi. They're not good men by any means, but they are realists. I believe that if they were released, they could form the nucleus of a group prepared to negotiate with the Tajiks and the Uzbeks and all the other groups to secure a peaceful future for Afghanistan. So I've been doing all I can to get them released. If the Pakistani intelligence services found out what I've been up to, it might cause difficulties."

"Why are you telling me this?"

"Because it's the truth; because you think I'm a liar, and I can't think of any other way to prove I'm not. I care about the people that work for me, Leyla. I keep tabs on them. In Ed's case, I made a mistake. I thought he was clean, that he could go over there without repercussions. But it turns out that he knows something valuable. It's not connected with his time in the Service. It came after. He may not realise what he knows, but he knows it nonetheless. It's unfortunate. It means I need to find out where he is. I need it as much as you need it. That makes us allies, of sorts."

Leyla laughed bitterly. "I don't think so."

"I'm concerned that his captors might resort to unpleasant tactics to get the information out of him."

33

The Toca

The gag reflex was almost, but not quite immediate.

There were a few moments when he could still breathe in gulps of air. The water ran everywhere, in his mouth, his nose, and his eyes. He tried, by tightening his throat, to let in as little water as possible, but he couldn't hold on. It felt like he was drowning, his body contorting as it heaved against the rack, his hands and his feet shaking uncontrollably.

"Enough," said a voice.

The water stopped, and they pulled the rag out of his mouth. One of the sandbag men punched him in the stomach until he threw up any water that he'd swallowed. And Noman, who squatted beside him throughout, consulted his watch and pronounced how long he'd lasted.

Fifteen seconds . . .

There was a quality to what followed that was not unlike a dream, a melting together that made it difficult to keep track. It felt to Ed as if time had come unmoored and the order of things was no longer certain. They came into his cell for two reasons only: prayer or punishment. They dragged him down the corridor to the cellar and led him to either the improvised rack or the prayer mat. It was impossible to calculate how often they came. The order of the daily prayers was jumbled and non-sensical, *al-Fajr* followed *al-'Asr*, *al-'Isha* preceded *al-Maghrib*, and the prayer mat pointed in a different direction every time. If he refused to pray, he was beaten with a bamboo switch.

On the rack, they waterboarded him. They strapped him to the V with his legs apart and raised above his head, and his arms bound at his sides. A rag was stuffed in his mouth and the water poured on his face from an old tin watering can. Later, they told him that the longest he'd lasted was seventeen seconds, though he had no way of telling if that was correct.

They wore the sandbags over their heads throughout, even the ones he recognised—the giant Mahfouz and Noman, who was as wide as he was tall. There seemed to be no purpose to it, any more than there was to the questions they asked. They looped and meandered and fixated on unexpected details, as if the questions themselves were deliberately intended to add to his disorientation. He remembered describing the problems they had in both Iraq and Afghanistan with suspect's names. They didn't even have a common way of writing Mohammed, so at times it felt like they had no idea who they were up against or who they had in prison. They seemed particularly interested in his mother and her lover's suicide pact—why they had cho-sen death over any other alternative? They seized on anger and shame, on anything that animated or needled him.

But there was really only one question that mattered, he understood that much. Noman whispered it softly in his ear, often just before they tipped the watering can . . . "Can I trust you?"

Back in the cell, they flicked the lights on and off at ran-dom, switching from total darkness to searing fluorescence, and one of the guards banged on the door at random intervals with a length of pipe.

At some point, he began to hallucinate. He couldn't tell if it was a natural product of his condition or if he had been drugged. It couldn't have been something he ate because they hadn't given him anything to eat. He was starving. Maybe the water was spiked.

In the darkness, it seemed that the cell filled with people.

He could hear them breathing and imagine their expressions: Tariq standing at the foot of the cot with a reproachful look on his face; Samantha Burns with her shallow smile; Jonah grimly blocking the door. There was Sameenah in a shell suit dancing from foot to foot; resentful Nasir; supercilious Totty with his red socks; and somewhere in the darkness behind him, in all her defiance, Leyla. All the people who had brought him here, even if they didn't know it. They were watching to see how he would acquit himself.

Just tell the truth. That's the beauty of it, Jonah had told him. *If you want to destroy Khan, you only have to tell the truth.*

It felt like he might die before he got the chance.

34

Cui Bono

The bolt was drawn back, and the door opened.

They lifted him up off the mattress and dragged him past the cellar door and up the steps to a room on the ground floor. Heavy blackout curtains covered the window, and the only light was from a bulb overhead. In the centre of the white-tiled floor, two wooden chairs faced each other across a wooden table with a meal of curry and naan bread laid out on it. The smell of the food was almost overpowering.

Noman was standing beside a sideboard with a bottle of Black Label on it. He had removed the sandbag and it lay beside him on the floor.

"Sit down," he said, casually. "Eat."

Ed needed no further encouragement. He shook off his captors and staggered over to the table. He tore off a piece of naan, and jabbed it in the curry before stuffing it in his mouth. He barely finished one mouthful before cramming his mouth again. He dropped into the seat and continued eating, shovelling the food into his mouth, pausing only to drink water from a metal cup.

Noman crossed over to him with a glass and the bottle of whisky. They sat across from each other. Noman poured himself a measure and sipped it.

"When you recruited him, how did you know that Tariq was due to return to Islamabad and join the Afghan bureau?" he asked, eventually.

Ed paused between mouthfuls. So now it had begun. He felt genuinely grateful to be able to answer Noman's questions. "Because that's what Burns told me when she called me at the embassy in Kabul."

He remembered that they had woken him in the middle of the night and escorted him to the embassy, put him in the secure room with the secure phone. He tried to recall her exact words.

"She said that an ISI agent had got himself in a fix on UK soil, and the situation was ripe for exploitation. She said that the agent was about to be called back to work for the ISI's Afghan bureau. She said, 'I don't need to tell you how important it is that we have an asset inside the Afghan bureau if we're going to get it right in Helmand. We need to get a handle on what the ISI are up to there, and we need to do it quickly.'"

"How did Burns know that Tariq was due to be recalled?"

Ed shrugged. "I don't know. I really don't. I guess it came from a wiretap. GCHQ were all across Tariq's communications."

"You saw a transcript in the file?"

"No. There was nothing about him going back to the Afghan bureau. But it wasn't the full file. It was something they pulled together just for me."

"You didn't think that was strange? They give you an agent to run, but you don't get to see the entire file? A key piece of information was given to you, and you accepted it without seeing any evidence?"

"It was short notice. The circumstances were unusual."

"Did you ever get to see the full file?"

"No." He was conscious that it was a feeble response and there was what sounded to his ears like a pleading quality in his voice. "Burns played her cards close to her chest. That's her way."

"And then you returned to Afghanistan?"

"That's right."

"And that's where you next met with Tariq?"

"That's right."

"Describe the meeting."

Ed closed his eyes, and the memories gathered around him like old acquaintances.

He wound black turban cloth around his head and under his chin, drawing it up over his nose to mask his face. The sun was low in the sky and the wind had got up; orange-tinted dust billowed over the Hesco rampart of the Forward Operating Base and in front of him the sheet-metal door rattled in its frame.

"I'll be back in a couple of hours," he shouted in the ear of the gate sentry, hoping it was true.

"You're a crazy man!" The sentry was a wide-eyed and buck-toothed boy from Tennessee who'd never seen someone walk out of the FOB alone and unarmed before. It was against every rule in the book. Beside the sentry, Dai gave him a nod that Ed had learnt meant both "Good luck" and "See you later for whatever passes for beer in this place." Not that there was any beer in the FOB. There was plenty of dimethylamine, but no alcohol. They would have to go over to the Afghan Police post for that. If he made it back. . . .

He slipped into the anonymity of the dust storm. Twenty minutes later, he was just one in the crowd hurrying to cross the border before it closed. The friendship gate was an unwieldy double-arched desert confection, which looked as if George

Lucas had assembled it from the salvaged parts of a second-hand space station, while the hooded and cowled figures struggling beneath it resembled Jawas and Tusken Raiders.

The gate was too precarious to admit traffic, and the long lines of waiting trucks were funnelled off the highway into a detour, a one-lane dirt road that snaked through a treacherous scree-covered ravine. By day, up to a hundred trucks carrying fuel and supplies for ISAF passed this way. But by night—when the crossing was officially closed—smugglers and their corrupt allies in the Afghan Border Police controlled it.

Ed set off on foot down the ravine, passing alongside the stationary trucks. Without warning, a man stepped out from behind a truck up ahead. It was Tariq, wearing the uniform of the Pakistan Frontier Police. He indicated for Ed to follow and ducked back into the shadows.

The tailgate was down on one of the trucks and ragged tarpaulin pulled aside. Ed climbed up and into the back where Tariq was waiting, sitting astride a pallet of fifty-kilogram sacks.

"This is the kind of shit you're looking for, right?"

Ed switched on his flashlight and inspected the cargo. No effort had been made to disguise their provenance: white sacks with the familiar palm tree logo and PALMTREE FERTILIZER LIMITED stencilled on them in black lettering and, below that, CALCIUM AMMONIUM NITRATE (CAN). The PalmTree factory was a sprawling forty-year-old complex of belching chimneys, rattling pipes, and rusting tanks surrounded by thousands of acres of mango orchards and cotton fields on the outskirts of Multan, in Punjab's agricultural heartland. Powerful and well protected landowners bought the three types of fertiliser produced by the factory, used the two safer varieties domestically, and then trucked the ammonium nitrate across the border to Afghanistan. It was easy to turn CAN into a bomb. Insurgents boiled the small, off-white granules to separate the calcium from the nitrate, mixed it with fuel oil and packed the slurry into a jug or box, and rigged it for detonation. Each sack could make up to four bombs.

"Four truck loads," Tariq told him. "That's a lot of dead unbelievers, right?"

"Where are they going?"

"Helmand. This is all they need for the spring offensive, right here. I've done well, right?"

Ed grunted. In his experience, all agents were insecure and out for approval. Tariq was no different to anyone else he'd run. The key was giving it to him in the right dose. Too much and he might get complacent and start taking risks, too little and he might run back to the ISI and confess his sins.

Tariq gave him a bewildered look, and said. "You're not tawhid, are you?"

Ed frowned. "No."

"I hoped you were some kind of believer."

He sounded depressed. Ed was surprised. Was that the impression that he'd given in the Oldham flat—that he was motivated by purity of belief and action? Was Tariq hoping that there was some kind of redemption in betrayal?

He reached out and grabbed him by the lapels.

"Listen to me," he said. "I'm not a mullah, or a guru, or a fucking Sufi saint. I don't care whether God is a Muslim, a Christian, or a Jew. I'm as fucked up as the next person, as fucked up as you. Yes, you'll save lives. British lives and Afghan lives. Well done. One day, we'll give you a medal. Meantime, tell me, who is this shit is going to?"

Two days later, a US Special Forces team backed up by a British Quick Reaction Force from 2 Para intercepted the trucks on the highway as they were being unloaded near Lashkar Gah. Four insurgents were killed, and a local businessman, with connections to the Provincial Governor, was arrested and airlifted to Bagram Prison for interrogation. Subsequent operations in Sangin and Musa Qala resulted in the arrest of several alleged Taliban sympathisers.

He could remember the jubilant reaction from London: Britain's security operatives, for too long starved of actionable intelligence, now had something to sink their teeth into. And the Americans could be invited to the feast. Signals intelligence from GCHQ and the American NSA was routinely shared under a bilateral agreement, but human intelligence was often subject to more of a barter process. By passing on intelligence from Tariq, the British were ensuring that they would be included if the Americans uncovered their own similar sources.

Noman poured cold water on it.

"Was there a decrease in the number of roadside bombs in Helmand as a result of the tip-off provided by Tariq?"

"Not much," Ed conceded. "But there wasn't an increase either. If we hadn't intercepted those convoys, a lot more soldiers would have died."

"How many shipments of ammonium nitrate did you seize?"

"Between 2006 and 2010, seven shipments as a result of information from Tariq."

"All from the same source?"

"Yes, from the PalmTree factory."

"But fertiliser still found its way to Helmand?"

"Sure. Tariq could only give us what he knew."

"Or what he was told to give you."

Ed looked at him. "You think that the information from Tariq was coming from a higher source?"

"Don't be cute with me," Noman snapped. "I'll send you right back down to the cellar. Tariq was a conduit, we both know that."

"It's what I always suspected," Ed conceded. "But I didn't have any proof. I didn't know the identity of the higher source."

"It's not difficult," Noman said. "Cui bono: who benefits. There are two factories in Pakistan that produce calcium ammonium nitrate," Noman told him. "PalmTree Fertilizers was initially established as a joint venture by the Pakistan Industrial Development Corporation and the Gulf Council Oil Company. It was privatised in 2005 and acquired by a consortium of the Noor Group and the Sharif Group. The other firm that produces CAN is Punjab Fertilizer Ltd., an enterprise privately owned by the Chuppa Group. You stopped the flow of CAN from PalmTree, but not from Punjab Fertilizer. You closed down one and opened a market for the other."

"You're suggesting that we got caught up in some kind of turf war between competing companies over the supply of nitrate to the Taliban?"

"Wake up and smell the coffee. That's exactly what I'm suggesting. And get this: the majority shareholding in the Chuppa Group is held by the Khan family, originally of Lahore. Javid Aslam Khan owns a 6 percent stake in the company."

"You think Khan was the higher source?"

"Don't you?"

There was a knock on the door, and a beautiful barefoot young woman with tiny silver bells on her ankles came in with a steel tray. She set the tray down on the table and loaded it with the empty bowls. Her movements were slow and deliberate, as if she had been drugged, and Noman watched her with a kind of lazy but predatory interest.

Ed realised that she must be Tariq's widow. He wanted to say something to her, but there was no consolation that he could offer. She picked up the tray and glided out of the room.

"Tell me about the next meeting."

35

The Sociopath's Address Book and Other Disappointments

They were in Kandahar, in the cemetery behind the Chowk Madad. Tariq came hurrying between the jumbled stone cairns and the ragged green martyr's flags with a turban disguising his face.

"What have you got for me this time?" Ed demanded, once he'd established they only had a few minutes.

"The nasty file." Tariq pressed a memory stick into his hand. "The sociopath's address book."

He left as swiftly as he arrived.

Bit by bit, Ed recounted the extent of the information in the Afghan bureau files that were passed to him by Tariq. The name and location and ISI point of contact for the leadership of some of the nastiest splinter groups in Afghanistan, Al-Qaeda affiliates, offshoots, and copycats, including the Lashkar-e-Jhangvi, the Zarqawis, and the White Taliban. In addition to the contact details, there was a breakdown of their sources of funding including, at the local level, extortion, kidnapping, and smuggling operations and, internationally, via wealthy donors in the

Persian Gulf. Ed's memory was good. He could remember the names of each and every ISI informant.

Noman interrupted. "Stop," he said. He was wearing the same stony, I'm-about-to-explode frown as when Ed described the provenance of the intercepted cargo of fertiliser. "That's all he gave you?"

"What do you mean?"

"A ragtag bunch of splinter groups that nobody would miss. That was your great coup?"

Ed shrugged. "It's what he gave us."

"Didn't you ask for more?"

"Of course we did. He said he didn't have access to better information. He didn't have the clearance."

Noman was incredulous. "Did you believe him?"

"I didn't know what to believe."

"Tariq was Khan's message-boy. He carried messages to everybody, from Mullah Omar to the Haqqanis, father and son. He knew everybody! He could have given you everything!"

Anger had been replaced by confusion on Noman's face.

The next memory stick was pressed into Ed's hand in a roadside culvert outside Jalalabad. They squatted amongst tangles of mottled bark sheddings that had been washed down from a eucalyptus plantation on the slope above them.

"They're going to wet themselves for this in London," Tariq told him with a sparkle in his eyes.

"What is it?"

"The enemy within," he said. "The alumni list."

The files on the stick identified the location of a dozen madrassas across the tribal areas providing weapons and explosives-handling training to eager young jihadis from English and other European inner cities, and with it, a list of the names and passport numbers of those who had graduated over a four-year period. British, Dutch, and German passport holders who might one day form the nucleus of a homegrown insurrection.

"And did they wet themselves?" Noman asked.

"Sure. Since the 7/7 attacks, preventing any further attacks on the homeland had become the highest priority."

"But?"

Ed sighed. "We couldn't find any of the individuals on the list. Don't get me wrong. They were real people. We could identify their families. Some of their friends and associates were placed under surveillance. A couple of arrests followed. Two of them turned up dead in Afghanistan, and another in Somalia. But there was no record of any of them reentering the UK. It was the same with the Dutch and the Germans. At Vauxhall Cross, it became known as the missing persons list."

"And the madrassas?"

Ed shrugged. "All the indicators suggested that the sites had been used as training camps, but by the time we got drones in the airspace over them, they had all been abandoned. Some just a couple of weeks before we received the intelligence."

And the confusion written on Noman's face had been replaced with dismay.

After that, it was an irrigation ditch in the Green Zone, the lush strip of dense vegetation that ran alongside the Helmand River. Ed went out of the medieval mud-walled fort that was FOB Inkerman with a platoon patrol from 2 Para. They dropped him off at a prearranged spot and agreed to collect him on the way back in. He slid down a reed bank into green scum-filled water. Tariq was already there waiting.

"What did he have this time?" Noman demanded.

"He told me a story," Ed explained. "He said it concerned a jihadi group in the tribal areas and its efforts to build a dirty bomb out of a cache of radioactive medical waste. When I asked where he had got the information, he refused to answer. He said he wanted to talk to Samantha Burns."

"He used her name?"

"Yes. I was surprised. Shocked, even."

Noman swore softly under his breath. "What did you do?"

"I called Burns." He'd waded along the ditch far enough to be out of earshot and called her on the sat-phone.

"How did she react?"

"She was unruffled. She told me to hand over the phone to him. I argued against it; caving into Tariq like that would only encourage more petulance. But I was overruled."

"So you gave him the phone?"

"Yes. She was my boss. It was an order."

It was Tariq's turn to wade along the ditch.

"Did you hear what was said?" Noman asked.

Ed shook his head.

"How long did they talk for?"

"Forty minutes."

"What did you do?"

"I waited in the ditch."

"And then?"

"Tariq handed me back the phone and took off into the foliage. Burns was still on the phone, and so I asked her what had been said. She told me not to worry about it. And she'd let me know what was going on in due course."

"And did she?"

"About two weeks later she called me in Kabul. She sounded relieved. She said it was a great coup, proof that our agent could deliver genuine major-league intelligence. She told me that the Americans had become involved, and a drone strike had been authorised. That was the last I heard on the subject, officially at least."

"And unofficially?"

"I know the strike went ahead. A rumour went around afterwards that the Americans weren't happy that the intelligence was from a single source. They were demanding evidence that there had really been a dirty bomb factory and that they hadn't been drawn into some private vendetta between clans."

Noman was shaking his head.

Ed described his final meeting with Tariq in the cemetery in Kandahar, in which he'd revealed the existence of an off-the-books surveillance operation watching a house in Abbottabad.

"I'm getting close to something," Tariq had told him, excitedly. "There's something hidden away up there, right under the generals' noses."

"I told him to steer well clear," Ed explained. "I told him his focus was Afghanistan, but he wasn't listening. The rest you know. As soon as he informed us that it was bin Laden who was being sheltered in the house, we passed the information to the CIA at Langley. But the Americans had beaten us to it. They were already watching the compound and had been for several months, and they were now absolutely furious at us for 'meddling.' The message from Langley was unequivocal: *stay out of it*. The Americans killed bin Laden and Tariq made a break for it. He got as far as Peshawar. Khan shot him in one of our safe houses."

"Of course he did."

"But why do that if Tariq was his agent?"

"You know the answer to that." Noman replied. "Tariq's cover was blown after the Abbottabad raid. He was on the run. If we had caught him, he would have revealed under questioning that he was the conduit for Khan's treachery. The only way Khan could ensure his own security was to have Tariq eliminated, and so he shot him."

*

Ed felt wrung out. But beneath the dejected façade there was a
sense of grim satisfaction. He had almost fulfilled his mission.
He'd done everything he could. Noman's insistence that Tariq
must have had a high-level collaborator and that all the evidence pointed to Khan was exactly what they had planned and
hoped for. It was at the heart of the scheme. But, at the same
time, there was something unsettling about Noman's conviction. As he unpicked each meeting, detail by detail, going back
and forth, Ed had found himself equally convinced that Khan
was the higher source. But if Khan really was a British spy, then
why was Burns betraying him?

*Because London had got tired of him and his self-serving
behaviour; because the intelligence provided hadn't matched the
promise; because spying was a profession of cold betrayal.*

But if that was true and London was prepared to deliberately sacrifice one of their own, then what did it mean for Ed,
who was alone behind enemy lines?

36

Under the Bo Tree

Noman burst out of the narrow stairwell onto the roof. The sky was a sulphurous yellow and a dusty smell hung in the still air. He could feel the air pressure building, a prickly, uncomfortable feeling in the hair of his forearms and along the back of his neck.

A storm was coming, in the next day or two, the first of the monsoon. Soon, purple-and-black thunderheads would pile up on the horizon. He was reminded of the storms of his childhood, when the orphans had danced in the streets as the rain soaked them and washed away the heat. He'd travelled a winding road since then, one beset with choices, difficult choices, and now he'd reached its most dangerous fork. What happened next would result in either his downfall or that of Khan. Nothing he had been told in the last few hours had made the outcome any more certain.

Khan had been passing information to the British—Noman was convinced of that. But did it make him a traitor?

He stepped between cement columns sprouting rebar-fingers and ducked under a line of drying bed sheets. There

were two bearded fighters of the House of War sitting in rotting armchairs with Kalashnikovs resting on their thighs. As
soon as he came into view, they rose from their chairs, lean as
wolves, and bowed to him in exaggerated deference.

With a curt nod, he strode past them to the parapet, a
three-foot-high brick railing running along the edge of the
roof. With both hands planted on the top of the railing, he
swung his legs up onto it like vaulting a horse. From there he
sprang upright, and for a moment he swayed out over the drop,
gripped by sudden plunging fear, before mastering himself.

He straightened up and began to walk along the parapet,
surveying his defences. As well as the two guards on the gate
and the two here on the roof, whose field of fire included the
entrance to the cul-de-sac, there was a guard posted at the front
door to the house and one in the kitchen, by the rear entrance.
Two more guards patrolled the grounds and loops of razor wire
had been added to the tops of the boundary wall. All outside
windows and doors were barred, and internal steel doors had
been added to the house. He had a room stacked to the ceiling
with ammunition.

He judged that things were as ready as they could be under
the circumstances and given the constraints against him. It
had been a calculated risk, running the operation without the
knowledge of his colleagues in the ISI and instead using Abu
Dukhan's fighters as foot soldiers. He had been forced to balance the danger of Khan learning what he was up to against
his reliance on the unknown quantity that was the House of
War. He didn't trust them. He didn't trust anybody, for that
matter, but for now, the interests of the House of War coincided with his. They were united by their hatred of Khan. And
he had no doubt that they would fight to the death if pressed,
not least because their leader was lying in one of the guest bedrooms. But defending themselves against attack was one thing;

bringing down Khan was another. He needed more than he had learned so far to move from defensive to offensive operations.

Closing down the flow of PalmTree Fertilizer to open up the market for Khan's own product was no more venal than the activities of any number of past and former Joint Chiefs of Staff. Facilitating the destruction of a few splinter groups that had refused to tow the ISI line was, by any reckoning, a practical move. The alumni list was patently worthless. He'd be surprised if any of the named individuals were still alive. As for calling in an American drone strike to take out the bomb-making capabilities of the House of War, there were powerful voices within the Joint Chiefs that would argue that, no matter the means used, it was the only available course of action in the face of a threat to the integrity of the nation.

Nothing that Ed had told him was sufficiently incriminating. If Khan was to be court-martialled as a traitor, then Noman required more. Without it, his plan was dead in the water. He would most likely die here, defending this house.

It felt like he was about to detonate.

He had reached the point where the parapet made a right-angle turn to the right and ran parallel to College Road. There was no sign of any watchers. No indication that their location had been compromised. The only person who knew they were here was the bootlegger who made weekly deliveries, and he could be trusted to keep his mouth shut.

Noman continued along the parapet to the next right angle. Here, the boundary wall backed up against the playing fields of a technical academy. There was a pipal tree against the wall, what the Buddhists called a Bo tree and where they believed the Buddha achieved enlightenment. It was old, much older than the house and too close to the perimeter wall. He regarded it as a weakness in the defences and had wanted to have it cut down, but since then it had taken on a new inhabitant. Sheltering between two of the ancient buttress roots in the shade of its dusty cordate leaves was a dark shape. Not Buddha. Bomb-boy.

Noman jumped down off the parapet and crossed the roof to the exit, passing Tariq's mother, who was pulling down sheets from the line. She shrank away from him and hissed like a cat.

Noman went out through the kitchens to the servant's quarters, pausing to pick up a bowl of meat in curry sauce and nodding to the guard at the back door as he passed. He walked between the raised beds of the abandoned cottage garden and across the dead lawn to the solitary pipal tree. He squatted down beside the boy and offered him the bowl.

While the boy shovelled the curry into his mouth with his right hand, Noman recounted the day's events. He shared with him his frustration and his fears, his sense that nothing was going according to plan.

The boy listened sympathetically.

Noman could have had the boy shot at any time in the last few weeks, a simple order and a sniper's bullet could have ended the threat long before the boy had any chance to press his trigger switch. The question was, why hadn't he? There was the matter of the *bamiyat*, the oath. But the truth was that he had come to enjoy these sessions. The boy was a ready listener, and in talking to him, Noman did not feel bound by the usual constraints. He felt able to say what he was really thinking. *This was what it must be like for Catholics in their confessional boxes*, he thought.

And why shouldn't he tell him whatever he liked? The boy was doomed, a self-shredding device. It didn't matter what was said. There was no security risk. It would disappear into the air.

He had even teased the boy's life story out of him. He was, as Noman suspected, an orphan. He'd grown up in a small village in Afghanistan, and his parents had died in an air strike.

At fourteen, he was sent by his uncles to the local madrassa, where he was told that Pharaoh had come to destroy Islam and it was his obligation to sacrifice himself in defence of it. After six months, he was sent for formal training as a suicide bomber in a desert city. It seemed likely to Noman that the city was Quetta, in Pakistan. From there, the boy travelled back across the mountains to fulfil his obligation. It was as he approached an enemy base that the car he was travelling in was stopped at a checkpoint. He was pulled out of the car and his suicide vest removed. He was sent to prison. The boy had described his shame at failing to complete his holy work. His uncles had disowned him, and the adult inmates had repeatedly abused him. He had escaped during a mass breakout organised by the Taliban. One of his abusers had dragged him out through a hole blown in the prison wall. He would not describe the time between the escape and joining Abu Dukhan's band of men, but the manner of his silence suggested some even deeper shame.

It was Abu Dukhan who had promised the boy a path back to redemption. He had offered him a blanket and a bed of straw in a hollow in a mulberry tree, which was as much kindness as anyone had ever offered him. Above all, he had offered the boy the opportunity, if he was patient, to put on a suicide vest again. While he waited, he had watched the men of the House of War building the bomb as day after day they shovelled radioactive shit into the smelter. He had watched them physically deteriorate. He had been there, watching the wedding feast from his tree, when the drone strike had happened.

In the aftermath of the attack, it was Abu Dukhan who had given him the suicide vest and told him that it was his destiny, as man-child, in accordance with the ancient prophesy, to destroy Pharaoh.

The boy believed that the index finger of his right hand was the *Shahadat*, the finger of Allah, and that he must use this finger on the trigger switch to be assured of a place in Paradise.

"You will have your vengeance," Noman promised him. "The traitor will be exposed and discredited, and then you can do your work. I'll do whatever it takes."

While he was talking, Raja Mahfouz approached. He stopped at a respectful distance.

"What is it?" Noman called out.

"We've found the girl."

37

With the Lahore Party Crowd

It was like being at the centre of a kaleidoscope, the spinning lights from the dance floor reflecting off the walls and the marble floors, the heat radiating out of her body. The music was a thumping remixed Desi collage, recently arrived, like Leyla, from London. All around her, the who's who of the Lahore party crowd were grinding against each other with long, lean bodies and huge grins on their faces. There must be some good ecstasy in circulation—proof, if any were needed, of the local aphorism that you could get hold of anything if you knew the right, i.e. wrong, people. The best you could say about it was that it was a Taliban nightmare come true.

It felt like she was the only one not in on the joke. She had no job to speak of, no money, and no wish to bag herself a prince from amongst their preening ranks. All she had was her determination to find Ed.

They'd eventually let her go at Heathrow, and she'd made it onto the flight as last call was announced.

She pushed out through French windows onto the back lawn. There was a pool with a few of the most wasted revellers splashing around in it, and on the far side, several people were chatting on their mobile phones. One of them nodded in recognition as she passed.

There were sprinklers at work across the vast lawn and it sparkled by moonlight like thousands of tiny mirrors. And there were fireflies, sudden traceries in the darkness, blinking at her, inviting her towards them.

She removed her Converse and luxuriated in the feel of the wet grass between her toes. There was no point even thinking about how much water was being squandered. It was the kind of calculation that made you want to scream. The father of the guy who was hosting the party was the Director of Export for Pakistan Ordnance Factories and responsible for a joint venture with the South Koreans to sell cluster munitions to tin-pot dictators. All the ingredients were present for a fin-de-siècle blog about the country going-to-hell-in-a-handcart. But that wasn't why she was here. She was looking for a bootlegger named Salman who ran a network of motorcycle couriers and *bolans*, second-hand minvans, delivering high-end foreign alcohol to the city's elite. All her other lines of enquiry had failed. The city police, who could normally be relied upon to cough up information in exchange for a generous *khancha*, had no idea of the whereabouts of Edward Henry Malik, recently arrived from London. A call for help on the Internet had yielded nothing but far-fetched speculation.

She'd tried everything. She was desperate. And so she had decided to use herself as bait.

The pounding of the music lessened as she walked in the direction of a distant grove of mango trees. There were times, like now, when she felt Ed's absence as a physical pain. It was hard not to go over and over it; it hung like a bloody albatross around your neck. They had been so good together. There was the laughter and the sex—how she missed that!—but the best part was the talking. She had been completely open with him. More open than she had been with anyone else before.

She had been devastated when he was abducted. Every day had been torture since then.

As she approached the mangoes, Leyla saw a young couple on a bench beneath one of the trees. She spotted the red coal of a joint being passed back and forth. She walked over.

"Hi guys," she said.

"Leyla," a familiar voice called out, clearly delighted.

It was her cousin Jamal, with his girlfriend Alia. They were drinking bottles of Murree beer and sharing the joint, presumably to even out the rushes from the ecstasy they'd taken. Jamal was the one who had got her into the party. He wasn't rich, not on the same scale as this crowd, but he was well connected.

"Enjoying yourself?" he asked.

"Not really my scene," she replied.

He offered her the joint, and she refused, though not without a twinge of regret. It would be great to be free from care for a while. On the bench they were giggling, Jamal stroking Alia's arm. She envied them their happiness. Jamal reached forward and kissed Alia behind her ear. Leyla could see that she should leave.

"I'll come back and check up on you in a bit," she said.

"Did that guy find you?" Alia asked.

"What guy?"

"Salman," Jamal added. "He's agreed to talk to you."

She pulled back slightly, and they were grinning at her, chemical wonder in their eyes. "You're serious?"

"I told you I'd fix you up," Jamal told her.

"He went that way," Alia said, pointing.

"I'll catch you later."

She walked in the direction Alia had pointed, trying not

to hurry, emerging from the mango grove onto another lawn. It was a cricket pitch. On the far side was the dark shape of a score hut and on the track beside it, a matte-black Bugatti Street Fighter. As she approached, he stepped out from under the eaves of the hut.

Salman was as unfeasibly handsome as she remembered. He was wearing low-slung jeans and a white T-shirt, pearly white running shoes, and a gold Rolex watch. He carried himself with the self-assurance of a dollar millionaire. There were various stories: he was fabulously rich, a twin, totally without scruples, so dyslexic he had never left a mark on paper and so careful he never spoke on a phone. Leyla's favourite story was the one where they were playing with sticks in the garden of his father's house. She was six years old and had recently demanded to have her head shaved. He was the same age and as quick as her with the stick. Later, he would become a Kendo master.

"Salman! It's time for Leyla to go," his mother had called from the veranda. "Say goodbye to her."

"He's not going! He's staying!"

"No darling, Leyla is a girl. She's going home."

She remembered the astonished look on Salman's face and could claim with some confidence that she was his first love. There were other stories of course, and they had been actual lovers for a while, in their early twenties. But she did not care to remember that time.

"How are you, Leyla?" he asked.

He had never forgiven her for leaving him and fleeing to London, of that she was sure.

"I'm looking for someone."

"I know."

Of course he knew, he always did his homework. Or someone did it for him, whispered the information in his ear ahead of any meeting. She knew he hated surprises. She got down on one knee, rolled up her jeans and peeled back the fastening on her ankle wallet. She retrieved a stack of dollars that amounted to just about everything she'd ever earned from blogging and stood up.

She offered the money. "Here."

"Put your money away."

She felt the blood rise in her cheeks. "It's everything I have."

He smiled wryly. "I'm sure it is."

"You're not going to help me?"

"You couldn't pay me enough to betray a client."

"So why are we here?" she demanded, angrily.

"I'm sorry," he said.

She spun around as a bull of a man stepped out of the shadows behind her.

"I am Noman."

38

Truth Serum

Ed opened his eyes. For a moment he had no sense of place; the mattress beneath him meant nothing. Then he shivered, and the world came back. He was in Pakistan, in a cell, beyond the reach of rescue. The bolt was drawn back, and the door opened. He looked up at the giant Raja Mahfouz, standing framed in the doorway.

"Noman is waiting."

He escorted Ed along the corridor, past the cellar door, and up the stairs to the ground-floor room they had used the day before. Noman was standing at the sideboard scowling, a vein in his forehead pulsing. He poured himself a coffee and palmed it in both hands.

"Do you mind if I have some?" Ed asked.

Noman shrugged. "Help yourself."

Ed filled a mug, and they sat down at the table. The coffee was strong and bitter, a jolt to the brain. There was something different about Noman, a harder line to his jaw. Ed contemplated throwing the coffee in his face.

"The British are looking for you. Interpol has issued a Red

Notice requesting your arrest and extradition. If the British are looking for you, then Khan will be too," Noman told him.

Ed shook his head. "This is so fucked."

"Let's go over what happened when you came back to London after Tariq's death."

"I told you."

Noman switched on the voice recorder. "Tell me again."

"I knew I was done for when they wouldn't let me past reception at Vauxhall Cross. I was told to report straight to Burns. She was waiting for me in a basement under Whitehall."

"Was Jonah there?"

Ed was surprised. "Yes."

"Did he show you the Khyber Collage?"

"How do you know about that?"

"You people think you invented espionage." He shook out a Gold Flake and lit it. "Is Khan still at the centre of the collage?"

"Yes."

"Why did they meet you there?"

"I don't know."

"What did Jonah say to you?"

"Nothing. Burns did all the talking. She said that getting out of Afghanistan took precedence over going after Khan. She said that with Tariq dead, I'd outlived my usefulness."

"How did that make you feel?"

"Just fucking dandy."

Noman slapped him hard across the side of the face. It was so fast, Ed didn't have time to react. He'd never seen someone move so quickly. He sat back in his chair with his jaw throbbing. The coffee cup was lying shattered in a corner of the room.

"I'm not in the mood for any of your shit," Noman told him. He casually finished his cigarette and dropped the butt on the floor, crushing it with the toe of his cowboy boot. "Why was Jonah in the meeting?"

"I don't know," Ed replied, holding the side of his face.

"When she introduced him, she said he was the only person in MI6 who had actually met Khan."

"When was he supposed to have met Khan?"

"Burns said it was back in 2005, when a terrorist cell tried to blow up a ship in the Thames Estuary. Jonah met with Khan in Peshawar. That's all she told me. I don't know what they talked about. If I did, I'd tell you."

"And Jonah didn't speak to you?"

"Not a word."

Noman reached inside the desk and took out something small. He tossed it on the table with a scowl on his face. A wrap.

Ed looked from the folded piece of paper to Noman and back again.

"Are you serious?"

Noman reached forward and unfolded the wrap. "I asked my dealer for truth serum. This was the best he could do." He tapped the cocaine into a mound on the top of the table and chopped it with a razor blade from his wallet. He drew off two lines and rolled a five thousand rupee note and offered it to Ed.

"It's not really my thing," Ed said.

Noman shrugged, leant forward, and snorted a line. He drew himself erect and wiped his nose with the back of his hand. He held out the note again.

"You don't get to choose."

After a pause loaded with menace, Ed took the note and snorted the remaining line.

"What did they do with you after that meeting?" Noman demanded, his fingers drumming a tattoo on the top of the table.

"Sure. Of course," Ed replied, his heart beating faster in his chest. He felt an expansive rush. "They suspended me. I shouldn't have hit that weasel Hagedorn. It was dumb, I know. I mean, what choice did I leave them after that? I was suspended, and my clearance was revoked. I waited a couple of weeks. Then there was the Board of Inquiry. I was dismissed."

"That's it?"

"Yes, that's it. I was out on my ear."

"You're sure?"

"Of course. Can I have a cigarette?"

Quick as a snake Noman was across the top of the table with his handgun drawn. He had a fistful of Ed's hair in one hand and his Glock in the other, squashing Ed's cheek against the table and screwing the muzzle of the gun into his temple.

"Fuck!" Ed yelled.

"You listen to me, you piece of shit. You haven't given me a single piece of information that I can use. You better start raising your game, or I'm going to blow your fucking brains out!"

Noman let go of Ed and strode back and forth in front of the table. Ed slumped in his chair. "What do you want to know?"

39

500g

The jittery smile on Noman's face vanished. He took his phone out of his pocket and called a number. He paused for a moment before holding it out to Ed.

"Here," he said. "Talk to your lady."

Sweat bloomed in Ed's palm as he took the phone.

"Ed?"

"Leyla?"

He was overwhelmed by a sudden plunging sensation like vertigo.

They've got her. They've got her. They've got her.

"Are you okay?"

"I'm sorry," she said. He could hear the fear in her voice. "I had to tell them."

"You're not hurt? They haven't hurt you?"

He had an image of her sitting with her knees drawn up on a mattress in a windowless cell.

"No, I'm not hurt."

Unharmed. He had to believe her.

"Don't be afraid," he said. "I'm going to sort this out. Everything's going to be okay. Where are you? Leyla? Leyla?"

She was gone. The phone snatched from her hand. Call terminated.

Noman was watching him. His face was strangely peaceful, his eyes lucid. It was as if he was feeding off Ed's desperation.

"You bastard!" Ed snarled.

"First, let me reassure you. She is completely unharmed."

Ed pushed himself up out the chair and set his fists on the table. "Let her go!"

Noman held up his hand. "You don't dictate terms to me."

"I'll kill you!"

"Don't make me tell them to do something to her," Noman said. "Slice her face or something."

Ed didn't answer. His head was pounding. It felt like something was tightening in his head and might at any time snap. In frustration, he flung the phone against the wall. He sank back into the chair.

"You know how this works," Noman said in the same even tone of voice. "You've spoken to her. You've established it's her. You know she's okay. I promise you nothing is going to happen to her if you cooperate. I've seen the room she's being held in. It's nice. Nicer than the one you're in. So stop bothering yourself. You can have her back and live happily ever after. All you have to do is cut out all the bullshit, and give me something I can use."

"You don't have to do this."

"You haven't given me a single piece of information that I can use."

Ed slumped in his chair. He felt utterly defeated. "What do you want to know?"

"Tell me about the courier job you did after you left the service."

"It was nothing, really. I delivered a briefcase to a woman in Dubai. That's it."

"What was in the briefcase?"

"Money. Fifty thousand dollars in hundred dollar bills in a single brick: five hundred grams in weight."

"Tell me in greater detail what you did."

"I collected the suitcase from a hotel suite at Heathrow and checked in for an Emirates flight to Dubai. A seat in business class."

"From whom did you collect the suitcase?"

"A service employee who worked for Informal Remittances, it's a department of the service that manages cash payments to international sources. I'd done this kind of thing before, in the build-up to the Iraq War, when we were paying relatives of high-up Baathists in Saddam's regime. We had an arrangement with the authorities who turned a blind eye. In Dubai, I cleared customs and was met in arrivals."

"Who by?"

"A former soldier named Dai Llewellyn. He'd been my bodyguard in Iraq and Afghanistan. Now he's based in Dubai. He's a big guy, knows how to handle himself. His job was to drive me to the hotel. He parked in the car park and waited while I went inside."

"Did he know what was in the briefcase?"

"He wasn't supposed to."

"But he knew?"

"He wasn't stupid."

"And at the hotel?"

"There was a reservation in my name. I collected the key card and went up to my room. I sat on the bed. Somewhere between forty-five minutes and an hour and half later, my room telephone rang."

"Who was it?"

"A Somali named Abdi. He told me his room number and invited me to join him. I went up in the elevator. He was in a much larger suite than mine. He answered the door and escorted me to a sitting area where the woman was waiting."

"Describe Abdi."

"He was a tall, thin man with an angular face and thinning on top. I'd met him once before when I was with naval intelligence. Amongst others, he represented an informal network of seamen who worked the dhows in the Strait of Hormuz and reported on the movements of Iranian shipping. He specialised in acting as an impartial third party; he facilitated secure meetings and counted money."

"Describe the woman."

Ed shrugged. "She was dressed from head to toe in a black niqab. She was wearing kid leather gloves and sunglasses. Black Louboutins. She smelled very strongly of Chanel No. 5. That's really about it."

"What happened?"

"Abdi used a money counter to count the money. When he was satisfied, he repacked the briefcase and handed it to the woman. She left with it. Ten to fifteen minutes after she'd gone, Abdi told me I could leave. Dai drove me back to the airport, and I got the next flight out."

"Why did you accept the job?"

"I'd just been sacked. I didn't know what else to do."

"Who offered you the job?"

"Jonah. He said I'd be doing him a favour. It was regular job, a monthly delivery. I just stepped in for someone. I did it once only and wouldn't have done it again even if they'd offered it to me. It was a job for a flunky, and I didn't want it to be my last memory of the service. I wanted an ordinary civilian job."

"Why is it that Samantha Burns doesn't want me to know you made that delivery?"

"I don't know."

"'He may not realise what he knows, but he knows it nonetheless.' That's what Burns said to your girl."

"You think it was a payment to a high-level agent in Pakistan?"

Noman stared at him, giving nothing away.

"What time of month did you make the delivery?" he demanded.

"Second Thursday of the month. That was delivery day."

"Tomorrow?"

"Yes."

"Is this some kind of trap?"

Ed shrugged. "I don't know, maybe."

"Fuck!"

"What was it you said to me yesterday. Cui bono? Who benefits?"

"I don't know who benefits," Noman replied. "That's the trouble."

"I've told you everything I know. Now let me see Leyla."

Outside, the sun was blotted out and the wind had picked up, whipping through the spaces between the huts with a rising howl. Noman ran from the kitchen, bent over to protect a bowl against the dust, to the pipal tree. He gave the boy the bowl and with it, a USB stick.

"Keep this safe," he said. "I'll need it when I get back."

The boy nodded.

Noman stood up. He smiled at the boy and messed his hair.

"I'm almost there," he said. He glanced back at Raja Mahfouz, who was waving from the kitchen door. The car must be ready to take him to the airport.

The end is in sight.

As he ran across the lawn, the first fat raindrops began to fall.

40 ❖

Intimacy

He lay in the darkness of his cell, imagining Leyla somewhere nearby, willing them not to hurt her.

The bolt was drawn back. Raja Mahfouz stood blocking the doorway with his meaty arms crossed on his chest. "Get up."

Ed climbed up off the mattress. "Where are we going?"

"That would spoil the surprise."

As he emerged from the basement, he heard the steady drumbeat of rain on the roof, the noise growing louder as they climbed two more flights to the servants' quarters at the top of the house. Raja Mahfouz led him along a corridor with a rough concrete floor and doors on either side. He unlocked one and stepped back for Ed to enter.

"In you go."

"Ed!"

The last time he had seen Leyla, at security at Heathrow, she had been wearing a dress, a rare event. Now she was dressed in the same grubby orange overalls as he was. Her eyes were darkened by fatigue or bruising, possibly both, and she looked thinner than he remembered. He was unable to think of a time when she had looked more fragile or more beautiful.

She jumped up from the bed and rushed into his arms.

"They kept telling me you were alive, but I wasn't sure whether to believe them."

Behind them, the door slammed shut. She drew him down onto the bed. In a few moments, they had stripped off their clothes. They snatched back intimacy from their captors.

Ed stood at the window and stared through the bars at the narrow cul-de-sac with its high-walled compounds. Below him, a guard in a poncho ran from the house to the sandbagged position at the gate. He glanced back at Leyla sleeping on the narrow bed. The look of exhaustion was now out of her face.

They had been confined together for several hours now, and during that time, there had been no let-up in the rain. Tariq's widow had brought them dinner on a tray and come again half an hour or so later to collect the dirty plates and plastic cutlery.

Ed had tried to engage the woman in conversation. "Can you help us?" But she had hurried back to the door and knocked on it to be let out. After that, Leyla had gone to sleep.

She hadn't been physically harmed. Apart from the loss of liberty, the worst she'd suffered was when Noman had escorted her down to the cellar and shown her the rack. She'd told him what the woman had said to her at Heathrow.

"That's what she wanted, isn't it?" Leyla said, clinging to him on the bed.

"Yes, that was what she meant you to do."

"You used me."

"Sleep," he'd urged her, and she had.

He'd prowled the room, opening the cupboards and peering under the bed. He'd stood watching from the window. Now he walked across the rough concrete floor to the bed and lay down beside her.

They were face-to-face on the narrow bed, with the tips of their noses inches apart. She had just woken.

"Are they listening?" she whispered in his ear.

"It doesn't matter if they are. I've told them everything I know."

"What is this about?"

"I was sent here to betray one of our own."

It was still difficult to believe that Khan, who he had regarded as his enemy for so long, was in fact a British asset.

"Why?"

"I think they grew tired of him."

"What's going to happen to us?"

"If this works out, they'll swap us."

"How can you be so sure?"

There was no avoiding what had gone before.

She frowned. "Nothing's real about you," she said. "You never stopped being a spy."

He wanted to tell her to stop and not pursue this any further. But he knew her well enough to know she would not be stopped.

"You came out of the blue, didn't you," she said, her eyes widening. "The saviour of J&K Cargo and Travel. Mum lost her license, Nasir was hit by a van, and Mohammed Akram ran off, and suddenly we needed a driver, and then, as if by chance, you were there. It wasn't chance though, was it? All the time you were working for my mother, you were preparing to come here, weren't you?"

He nodded.

"My mother loved you. You were my rescuer. Damn!" He saw that she had worked out what he had most hoped to prevent her from discovering. "The attack on me in London, it was a sham, wasn't it? It was all a bloody sham."

He nodded.

There were tears in her eyes. "Everything about you is a lie. You stole my heart."

"I love you," he told her.

41 ❖

Sodom-sur-Mer

A six-foot blonde slid onto a bar stool next to Noman, the split in her skin-tight, low-cut evening dress running all the way up her tanned leg to the top of her unblemished thigh.

"Where are you from?" she asked, not even looking at him. Her voice was startlingly beautiful, bell-sweet. "How long are you here? Where are you staying?"

Every woman in the place was a prostitute, the eastern European hookers gathered at one end of the bar and the Chinese at the other, with an invisible line that might as well have been an international border running between them. Selling sex was forbidden in Dubai, but the Emirate's ruler Sheikh Mo took a laissez-faire attitude and the authorities rarely did anything about it. Occasionally, an establishment would break some unwritten rule. Cyclone, a notorious whorehouse near the airport, had been closed down after it went too far—a special area of the vast sex supermarket had been dedicated to in-house oral sex. It was said that it had offered the best blowjobs west of Bangkok.

Noman had come straight from the airport, and he hadn't

figured out yet where he was staying. Looking at the woman and her swollen silicon cleavage, it was easy to see how the night might pan out.

"Tell me about yourself," he asked.

"I'm a Nobel laureate of sex," she replied, turning her eyes on him, widening them. "I'll show you things you have only ever dreamed of."

He figured that business must be slow if she was making a move on a Desi guy like him this early in the evening. She glanced over his shoulder, and he watched her face change, a mask of wariness descending, like the shutters going down.

"Later," she said, and slipped off the bar stool and walked away without looking back. He was almost sad. Her place on the stool was taken by a diminutive man in a long, white Indian shirt with the sleeves rolled up over thick, veiny forearms, baggy white trousers, and a small white cotton hat perched on a cannonball of a head. He gestured for the barman and ordered a whisky.

"Little Man," Noman said.

Little Man was an "independent trader," a Kokani Muslim who'd grown up as a sadistic street-hood in the chawls of the dirt-poor Dongri district of Bombay, hiring himself out as muscle before graduating into the role of assassin. He'd made a name for himself for his proficiency with the notoriously tricky *kutta*—a pistol manufactured in Uttar Pradesh whose barrel had a tendency to blow up. You had to admire the balls of a man who used a weapon that was good for one shot only. Little Man had cleared out of Bombay in the midnineties and set himself up in Dubai as a narco-trafficker, smuggling Afghan heroin into the ports and bays around Bombay. And in this part of the world, if you wanted to guarantee the success of a narcotics business there was one organisation that you needed to keep sweet—the Directorate of Inter Services Intelligence. In return for the ISI's good favour, he had, on several occasions, made his routes available for the transport of explosives to rebel groups in India. But that was not the full extent of his links to the organisation.

"How is my brother?" Little Man asked, calmly, once his drink had been set in front of him.

"Safe," Noman grunted. Little Man's brother was in Karachi, living in the opulent hill district of Clifton under the protection of the ISI. That was the problem with Dubai: you were always a guest and Sheikh Mo could kick you out at any time. It was prudent to have a bolthole ready. For Little Man and his family, that meant Pakistan. And the Pakistanis didn't offer asylum without conditions attached.

"I've got the information you requested," Little Man said. "You understand how the visa system works here? If you're an Emirati, you get an allocation of visas, so it's common to offer them to a broker who sells them on. There is a broker who specialises in selling visas to Somalis. He says that the man you are looking for operates out of this address."

He put a folded piece of paper on the bar-top.

"Thank you," Noman said.

Little Man nodded, drained his glass, and hopped down off the barstool. Noman ordered another drink. A couple of minutes later, the tall blonde rejoined him at the bar.

"Where were we?" she asked.

"We were talking about my dreams."

Early the following morning, Noman sat in the back of a white Mercedes taxi with the meter running and the radio turned down low, fading between local stations.

A blue glass eye, a ward against devils, swung above the dashboard, and in the rearview mirror Noman could see the driver's eyes. He was an off-duty cop from the Department of Punitive Establishment. A prison warden, really. He was singing along to the radio absentmindedly. They hadn't talked since the initial exchange outside the hotel when he'd picked Noman up.

Now they were parked across the road from a shuttered shop front in the Deira district of downtown Dubai, the address given to him by Little Man the night before. Behind them there was a "borrowed" surveillance van with four more off-duty cops in civilian clothes.

Noman was nursing a brutal hangover and trying to decide which of the various drugs in his arsenal to deploy against it; something powerful enough to wipe away the pain but not so powerful that it reduced him to a quivering jelly. This was no time for dosing errors. He kept getting flashbacks of the night before: the whore licking cocaine off his Viagra-stiff cock in the bathroom of his hotel suite, the two of them jumping up and down on the bed like it was a trampoline, her endless legs crossed behind her ears while he rammed into her like some kind of assembly line automaton. He hadn't been able to come, of course, but he'd gone on banging away for ages. Finally, she'd had to beg him to stop. He'd kicked her out and spent the rest of the night with dreams of fiery infernos flickering like strobe lights behind his eyes.

Now he was exhausted. He decided that he would have to forego further drugs and bear the pain.

He really needed the Somali to make an appearance; without him, he was scuppered, open to counterattack. But if Noman could prove that Khan was taking money for the information provided, he could go to the joint chiefs and demand his arrest. It wouldn't matter how flawed or self-serving the information was, the fact of accepting money for it would seal Khan's fate. He'd be court-martialled as a traitor.

At 5:45 p.m., the Somali emerged from the shop and got in the back of a cab. They followed him to the Al Manzil on Sheikh

Mo Boulevard, where he checked into a room on the top floor with a view of the Burj Khalifa.

Noman took a seat in the corner of the lobby and surveyed the entrance, while his friends from Punitive Establishment made themselves known to the hotel staff. Half an hour later, a pink ladies taxi pulled up in front of the hotel, and a woman in a voluminous black hijab and stilettos got out. As she crossed the foyer, he caught a glimpse of the distinctive red-lacquered soles of Christian Louboutins.

She spoke to one of the receptionists, who accompanied her to the bank of elevators. She took one to the top floor. Fifteen minutes later, Noman received a call telling him that the Somali had made a call from his room to another room on the second floor. Its occupant was an Englishman named Totty, who had arrived with only a briefcase.

Totty rode the elevator to the top floor and entered the Somali's suite. Another ten minutes passed. The elevator in the lobby pinged open. The fully covered woman strode out holding a briefcase, and the doorman summoned her a pink taxi.

Noman hurried out after her and got in the waiting Mercedes.

"Follow that car," Noman said, his hangover forgotten.

From the hotel, they followed the pink taxi to a bank, and watched and waited as the woman in the hijab went inside and emerged again ten minutes later, without the briefcase. The taxi dropped the woman outside one of the entrances to the Dubai Mall. Noman abandoned the Mercedes and followed her inside. He was immediately confronted by a massive indoor waterfall four storeys high, like a plunging curtain of molten silver, with fibreglass castings of plummeting human divers suspended above it. It made his head reel. He almost lost the woman in the milling crowds. Suddenly, it seemed there were women in hijabs all around him, but then he caught another glimpse of her red soles and set off again in pursuit, following the signs for Fashion Island.

He watched her enter the Versace shop.

Twenty minutes later he observed his wife, Mumayyaz Khan, emerge from the shop and saunter casually across the polished marble floor in a sumptuous black cat suit with pantaloon legs and a plunging neckline that was adorned with gold necklaces as thick as rope.

"Howzat!"

42

Noman's Choice

Noman waited for the maid's trolley to turn the corner at the end of the corridor and then rapped his knuckles on the door in front of him.

"Room service."

He stepped back a pace and waited. He was in the Palace Hotel, on the lake. He hadn't realised that Mumayyaz had such expensive tastes.

The door cracked opened a couple of inches. An Arab with a towel clutched around his waist stared indignantly out at him through the gap. According to Noman's contacts in the local police, the man was a Kuwaiti property dealer, a conjuror of skyscrapers out of barren sand.

"We didn't order anything."

Noman kicked the door open, sending the man sprawling. He stepped over him into the room. There were clothes scattered across the floor, and his wife was tied to the bed, lying face down with her ample buttocks raised by a stack of crisp white pillows. He paused long enough to reflect that she really did have a magnificent ass before scooping up the man's trousers and shoes and throwing them out into the corridor.

"Get out," he snarled, helping him on his way with another well-aimed kick.

He slammed the door and stood for a moment with his back to it. This was no time to let his actions be ruled by emotions. He crossed the room and threw himself down into an armchair facing the bed. He lit a Flake.

"How long has this been going on for?"

"I should have known you'd come busting in," she said, her head turned to one side so it appeared as if she was speaking into her armpit. "This is a non-smoking room."

"How long?"

"This one? He's new. A couple of months."

"I mean the money." She'd been making the monthly visit to Dubai for as long as they had been married and burning his salary on clothes she never wore. "How long have you been collecting the money?"

"Six years. There is about three million dollars left in the account. I've spent some of it, obviously."

"Shit!" He didn't know what was more shocking, the act of betrayal or the fact that she'd been able to pull it off for so long without him realising it.

"Are you going to untie me?"

Seeing no reason not to, Noman undid the straps, and Mumayyaz rolled over onto her back and kicked the pillows away. She swept her hair out of her face.

"You're in a lot of trouble," he said, sitting down again. "You'll be lucky if they don't hang you alongside your father."

"Is that what you want?"

"Tell that to the Joint Chiefs."

"You really think this is going to see the light of day?"

"Your testimony, alongside that of an MI6 officer named

Edward Malik, will leave the Joint Chiefs with no alternative but to court-martial your father."

"Don't be so bloody naïve. This will never go to court. No senior officer has been convicted of treason in the entire bloody history of Pakistan. You think they're going to shame themselves in public like that? You, of all people, should know them better than that."

"They'll hold a closed session. They'll do it in the cantonment."

She rolled over onto her stomach and rose up on her elbows, cupping her face in her hands. As usual he found himself distracted by her cleavage, its dark inviting crevice. "Darling, they'll hush it up. You know they will. I'm not saying there won't be consequences. Most probably, Papa would have to retire. Frankly, it's about time he did. But more than that? Really? I'm sorry to say this, but you're the one that's most likely to suffer."

"How do you figure that?"

"No one is going to believe you weren't in on it. They've been waiting all their lives for a reason to discredit you. In their eyes, you're a filthy outcast and you always will be. They'd seize on it as a means of discrediting you. No, I really don't think it's in your best interests to make a fuss. I have a much better plan."

"You do?"

"We keep the money. I'm tired of sharing it with Papa."

"I'm sorry?"

"The British have agreed. All you have to do is release some smelly old Taliban for talks and cancel next year's fighting season in Afghanistan. Let them get out without any fuss. They'll be so grateful, and the Americans too. They've offered to double the money."

"They have?"

"They're furious with Papa right now because of him not

telling them about bin Laden and lying about this and that and not giving them any proper secrets, but they're prepared to put that to one side. They're realists. You give them the promise of a smooth exit from Afghanistan, and I guarantee they'll make it worth our while. We only need another year or so, and then we could retire. We could settle here." She wagged a finger at him and her eyes lit up. "You love it here. You know you do. And you could have it all—girls, boys, drugs—anything your heart desires."

He shook his head. "You really are a piece of work."

"Everything has been arranged. I've spoken to Samantha Burns."

"And what about your father?"

"That's the beauty of the plan. You confront him with the evidence you've gathered. Tell him he's a traitor to his face. Be as angry as you like. But then, and this is the genius, you relent. In recognition of his years of service, you tell him you've decided not to blow the whistle. In return for which he must do the honourable thing. It's time for him to retire. Not pseudo-retirement, the real thing. You tell him that in return for your silence, he is to nominate you to take his position in the shadow government. You step into his shoes."

"And you've cooked this up with the British?"

"They're reasonable people. They very much like the idea of you. They love a boy with a chip on his shoulder."

"What about Edward Malik?"

"It was a journey of discovery," she explained. "I couldn't just present you with the facts. You'd have freaked out. You know how obstinate you can be. We had to reel you in."

He shook his head. "I don't believe this."

"Come on, darling. You're a realist, above all, that's what you are."

"You're asking me to betray my country. I love my country."

"It does *not* love you."

"Get dressed," he told her, grim-faced.

"What are you thinking?"

"You father is a traitor and so are you."

"Darling, you're not thinking straight."

"We're going to the airport."

"We'll lose the money!"

"I don't care."

He'd never seen her so angry. "You really are a loathsome little Hindu!"

They flew into a storm. As the plane crossed from sea to land, it was shaken by turbulence, and forks of lighting stabbed the clouds. By the time they began to descend into Islamabad, half the passengers were screaming, and the aisles were running with vomit. It wasn't so much a landing as a slam dunk. They skidded down the runway with a torrent of water running off the wings and came to a sudden halt on the taxiway.

Staring out through his window seat, Noman could see what looked like a line of army jeeps and a huddle of soldiers in ponchos in front of them. While the engines idled, a set of steps was manoeuvred alongside the plane, and twelve Military Police officers in their distinctive red berets came aboard. They marched up the aisle in single file and stopped at Noman's row. He was sitting with his fists clenched on his knees, energy coursing in every part of his body.

This wasn't meant to happen.

"Colonel Noman Butt, I am arresting you on a charge of high treason," the senior redcap said and issued a *Danda* warning informing him of his constitutional right to protection against self-incrimination and his constitutional right to the services of a legal practitioner.

"I'm sorry, darling," Mumayyaz said, "I did try to warn you."

Noman burst out of the seat like a jack from a box, power

swarming in his shoulders as he flung open his arms. He scrambled hand over fist across rows of seats, kicking and stamping on passengers, cracking bones and scattering sick-bags and in-flight magazines. Plunging into the aisle, he seized two redcaps' heads and slammed them together, skull-to-skull. He trampled the bodies with his boots. Another redcap lunged forward, and Noman grabbed him by the cheeks and bit off an ear. He snorted and rolled his head and spat out a mouthful of blood and gristle.

A Taser was fired at point-blank range at the back of his neck, and he was dragged from the plane convulsing.

43

Ed Kills

In Lahore, it had been raining all night, a roaring downpour pounding the roof and rattling the windows in their frames, and then a couple of hours before dawn, it stopped. The sudden silence brought Ed abruptly awake. He was still awake an hour later, in the creeping damp of tangled sheets, when the crack of a rifle shot echoed amongst the high walls of the cul-de-sac. He instinctively rolled out of the bed and dropped on all fours. He grabbed his watch and stared at the luminescent dial.

Four a.m. An extended staccato of automatic fire: the window shattered, the curtains billowed, and glass spilled halfway across the floor. He pulled Leyla down beside him.

She was shaking her head. "What?"

"We're being attacked," he said. "Stay low." He scrambled across the floor to the wardrobe, pulling her along behind. There was shouting from outside and the rattle of answering fire from the direction of the gate. Reaching up, he pulled their coveralls off the hangers. Apart from the strobe of muzzle flashes, it was almost pitch black.

"Get dressed."

Lying on their backs, they pulled on the coveralls. Under different circumstances it might have been funny, the two of them fishtailing on the floor. Their flip-flops were by the door; he thrust hers into her hands and then reached beyond her and grabbed one of the fallen hangers. He crouched by the door with his back pressed to the wall, bending the hanger, pulling it out into a diamond shape and pushing it back together, folding it into a hand-grip. He straightened the curved end and started sharpening it against the concrete floor.

It went silent for a moment, and in his heightened sense of awareness it felt like someone had hit pause. Then there was the startling roar of a diesel engine starting up, followed by the distinctive clatter of caterpillar tracks in the cul-de-sac.

Seconds later, there was the scream of tearing metal. He guessed they'd rammed the gate. Whoever they were, they were now in the compound.

The door was flung open. A large man with a flashlight rushed into the room and stopped at the foot of the bed. Before he had time to react, Ed had risen up behind him, taken two steps, reached around, and put his hand over the man's face and stabbed him in his neck. The sharpened point of the hanger went in smoothly, without resistance. The man gave a gasping exhalation and dropped the flashlight. He tried to raise his hands to his neck as if to pull out the hanger, then fell forward onto the bed. Ed picked up the flashlight and pointed it at him. The man was lying face down with the hanger sticking out of his carotid artery, blood pumping out and soaking the sheet. Ed lifted his head. It was Raja Mahfouz. Ed reached into the holster at Mahfouz's belt and took out his pistol, a Heckler and Koch 9mm. He made ready, pumping a shell into the chamber. He would have preferred a larger weapon, but it was better than a coat hanger.

"Get ready to move," he told Leyla.

When she didn't reply, Ed flicked the flashlight in her

direction. Her face was so pale and wild looking that he wondered for a moment if she'd been hit by a stray round.

"You killed him," she whispered.

"He might have killed us," he replied, gently. "Wait here until I call for you."

With the gun in both hands, he risked a glance out into the corridor. There was no movement. The shooting was coming from the lower levels of the house now, and he got a whiff of tear gas rising in the stairwell at the closest end. Taking another glance, he looked back the other way. There were three other doors, two rooms on either side of his, and at the far end a narrow stairway that he assumed led up to the roof.

He quickly crossed the corridor to the first of the doors. He went in fast, with the flashlight pointing from his shoulder and the gun out at arm's length in front of him. The smell of rotten flesh made his head reel. A woman was screaming. As he pointed the light at her, he realised it was the mad old woman who had spoken to him when he first arrived. She was on the floor in the corner, grabbing fistfuls of her hair with her hands. On the other side of the room, a bandaged man was lying on a bed with one mangled hand raised.

Ed ran to the window and looked out through the bars at the back of the house and the silhouette of a large tree beside the boundary wall. It was dark, and there were no signs of movement or muzzle flashes. If they could get out there, he might find a means of escape. He would have to move fast, though— the tempo and proximity of gunfire was increasing all the time.

He darted back out into the corridor.

"Leyla!"

She rushed into his arms, burying her face in his chest. He swung round, bringing up the pistol, pushing her against the wall, and fired at the shape at the top of the stairs: a commando in a gasmask. The bullet went into the mask's filter, the man's face sucked inwards by the gauge of the bullet. He toppled, falling back on to his colleagues.

Ed turned and ran in the opposite direction, tugging Leyla along with him. They climbed up the narrow staircase and emerged onto the roof.

"Stay low," he told her.

They dashed through the cement columns, splashing through pools of rainwater. The body of one of the guards was lying in a dark puddle. The other was firing over the parapet. Ed ran up to him and put three bullets in him at close range. He took a quick look over the parapet. Three stories below, a bulldozer had come to a halt at the foot of the steps with the crumpled gate beneath it. There were several bodies on the steps and across the compound, some in black commando uniforms. Tear gas was drifting out into the street.

As he ducked back down, bullets hit the concrete beside him. He stuck the pistol in his waistband and picked up the dead guard's Kalashnikov.

They ran to the farthest side of the roof that overlooked the tree, the wall, and beyond it, the playing fields. Looking down, Ed saw that it was too far to jump. The only hope was the main spoil pipe. It looked like cast iron, rusty but substantial. Maybe it was strong enough to carry them. He glanced back and saw the first dark shape flitting between the columns. There was no alternative.

"Over you go," he said, "Climb down the pipe. I'll follow."

He raised the Kalashnikov and fired two bursts. The bolt clicked empty. He flung it away and jumped up onto the parapet. He grabbed hold of the pipe vent and swung his legs out over the drop. The pipe shifted and groaned. His feet scrambled at the brickwork. He looked down. Leyla was descending in a barely controlled slide. He set off after her. Twice he was able to slow his descent at the junction with smaller feed pipes. He barely felt the pain in his hands.

Arriving at the bottom, he crouched against the wet ground and surveyed the terrain. His mind was racing. They were next to a row of huts, and ahead of him there was an open space and the dark outline of the pipal tree by the wall. It was a huge old fig, with a trunk like writhing cables and limbs that looked easily strong enough to hold their weight. They might be able to use one of the upper branches to cross the wall to the other side. How to get there? They were safe where they were, for now at least, protected by a slight overhang, but if they moved, they would become visible to the gunmen on the roof. Unless they stuck to the shadows cast by the row of huts.

He looked at Leyla. She was watching him, holding her hands, bloodied from the descent, in her lap.

"Ready?"

She nodded.

"I love you," he said.

"I love you, too," she replied without hesitation.

"So it's going to be fine . . ."

"You think?"

He drew the pistol from his waistband. "Come on!"

He led her along the backs of the huts, sprinting across the space between each one. Within seconds they had arrived at the comparative safety of the wall. They moved swiftly alongside it towards the tree. Reaching it, they saw that the back of the tree was dappled with pale freshly sawn stumps. Someone had cut off all the overhanging branches.

"Damn."

Looking around, he saw a small recess in the wall, with three concrete steps that led down to a metal door. It was locked, and it would not budge when he put his shoulder against it. Behind him, there was a lot of shouting and calling out as the gunmen moved from room to room in the house, but the firing had stopped. If he tried shooting out the lock it would immediately draw their attention.

"Here," said a voice, in Pashto.

With a start, Ed realised there was a small boy squatting at the top of the steps. He was wrapped in what looked like a ragged black cloak and was holding out a key in his hand. Ed took it and it worked. The door opened onto the playing fields. When he looked back to thank him, he found that the boy had disappeared. There was only Leyla, with an incredulous expression on her face.

"Come on."

They were about halfway across the pitch when they were lit up. From directly in front of them, a pick-up truck switched on its rack of floodlights. They were blinded. Pinned like moths. Then he was being shouted at through a loud hailer.

"Put down the weapon!"

There was no alternative he could think of, and so he flung the pistol away.

"Get down on your knees, and put your hands up!"

They sank onto the soft wet grass with their hands in the air, and as they knelt there, squinting, he became aware of a man, in silhouette, approaching with his arm raised and something stick-like in his hand.

Ed swore softly.

When his vision adjusted, Javid Aslam Khan was standing over him. His appearance was entirely consistent with his reputation. He was ramrod straight despite his advanced age, wearing a three-piece tweed suit and polished brogues, and in one of his hands he was holding a leather-covered cane.

"You think I don't know what Burns is playing at, young fellow?" he said, tapping Ed on the soft skin of his temple with the end of the cane. "She's an insightful woman, I'll give her that. She knew that Noman would fall into her trap. What I don't understand about this whole foolish business is *why*? What was she trying to achieve?"

"A different outcome," Ed replied.

"She wanted Noman in charge?"

Ed laughed. He remembered what Queen Bee had told him about wanting to change the choice architecture. "I think anyone but you."

44 ❖

The KSM Suite

Several hours later Khan and his colleague Farrukh Meghwa from the Committee of the Joint Chiefs of Staff, stood behind glass in the viewing area of the KSM Suite, named for the 9/11 mastermind Khalid Sheikh Mohammed, who was interrogated here in 2003. They were underground, in the prison complex beneath army headquarters in Rawalpindi, and Farrukh was wearing the uniform of a major general.

The oldest cells in the complex dated back to the pre-colonial era, and extensive work had been undertaken in the last decade to modernise them, adding cameras and recording equipment. And, in the case of the KSM Suite, a hole had been cut in a stone wall that divided two cells and a pane of mirrored, one-way glass added. It allowed visitors, Americans and representatives of other intelligence agencies, to observe interrogations anonymously.

On the far side of the glass, Mumayyaz was sitting at a metal table in a cell. She had been brought straight here from the airport and was wearing her travel clothes, a midnight blue *shalwar kameez* with a white silk headscarf. Her lipstick was a deep, dense red, and her nails were painted to match. Tufail Hamid was sitting opposite her, with his white-gloved hands resting, palms down, on the surface.

Tufail spoke softly. "Please state your name."

She tucked a stray lock of hair into her scarf and nodded demurely. "I am Mumayyaz Khan."

"Can you confirm that since 2006, you have travelled once a month to Dubai, ostensibly on a shopping expedition?" Tufail asked.

"Yes."

"Can you confirm that in Dubai on your monthly trip, you attended a suite in a hotel, and on each occasion you received fifty thousand dollars in cash?"

"Yes."

"Speak up!"

"Yes."

"What did you do with the money?"

"I paid it into a bank account in my name."

"Where did the money come from?"

"I had no idea." She was crying, tears rolling down her cheeks. "I did what I was told to. That's all. I was told there was no hope for Pakistan, and one day we would have to leave the country. The money was for our future together. How could I refuse?"

Khan removed his glasses and used a handkerchief to wipe the sweat from his eyes. He resisted the urge to loosen his tie.

"What is your relationship to the accused?"

She paused, milking it for full dramatic effect. For a few seconds, Khan thought he might have a heart attack.

"He is my husband."

"Soon he will be her ex-husband," Khan explained to Far-rukh, once the pounding in his chest had stopped. "*Talaq* has been pronounced, and written notice has been submitted to the Union Council. I can assure you their divorce will be finalised within ninety days."

Farrukh nodded inscrutably.

"Why did you turn him in?" Tufail continued.

"Because he admitted that he was a traitor. He had been hiding out in Lahore and now had fled to Dubai. He confessed to everything, every sordid little detail, his unnatural relationship with Tariq Mahoon and Tariq's wife, and how together they sold secrets to the British."

"We believe that for five years Noman used Tariq as a conduit for information, including details of assistance to our allies in Afghanistan," Khan explained. "Noman was in Abbottabad at the surveillance house the night before the Americans launched their operation against bin Laden. He may have warned Tariq of what was coming."

"He begged me to run away with him," Mumayyaz sobbed. "He asked me to withdraw the money, every last dollar, and hand it over to him."

"How did you respond?"

"I refused. I told him it was out of the question. I love my country. And I love my father. I simply couldn't."

"Then what happened?"

"While he was sleeping, I made a call to my father. I told him everything. Everything! I couldn't bear the thought of Noman's treachery and how it might bring shame on my family."

"And how did your father respond?"

"He told me it was vitally important to persuade Noman to return to Pakistan. He advised me to tell my husband that, although I was not ready yet, I might agree to hand over the money in the near future. I made my case, and reluctantly, Noman agreed to travel back with me."

Farrukh was causing Khan some anxiety. Despite Mumayyaz's performance, it was a thin story, and if Farrukh didn't buy it, Khan could find himself hanging at the end of a rope. The whole thing was a mess, a bloody great mess. He would have to draw heavily on his reputation for efficiency and integrity if he was to survive.

"She will have to hand over the money," Farrukh said eventually. "You can make the payment into the Army Relief Fund."

Although it was not unexpected, Khan was still extremely angry. More than three million dollars saved up and now lost. He was careful not to show it, though. It was imperative that he did not seem upset in front of Farrukh.

"Of course," he agreed.

Under different circumstances he might have left the country at the first opportunity, and even if some amongst the Joint Chiefs entertained doubts, they might have been prepared to see him depart without any fuss. After all, others had left under a similar cloud. But without the money, it was out of the question. He was going to have to keep on going, outplaying his enemies, relying on his determination and fortitude.

Meanwhile, there were loose ends still to be sorted. Ed Malik must be disposed of, and Noman too, preferably without the embarrassment of a court-martial. Then there was the question of repairing his relationship with the British.

"I'll handle the clear-up," he said.

"That would be best for all concerned."

"You can rely on me," Khan replied. His uneasiness began to dissipate. Perhaps it was all going to be okay after all.

45 ❖

#TheHiddenHand

Leyla waited for the army to collapse the cordon and leave before getting out of the car. Crossing the road, she ducked under the incident tape at the entrance to the cul-de-sac and cautiously approached the Gulberg house, skirting potholes filled with muddy rainwater.

She had spent the last couple of hours in her aunt's Volkswagen, within sight of one of the roadblocks, waiting to get back inside. After they were captured, she was separated from Ed and driven back to her aunt's place and dropped outside. She'd ditched the orange coveralls, thrown on some new clothes, taken her aunt's car without asking, and driven straight back. Since then, she'd watched unmarked black vehicles come and go. She'd kept an eye on Twitter. At the time of attack, several Gulberg residents had commented on the gunfire and what sounded like a tank in the road, and later, others chipped in with details of the road closures. A Lahore-based news site was reporting that a major anti-terrorist operation was underway in the city.

Now it was eerily quiet.

She squeezed through the gap between the gatepost and the bulldozer and clambered over the flattened gate into the compound. There were spent cartridge cases scattered everywhere and scorch marks on the walls. She saw several large bloodstains and bloody drag marks in the sand that suggested bodies had been removed.

She climbed the steps and went in through the front door. She walked from room to room, hoping for some clue as to where they had taken Ed and why.

Half an hour later, she was sitting on the kitchen steps at the back of the house, trying to work out what to do next, when the boy appeared. One moment she was alone and the next he was there, standing watching her from beside the pipal tree, a malnourished-looking teenage boy in a long black coat—the same boy who had given them the key the night before.

"Hello there," she said, getting to her feet.

The boy shrank back into the shadows.

"I mean you no harm," she said, walking slowly towards him.

The boy remained where he was.

"I'm looking for my friend," she told him, "the man who was with me last night. They've taken him somewhere. I don't know where."

The boy nodded, solemnly.

"Do you know where he is?"

"Pharaoh has taken him."

"Pharaoh?"

The boy reached inside his jacket and took something small out of his pocket. He held it out on his palm. On it was a plain black USB stick.

"What's on it?"

The boy shrugged.

*

She sat cross-legged in the back of the Volkswagen with her MacBook on her lap, gave a prayer to a protector she didn't believe in, held down the shift key to disable auto-play, plugged the USB stick in, and ran a virus scan. Nothing. She breathed a sigh of relief.

A folder of audio files. She settled back and listened to the voices. Ed's softly delivered account of six years of clandestine meetings in ditches and graveyards and Noman's questioning, by turns encouraging and hectoring, and always that name . . . Khan.

She listened and listened again, and the rain came, at first gentle and then torrential, while it hammered on the car's roof, she swapped the USB stick for a dongle, and started doing what she knew best: digging around on the web. There were plenty of surface markers, some of them as large as roadside advertising hoardings—library photos of Khan, beaming like a talent scout, alongside the Mujahideen warlords Gulbuddin Hekmatyr and Jalaluddin Haqqani.

She delved deeper, rummaging amongst the bluster and paranoia in chat rooms, micro-blogs, and social networks, and she came to know him by the name bestowed on him in equal measure by admirers and detractors: *#TheHiddenHand*. She learned that Khan was the former head of the Afghan bureau of the ISI and in that capacity, was credited with driving the Soviets out of Afghanistan. Some said he was responsible for the murderous civil war that followed the collapse of the communist regime when the same warlords fought each other over the rubble of Kabul. Everyone seemed to agree that he was the one who spotted the Taliban in its infancy and nurtured it and launched it on its cleansing path. Some wag from the Association of Afghan Blog Writers had mocked up the identity parade from the film *The Usual Suspects* with an assortment of Taliban

fighters and the banner headline: THE GREATEST TRICK KHAN
EVER PLAYED WAS THE MYTH OF MULLAH OMAR.

She found company records listing him as shareholder in
the Chuppa Group, supplier of bomb-making materials to the
Taliban. There were rumours of links from Khan to Al-Qaeda
and its affiliates. It was Khan who had stashed bin Laden away
in Abbottabad after he'd fled Afghanistan.

Khan was the sworn enemy of the West . . .

. . . and its secret friend.

According to the audio files in her possession, Khan had
been playing for both sides. Enriching himself at everyone's
expense. She wondered what the blogosphere would make of
that. And in the silence following the temporary end of the
rain, an idea came to her and, the more she thought about it, the
more convinced she became that it might work.

46

The Pit

"You should drink your tea." Tufail told him from the other side of the desk.

Ed regarded the glass of masala chai with distaste. It hadn't improved in appeal in the ten minutes since they removed his blindfold. There was a layer of milky scum on its surface as wattled as the pouches beneath Tufail's eyes.

"Where am I?"

"You are in an interview room in the stockade at military headquarters in Rawalpindi. We have every manner of miscreant here: religious extremists, separatists, communists, wreckers, revanchists, and saboteurs. We even have high members of the Afghan Taliban."

"Why am I here?"

"Your accomplice, Noman Butt, is a traitor, and it must yet be decided if you are also a traitor."

Ed studied the mirrored pane of glass set in the rough-hewn stone wall and wondered if there was someone standing on the other side watching him

"How can I be a traitor? I'm a British citizen."

"You are a Pakistani. And you cannot be a Pakistani and something else."

Someone tapped on the glass. Tufail sprang up out of his seat and knocked on the door to be let out.

Ed pushed the glass of chai to the far side of the desk and waited.

The door opened again. Tufail beckoned him with a finger. "This way."

Ed followed him along a windowless corridor past cell doors, through barred gates manned by guards, down several flights of stairs, into an older damper part of the prison, until he was so far underground that he wondered if he would ever see the sun again.

He was lying flat on his back on the concrete slab that served as a bed and staring into the impenetrable blackness, desperate for a sound, blackness so acute it hurt his ears.

Time passed without measure. When a key turned in the lock, he cried out in surprise. The door to the cell was opened, and he was blinded by flashlight.

"Who is it?"

"It is Khan."

Ed was blinded, dancing prisms of light at the edges of his perception. Abruptly, Khan pointed the flashlight away from his face and at his feet, a pool of light on the flagstones.

What was he waiting for?

Ed rolled off the slab and onto his feet, feeling the energy coursing through his veins and muscles and surging into his hands. He prepared to launch himself at Khan and slam his head against the stone. He was an old man, easily overpowered.

"I've come to get you out of here," Khan said.

Which was not what Ed had expected. He held himself in check, suddenly not knowing what to do. "Why?"

"Because Noman will not stand trial," He stepped out of the cell and hissed, *"Jaldi, jaldi!"*

Cautiously, he followed. Khan relocked the door of the cell behind him and then pointed the flashlight down the corridor with its rows of steel cell doors. "This way."

Ed followed him along the corridor and down a further flight of stone steps. The further they descended, the colder it got. At the bottom, Khan unlocked a small metal door. Behind it was a tunnel with a low, arched ceiling that was so narrow they had to turn sideways to advance through it. It was a long way before they got a taste of the outside air. When they did, Khan switched off the flashlight. They emerged onto a metal grille in a round brick-lined chamber. They were in a well with water beneath the grille and a view of angry clouds rushing overhead in the moonlit sky. There was a metal ladder leading upwards, and Khan started up with Ed following, his hands gripping the wet rungs. As he climbed, he saw that the brick-work was covered in thousands of tiny snails.

The top of the well was at the intersection of four tree-lined pathways at the centre of a formal garden that was trans-formed into a sea of mud and puddles. As he eased himself over the parapet, the humid monsoon air pressed like a damp cloth against his face. There was a distant rumble of thunder. More rain was coming. Khan beckoned and led him down one of the paths. An effort had been made to clear the way, and the mud was piled up on either side against the white-painted trees.

At the end of the path, there was a gate formed by two artillery pieces. Parked in the gateway was a silver Mercedes with Tufail at the wheel.

"Get in the back of the car," Khan urged. "There isn't much time."

The car took off across the army base. They passed rows of single-storey barracks and waterlogged playing fields and a squad of Pakistani soldiers in tracksuits and fluorescent jerkins splashing along on the road.

The car slowed as they approached the main entrance. The driver stopped and waited for one of the sentries to approach.

"Don't say anything," Khan whispered.

The sentry was wearing a poncho and carrying a flashlight, which he pointed at each of them in turn. When he saw Khan's identity card he stepped back and saluted.

"I'm sorry to bother you, sir."

"That's quite all right," Khan told him.

Within minutes, they were speeding down the main road out of Rawalpindi.

"Where are we going?" Ed asked.

"You'll see."

Not long after Islamabad, they turned off the highway and followed a potholed road that turned into a rutted track, which climbed into the hills. They parked alongside a jumble of rocks beside a wizened mulberry tree, its trunk bent, growing horizontally, just a couple of feet above the ground.

They got out and stood beside the car. Tufail drew a pistol from the holster at his belt and pointed it at Ed.

"Come on," said Khan.

He placed a hand on Ed's shoulder for balance, and together they advanced down a path between the rocks with Tufail following.

"You've caused me a lot of trouble, young man," Khan said. "If it wasn't for my daughter, you might have succeeded."

They emerged into a muddy bowl with sheer rock walls. There was a pit at the centre of it. As they approached the edge, two men climbed out of it. They were covered in mud from head-to-toe, and only their teeth and the whites of their eyes shone out of their blackened faces. They dropped their spades before heading off up the path.

"As it stands, I've lost a lot of money," Khan told him.

Ed glanced back at Tufail, who was watching him down the barrel of the gun with his forefinger curled around the trigger. He supposed it must be easier to kill him out here and dump him rather than hang him in the cantonment, a way of avoiding embarrassing records. He stared into the bottom of the pit. The one thing he really regretted was that he hadn't had an opportunity to make peace with Leyla.

What he wouldn't give for another punch.

"But I'm prepared to let bygones be bygones," Khan said.

Ed frowned. "What do you mean?"

There was a shout from amongst the rocks behind them.

"This way!" Tufail called out in response.

Two soldiers emerged, dragging a prisoner between them. He was manacled at the wrists and ankles and had a sandbag over his head, its pointy ends like a devil's horns.

"Your partner in crime," Khan said.

Judging by his shape and size, it was Noman. Ed reflected that the hole was easily large enough for both of them.

47

Kill-and-Dump

Squinting downwards with sweat-matted eyelashes, Noman could just about see through a gap at the bottom of the sandbag. He could make out the shape of a spade lying in the mud at his feet. He considered trying to make a grab for it, but there was little enthusiasm in him for a pointless act of defiance. He was a realist, ferociously a realist, and there was nothing he could do to get him out of this situation. He was still struggling to comprehend how thoroughly he'd been out-manoeuvred. He'd seriously underestimated Khan and now he was going to pay for it.

"When I'm done with you here, I'm going to erase your file," he heard Khan say in matter of fact tone. "It will be as if you had died in that hut with your mother."

He was recalling the words of Khan of ten years ago, not long after he had brought him into the ISI and taken him under his wing:

The only thing I will not tolerate is disloyalty.

He should have paid more attention. The sweat in his eyes was making them smart. Through numb lips he contrived a smile. It was said of condemned men that they sometimes experienced moments of elation. What was the worst they could do to him?

"Kneecap."

Crack.

Noman let out a shriek of agony and toppled. His shriek rebounded off the rocks.

When he opened his eyes again, he realised that he must have passed out for a few moments. He could hear the rumble of distant thunder. More rain must be coming. He reached out and touched the mauled flesh and bone shards of his shattered knee. His hand came back wet and sticky.

It's time to climb the mountain.

That's what they used to say in the Special Services Group. Commandos! Don't give up until you reach the top. You're a black stork. Don't let them know you're beaten.

He would not give them the satisfaction of dying quietly. He struggled up onto one knee, gritting his teeth against the pain. His other leg was hopelessly twisted, sliding in the mud at an unnatural angle, only held on by the manacles. He grabbed the spade and tried to use it as a crutch to lift himself further up.

A shadow fell across the sandbag. Cursing, he tried to grab behind him, clawed hands grasping at air. A boot in his back propelled him into the pit. He landed face down at the bottom.

"Fill in the hole," said Khan.

Noman heard Ed protest. "He's still alive."

"Do it, or you'll go in after him."

There was a pause. Then Noman felt the thump of soil landing on his back, like a gloved fist into a punch-bag.

"Quickly!"

Each loaded spade a further punch. You never quite knew where it was going to land. A spade-full landed on his destroyed knee—pain within pain. A wrenching that caused his mouth to

open and filled it with the sodden hessian of the sandbag. Soon
he was unable to move his arms above the elbow, and he struggled to raise his head. He spat muddy water out of his mouth.

It was like being back on the Siachen Glacier when the
avalanche buried him, and he had to dig his way out. It was
the worst time he ever had. Worse even than the battle that
followed it. He remembered desperately moving his hands to
create some space for air to collect in. It was the same now. It
was all about air. Without air, he'd lose consciousness in a couple of minutes, and brain damage would soon follow. He had to
keep moving, keep creating space, his frantic hands scrabbling
at the dirt.

There was only one truly depressing thought, one wretched
piece of thinking. He'd never pull it off a second time. Climbing up out of the avalanche was one thing, but this was a whole
different matter. He felt an incredible weight pressing down on
him.

Look at me, Mumayyaz. My wife. I'm down here in this hole,
in this terrible place. Is this really what you wanted? Was there no
softness in your heart?

He was in the orphanage, the owner rapping his knuckles.

"You filthy little Hindu!"

He was with his mother, who was washing pots in the
kitchen.

The dirt burned his eyes. There was nowhere to look. Only
blackness. It was tempting, but he might disappear into it, pass
out, and die.

Then there was a kid with him in the hole, a kid from the
orphanage who made up stories, a know-it-all kid using up
valuable air.

"What are you doing?" the kid asked.

"Burrowing, " he replied, his fingers screaming from where
the nails had ripped off.

"My father's a dacoit," the kid told him. "He's the most

feared bandit in the whole of Pakistan. One day he's going to come rescue me."

"You can't fool me," Noman said. In the orphanage, they had all lied about themselves. "You've got no dad. I can see through your lies."

"No one calls me a liar."

"I just did. Everyone knows you're a liar. They'll give you everything you want, but they won't believe a word you say. You name it, guns, dope, pussy, and ass . . . whatever you want!"

The kid grinned. "Bring it on. I'm going to join the army."

"Of course you are, whether you want to or not. When you get to basic training, you'll recognise the other orphanage rats because they lie and steal."

He felt suddenly very cold. His teeth were chattering and his knee was throbbing again.

"You're dying," the kid said.

"I know who you are," Noman told him. "I wish I didn't. You need to sort yourself out, stop the whining and the bed-wetting. I don't want to watch you do it. It makes you look weak. Who do you think you're whining *to*? Muslims? Punjabis? Nobody cares. Go find your own hole."

The kid laughed. "Who are you trying to fool? They'll make me an officer."

"But they'll never trust you. You'll always be a dirty little Hindu with a swarm of angry gods buzzing around you like flies with shit on their feet."

Remember where you are, Noman told himself—*flex the tips of your fingers and flare your nostrils*. Keep it moving. Stop talking to ghosts. There's no one else. Just the cold, dead earth. The weight was unmanageable. A lesser man might have given up by now.

"You were always happiest in the dirt," his mother said. "As soon as you could crawl, you were covered in filth from head to foot."

That was funny. So funny it hurt.

"You deliberately set out to live your life in the wrong way," she said. "You always fought being a human being."

"I wasn't given a chance," he protested.

"Don't give me that! Even as a tiny child, you were a monster. From the first moment you opened your eyes, I knew you were evil."

Remember why this happened, he told himself, *because you believed in your country, but it did not believe in you.* Nobody starts out evil. You're just an ordinary man with a child at your core. They made you this way. They twisted you and turned you like putty.

"Look at you," his mother said, sadly. "You can't even die with dignity."

"Leave me alone!" he screamed. "You don't exist. You're just a ghost.'

The pain was so much worse. It was getting away from him, unravelling into the void.

"Where you're going, Noman, there are only ghosts."

48

The Patriot's Way

Khan had always regarded his first duty as the protection of Pakistan, by which he meant the Indus Valley and its neighbouring deserts, mountains, and swamps. He considered the ISI to be the moral guardian of the state, defending it against corrupt bureaucrats, judges, and politicians. He therefore saw nothing wrong in the ISI interfering in the running of Pakistan, or anywhere else for that matter.

He liked to explain it to people by saying that the ISI was a tool, and it was the way you handled it that counted. It was like a knife—it was sharp, which was efficient, and it just depended on whether you cut vegetables with it, you slit somebody's throat or you committed hara-kiri with it. Anything was possible. It was up to him to decide how to wield it.

A large part of protecting Pakistan involved preventing India from extending its influence in Afghanistan. The worst-case scenario was Afghanistan as an Indian client state ruled by its non-Pashtun peoples. There was nothing that frightened the Chiefs of Staff more than the prospect of encirclement. To prevent it, the prevailing consensus was that the tribes of

Afghanistan must be kept in a state of turmoil. It was a practical matter. Not meddling for the sake of it, as some suggested, but as a deliberate policy of keeping Afghanistan on the boil. That had been as true during the Jihad against the Soviets, the subsequent civil war, and the period of Taliban rule as it was now during the American occupation.

His role in creating the Taliban did not signify ideological approval of them or any desire that Pakistan should experience a Taliban-style revolution, any more than his support for Mujahideen in the 1980s implied much liking for them. In his mind, the Afghan Taliban were no worse than the Taliban's old enemies the Afghan Northern Alliance, with whom the West had, in effect, been allied since 2001. The atrocities and rapes committed by the Northern Alliance in the 1990s and their looting of western aid and revival of the heroin trade in the 2000s had helped cement Pashtun support for the Afghan Taliban. There were times when Khan was staggered by the naivety and hubris of Western politicians who had aligned themselves with a gang of murderers and narco-traffickers, and yet seemed to genuinely think they had right on their side.

Khan had been studying the Americans and the British for his whole career. Since 2001, he had watched them drawn into quagmires in Iraq and Afghanistan. He had watched them expend blood and treasure for no discernible profit. He had talked to colleagues from intelligence agencies in Syria, Iran, and Saudi Arabia. And in the process, he had come to what was perhaps a surprising conclusion.

He had come to realise that it was not the Americans or their little cousins, the British, who threatened his faith; they were not the ones who threatened his way of life or his liberty—it was the radical Islamists, Al-Qaeda, and their allies in the Pakistani Taliban who presented the more mortal threat. They were the ones that would rip apart the fabric of the country that he had pledged to protect.

He decided it was time for Pakistan to rescue Islam from the Islamists. And it was for this reason he had decided to start channelling information to the British Secret Service. He preferred to deal with the British than the Americans. You never knew where you stood with the Americans. They had an unnerving habit of learning from their mistakes, which could never be said of the British.

He had happily provided Tariq with information for the British. He had no qualms about revealing the location of terrorist training camps in the Pakistani tribal areas. He viewed the drone strikes as a useful means of achieving his aims. And when it came to giving them a helping hand in Afghanistan, it was a question of balancing the opposing sides. At times, it was necessary to support both sides in a conflict. After all, the objective was to keep Afghanistan on the boil, not for it to boil over.

He did not consider himself a traitor. Far from it. He viewed himself as a patriot.

On balance, perhaps, he should have provided better-quality information to the British. If he'd given up bin Laden earlier, for instance, he might have avoided this ridiculous and petulant plot against him, and he might not have had to give up the three million dollars accrued, but all was not lost. It wasn't unremittingly bleak. There were some advantages. He had rid himself of a dangerous subordinate and, as well as offering to resume the payments, the British had pledged to assist with relocation. It was reassuring to know that there were options in hand in the event that the forces of discord prevailed and it became necessary to leave the country.

He could not be sure that he would succeed.

49

The Road West

"That's it." Ed threw down his spade and stared at him across the disturbed earth. "I've done your dirty work for you. What now?"

"Come here."

Khan put his hand on Ed's shoulder, and together they climbed back up the path to the car, with Tufail following.

"Tariq spoke highly of you," Khan told him, as Tufail eased the Mercedes along the ruts in the track. "Tariq said that at the beginning of a meeting you always asked the same question, it didn't matter where you were or how difficult the circumstances, you said 'How long have you got?' And provided there was more than fifteen minutes, you always took the time to ask after his family, his wife, and his mother. He appreciated that. I appreciated it, also."

"He was my agent."

"And mine too," Khan said.

"You killed him."

"It was regrettable, but necessary. He would have revealed

everything if he had been captured. The consequences of that would have been disastrous for me and you."

Ed didn't bother to reply. They bounced up off the track onto a tarmac road.

"I have given much thought to the subsequent actions of Samantha Burns," Khan said. "I can see now that perhaps I should have been more generous with the provision of information. I could have done more to explain the danger posed by the House of War. After all, it was a genuine threat. And I could have given up bin Laden earlier. I acknowledge that. I made mistakes. I am genuinely sorry for that."

The car turned off onto a muddy esplanade within sight of the junction with the Grand Trunk Road. There was a car, a battered white Corolla, parked alongside a small boarded-up kiosk. In the background, trucks trundled by on the highway.

"I have spoken to Jonah," Khan told him. "I sent my regards to Queen Bee. I said to him, 'Tell her that I forgive her.' We agreed that there is no need for further unpleasantness. We identified an opportunity to put the relationship on the right footing again. I've offered to help with the exit from Afghanistan."

"I'm sure they'll be thrilled."

"Everything is going to be back on an even keel."

It was so brazen it was breathtaking, Ed wanted to clap: a slow handclap in ironic tribute to the Hidden Hand.

Khan reached into the inside pocket of his blazer and took out a dark-green passport and handed it to Ed. He looked at his watch. "We're about three hours from the Torkham border crossing. The guards have been told to let you pass."

"You're letting me go?"

"Yes, I am. You know you're a lucky man. I don't think the British would have gone to such lengths for you. In fact, I'm sure of it. Tell your friend that I'm relying on her to keep her word."

"What are you talking about?"

"You'll see."

Ed hesitated with his hand on the door lever. It seemed possible that he was about to be shot while trying to escape.

"Good-bye," said Khan.

Ed got out of the car and closed the door behind him. When he looked up, he saw that someone had got out of the Corolla. It was Leyla. Without a backward glance, he ran through the mud towards her.

They embraced.

"What's going on?" he said. "Why is he letting us go?"

She put the car keys in his hands. "You drive."

He got in the driver's seat and started the car. Soon they were driving fast, heading west along the Grand Trunk Road, the needle showing 120 kilometres an hour.

"What's going on?"

"I swapped you for a USB stick," she replied.

His eyes kept flicking to the rearview mirror. The road was empty. As far as he could tell, they were not being followed.

"What was on the stick?"

"You were. Recordings of your interviews with Noman Butt; I threatened to spread them all over the web."

"You blackmailed Khan?"

"Sure."

He laughed. "Did you keep a copy?"

"Of course."

"I love you," he told her.

For a few minutes, he dared to imagine that they might make it. He could see that the information on the recordings would cause Khan considerable embarrassment and cast doubt on Noman's guilt, but it would only be effective if it was substantiated by witness statements from those present, and one of them, Noman, was already dead.

"It's not enough," he said, eventually. "We know too much."

"So why did Khan let us go?"

"Because he thinks we're not going to make it. My guess is he's issued orders for us to be shot at the border, or maybe even at the checkpoint outside Peshawar. Later, he'll tell London he tried his best. That's assuming anyone in London gives a damn." He'd never had such a strong sense of how expendable he was. "We don't have any value."

She looked at him, a mixture of fear and exhaustion written on her face. "How can you be so calm?"

"Because I'm not going let it happen," he said. "You won't die tonight, I promise you that. We're going to get off the highway and find another way over the border."

After ninety minutes of driving, they turned off at the locomotive factory at Risalpur and headed north on the Malakand-Mardan Road. It was raining harder now.

"We've got about an hour before we're overdue in Peshawar and they raise the alarm."

50

The Devil You Know

At lunchtime, Samantha Burns stepped out of the cabinet office and walked north along Whitehall past the Scotland office, wearing a pair of pink running shoes from the bottom drawer of her desk. She had just received word that Noman was dead and Khan's position was assured. Ed was missing. Under any other circumstances, the operation might be considered a disaster, but really, it had all turned out rather well. She felt a great sense of relief and with it, the desire to stretch her legs.

She turned left into Horse Guards, walking through the gate past the mounted sentry of the Household Cavalry. There was the usual gaggle of tourists having their pictures taken beside the horses. More and more of them seemed to be Chinese. China was on her radar, of course, for the usual geopolitical and economic reasons. She kept a watchful eye on the Straits of Taiwan and disputed islands in the East China Sea, the dinosaur regime in North Korea. Reports of industrial espionage crossed her desk. But mostly, if she was frank, she left the business of worrying about the Chinese to her successors.

She went through the arched gate and onto the broad

expanse of the parade ground. Crossing on the south side, she came under the censorious gaze of Field Marshal Frederick Roberts, hero of the Second Afghan War. His bronze monument stuck like a fishbone in the throat of their current endeavour—the vigilant old soldier astride his horse, its hooves splayed with its front legs locked, and its head turning away as if to say *"Thus far and no further."* You could never escape from history in London. Despatched in 1879 to seek retribution for the death of the British envoy at the hands of an angry mob, Roberts had quelled an uprising in Kabul, and then marched his army south to avenge the loss of a thousand British and Indian troops at the battle of Maiwand. He had routed the Afghans at the battle of Kandahar and then, astonishingly, against all expectations, had marched his army straight back out of Afghanistan.

It was Roberts who had said: "We have nothing to fear from Afghanistan and offensive though it may be to our pride, the less they see of us the less they will dislike us."

It had been a terrible mistake to stay in Afghanistan for so long. Afghanistan was a trap. It was easy to get in, but almost impossible to get out. The Soviets had learned that and the British in the nineteenth century before them. Only a few far-sighted individuals, Roberts among them, had warned against the trap.

She entered St. James' Park by the Guard's Division Memorial. The park had been out-of-bounds for a while, after that fool Fisher-King was found poisoned on a park bench back in 2005, but it was back in-bounds again now.

She took her customary route around the lake: a figure-eight loop, starting on the south side, passing Duck Island Cottage, the fountain, and the massive old willow, with a nod to the orange-billed pelicans that were introduced to the park as a gift from the Russian ambassador in 1664. Back then, there had been rumours of witchcraft, that the large and ungainly creatures with sinister yellow eyes were Russian spies. She had once seen one swallow a pigeon in one gulp.

She had decided that a celebration of sorts was in order, and before she left work she would call her husband and ask him to pick up a two-inch thick piece of sirloin and open a bottle of Clos de Vougeot laid down four years before. It was the last of the bottles left over from her daughter's wedding. She'd been saving it for just such an occasion as this. She would eat the steak and drink a couple of glasses of the wine and was confident that she would sleep well.

She did not often sleep well. There was so much to worry about: the rise of militant jihadists from the Maghreb to Eastern Libya, from Egypt's Sinai desert to the battlegrounds of Syria's civil war; the danger of the Israelis launching a pre-emptive strike and the Iranians retaliating by blocking the straits of Hormuz; further disintegration in the Horn of Africa and Yemen; civil war in Afghanistan post-2014. But it was Pakistan that kept her awake most often at night. It was Pakistan that she regarded as the most dangerous place on Earth. Not just because of its out-of-control intelligence services and nuclear weapons, its radicalised madrassas and failing civil institutions, its terrorist training camps and unregulated arms markets, but also because of its large British-based diaspora.

It was Burns' belief that the key to preventing a recurrence of the 7/7 London bombings in 2005 was a strong and stable Pakistan, with its government (military or civilian) prepared to take control of its ungoverned spaces and rein in its extremist elements. How to achieve it? It was necessary for Britain to exert pressure, of course. But there was an equal need to be careful, to ensure that the pressure did not become so overwhelming that it undermined or destroyed Pakistan's government by humiliating it in the eyes of its own people. The orthodoxy at Vauxhall Cross was that it was only legitimate Muslim governments and security services that could control terrorist plots on their soil. And so they had convinced themselves that the help of the Pakistani intelligence services to Britain, particularly the information passed by Khan via Tariq, had been absolutely vital to identifying the links between extremist elements in Britain and groups in Pakistan and to preventing more attacks on Britain, mainland Europe, and the USA. The information that he provided had allowed the great uninformed mass to slump safely in front of their television sets and watch whatever passed for importance these days, *Britain's Got Talent* or *X Factor* or whatever.

As a source, Khan was of "unparalleled value."

In truth, he was a fucking disaster. The Americans had described the contents of the USB stick known as "the sociopath's address book" as "cannily compiled and heavily redacted." They accused MI6 of being the credulous dupes of a foreign intelligence service. They were right. It was the same with the "alumni list." Vauxhall Cross had been right royally screwed. The fish had reeled in the fisherman. Khan had repeatedly used them to enrich himself and pursue what seemed like private vendettas. The Americans were still demanding information on that bloody drone strike. Nobody really believed in the dirty bomb. By 2010, enough was enough. Burns had spent half-an-hour on the phone with Tariq while he was squatting in a ditch in Helmand, telling him that the information from Khan had to bloody improve or else.

Or else what?

Or else we shut off the money and find someone else to do business with.

The final straw was the realisation that Khan must have known the whereabouts of bin Laden for several years before revealing it to them.

She'd never mistaken him for an angel. There had never been any doubt in her mind that he was a bad man, an unscrupulous manipulator who bore more responsibility than almost anyone else for the rise of Islamic extremism in Afghanistan and Pakistan. But she had expected him to honour the deal, the deal offered to him in 2005 when he agreed to provide information to Her Majesty's government.

As far as she was concerned, he had broken that agreement, which was why she had felt no qualms in acting to get rid of him. After all, spying was a profession of cold calculation. The West was probably going to fail in Afghanistan, leaving civil war and anarchy behind, just as it had after the Soviet withdrawal and the collapse of the communist regime. The last time around, the anarchy had given birth to Al-Qaeda, which had risen like a ghastly phoenix from the ashes. Who knew what might be born this time around? Ensuring an improved flow of information from Pakistan was therefore vital. Burns did not count herself amongst those who argued that electronic surveillance and drones were sufficient to protect Britain against its enemies. There would always be a need for human intelligence.

She stopped at the centre of the Blue Bridge, with its view of the East Front façade of the palace.

It was standing here beside Jonah, in the immediate aftermath of the death of bin Laden and the exposure of Tariq as a British spy, that she had raised the possibility of discrediting Khan. At the time, she had been under considerable pressure from No. 10 to deliver some form of nudge that would allow for a swift exit from Afghanistan. Something had to be done. It had been her hope that by removing Khan from his position of power in the ISI it would allow more malleable elements to rise to the fore. It was Jonah who had suggested Noman Butt as the poster boy for a post-Khan future. It was an elegant solution, with a minimum of fuss. Mumayyaz would remain as the recipient of the funds and ensure that her ambitious husband delivered a better product than her father had. Together, they had drawn up the plan to ditch Khan and empower Noman. Ed

Malik was the obvious choice to execute it, and his assault on the CIA head of station in Kabul had provided a helpful pretext for his subsequent downfall.

The plan had failed, of course. Noman had proven to be less malleable than promised, but at the same time, it had exceeded her expectations. Khan had been given a timely reminder of how vulnerable he was and notice that it was time to deliver on old promises.

The indications were that he had learned his lesson. There was even a chance that her predictions of failure in Afghanistan might be turned around. By inadvertently entrenching Khan's position, she had perhaps created space for a deal with the Taliban.

In his conversation with Jonah, Khan had pledged to arrange for Pakistan to free the senior Afghan Taliban officials that it was holding in Rawalpindi, releasing them to the care of the Afghan High Peace Council, which was tasked with opening talks with the Taliban. He had pledged not to interfere if the Afghan Taliban and the Afghan Council went to a third country as a venue for future talks. And if these initial steps bore fruit, he had promised to put pressure on hundreds of Taliban commanders fighting Western and Afghan forces inside Afghanistan to support reconciliation talks with Kabul. If Khan delivered on these promises, then it might be possible for America and Britain to withdraw from Afghanistan without it turning into a rout. And in return, all he had requested was that the money continued to be delivered as before.

She took a left turn past the Nash Shrubberies and walked counterclockwise past the playground.

It was unfortunate about Ed, of course. It wasn't completely hopeless, but it was necessary to be realistic. He was probably dead by now. Burns had agreed to send Jonah out to Afghanistan to see what could be done, even if it was just a question of recovering the body. She would ensure that Ed received some form of posthumous recognition.

It was necessary to balance the destruction of one man—Ed—with what had been achieved. It was a matter of the greater good of the British people. They were fighting against an amorphous enemy that killed thousands with suicide bombers, that used torture and intimidation. It would be absurd to be squeamish when the stakes were so high.

51

Into the Tribal Areas

As they approached the bridge over the River Swat, Ed could see lights haloed in the driving rain and dark shapes moving in the road ahead.

"It's a checkpoint," he growled. "Hang on!"

He floored the accelerator. He caught a brief glimpse of soldiers in ponchos scattering. The car struck an oil drum with a glancing blow and fishtailed on the road before righting itself.

Then they were on the bridge with the immense roar of water below them, the only light from the muzzle flashes behind them. A spray of bullets struck the back of the car, and the windshield cracked and spider-webbed in front of him. Ed cried out in pain and anger. The car grazed the parapet at the side of the bridge in a flurry of sparks, slid sideways, and struck the other side before bouncing back into the centre of the road.

The road climbed after the bridge in a series of precipitous switchbacks. The windshield was almost completely opaque and he could only see to steer by sticking his head out the side window.

"Are they following?" he asked her.

She turned in her seat. From this height she could see back down the route they had travelled and the bridge far below.

"No."

After a few minutes, he pulled over to the side of the road. He got out and picked up a rock with his good right hand, and used it to knock out the windshield.

"You've been hit," Leyla said.

He was breathing heavily, and blood was running down his sleeve. The adrenaline was already deserting him, and he knew he would soon feel the pain.

"Give me your belt," he said. She pulled it out of its trouser loops. He fed the tongue of the belt through the buckle, slid it up over the wound onto his upper arm, and tightened it.

"You drive."

He crossed to the passenger side. She got in beside him in the driver's seat. She restarted the engine and pulled out into the road with her scarf drawn tightly across her face so that only her eyes were exposed. He ripped away the sleeve on his wounded arm and tore it into rags for a dressing with his teeth. He started winding them around his arm. When he was done he let himself sink back into the seat. He was cold, and he could feel his heart pounding as it tried to keep feeding oxygen to his brain.

"Where are we going?" she asked.

"I'll tell you when we get there."

"Why aren't they following us?"

"Because it's too dangerous on the roads for the army here."

"What about us?"

"It's dangerous for us too."

The road had been damaged by flooding or earthquakes, and in places, the tarmac had buckled and cracked. Some parts had washed away and been replaced with meandering detours through dynamited rubble. Several times they had to slow to a crawl and weave between boulders that had tumbled into the

road. The landscape appeared to have been torn apart by ele-
mental energies.

There was a scintillating pattern in the rain, like falling strings
of code not visible to the focussed eye. A drumbeat on the bonnet, stinging needles of rain striking his cheeks, the foot-well
awash with bloody water.

The headlights barely pierced the storm, but his retinas
were filled with light. The car slammed to a halt. The falling
rain swelled and contracted like a kaleidoscope.

"You keep passing out," she said.

He gripped the dash with his good arm.

"It's after the next river crossing," he said, loosening the
tourniquet.

"You're sure?"

"I've been here once before," he laughed, sending shooting
pains up his arm and into the base of his skull. "Two miles after
the crossing, there's a lay-by and a rock that looks like a raised
fist."

"I can barely see the road ahead."

"Don't worry," he told her.

Water was running across the surface of the bridge when they
got there.

"Hold tight," she said.

The car surged into the water, creating a bow wave. For a few
precarious moments, the car drifted sideways, and it seemed as
if they might be swept off the bridge into the ravine, but then
they were through to the other side.

He watched the milometer tick by.

"Here," he said.

She rolled to a halt and switched off the engine. Together they peered into the swirling darkness.

"There," he said, "the Gonzo fist."

"It really does look like a fist," she said.

They got out of the car.

"This way," he said.

They slid down the muddy shoulder of the road with Ed in front. There was a half-hidden trail leading away between two large spurs of rock. They went carefully between the two and followed the trail down into a ravine. Around a boulder, they came in sight of an old Soviet command trailer on a Zil chassis with the skeletal remains of a radar dish at its front end. Its windows were lit by firelight, and shadows danced in the windows.

"Come on," he said.

She followed him into a muddy yard filled with stacks of tires and car parts and what looked like the tails and nose cones of several missile systems. There were a number of vehicles behind the trailer, but it was difficult to judge how many.

"I know these people," Ed told her.

He moved into the shadow of the trailer and close along-side the window. He climbed up on an old ammunition crate, and from where he stood, he could see most of the interior. There was a fire in the stove and an oil lamp hanging from a hook. A young woman in a headscarf was kneeling by the stove, and sitting against the wall behind her was an old man wearing a white turban. It was Hakimullah, Tariq's manservant. He was smoking a long-handled pipe. The young girl was his granddaughter.

Ed found Leyla squatting in the darkness by one of the wheels and pulled her to her feet.

"It's okay, they're friends."

He climbed the steps and knocked on the door. He didn't

want to surprise them. He pushed it open and stepped inside. The girl issued a stifled scream.

"Who is it?" Hakimullah called out in Pashto.

The girl on the floor stared at him with fearful, addled eyes. Hakimullah climbed to his feet and came towards them.

"I didn't recognise you," he said. He was smiling, his voice slurred by opium. "You look like a ghost."

"It's been a long night," Ed replied in Pashto.

"I didn't expect to see you again."

"Well, I'm here now," Ed told him, collapsing into one of the chairs. He saw that the girl was looking towards the door where Leyla was standing. He was pleased to see that she didn't look scared.

"She's my friend," he said.

"You're bleeding," Hakimullah told him.

The dressing on his bicep was dark brown and saturated with blood. More blood had crusted in patches all down his arm.

"I got shot. I think it's gone all the way through. Can you stitch me up?"

Hakimullah shrugged, "Of course."

"Have you got something you can clean it with?"

Hakimullah nodded. He pulled aside the rug and lifted one of the wooden planks, revealing a metal box beneath. From it, he removed a bottle of clear liquid covered in Cyrillic writing.

Vodka.

"Let's have a celebration," Ed muttered.

Hakimullah removed the dressing, peeling it away from the entry and exit wounds, and poured vodka on them. Ed winced at the sting. Then they passed the bottle back and forth, taking swigs, while Hakimullah stitched the wounds with a sewing needle and some dark thread.

"I need you to get us over the border," Ed told him.

Hakimullah paused with the needle in his a hand and the thread between his teeth.

"We have a car that can get us most of the way," Ed explained. "If you've got some fuel."

Hakimullah finished sewing before replying. He tied off the ends and made a fresh bandage from strips of cloth cut from a white turban. He took a final swig at the bottle.

"Let us go now," he said. He gave them blankets to fashion into cloaks.

They went out again into the rain. Hakimullah and his granddaughter were clutching two-litre soda bottles filled with petrol in each hand. They crossed the yard and followed the trail back up onto the road. The car was still there.

As soon as the petrol had been dispensed they set off again, Hakimullah driving this time with the young girl beside him, Ed and Leyla in the back with a blanket over them.

"Try to get some sleep," Ed told her. "We've got a long walk ahead."

52

Crossing the Durand Line

They had been walking for a couple of hours when they heard the noise of the helicopter carried on the wind. It had stopped raining, and they had made reasonably good speed, but dawn wasn't that far off. For the last hour, the forest had blocked their view of the valley as they climbed. It had been dark under the fir trees, like being in a long tunnel, and silent, their footsteps swallowed by the soft carpet of needles. Then they emerged onto an exposed ridgeline, and it was as if they were on the roof of the world. Deep gorges and jagged peaks stretched away in every direction. There was a sprinkling of stars to the west, but most of the sky was dark.

The cloud cover wasn't low enough to inconvenience the helicopter. It was heading towards them, but wasn't flying in a straight line. It was criss-crossing the valley, and every now and then, its searchlight would pinpoint one of the isolated farmsteads. It was looking for movement, any kind of movement.

As it approached the edge of the valley and climbed towards them, they took refuge in a hollow at the base of a rock. It passed almost directly over them. They waited breathlessly for it to turn back, but the sound of its rotors was abruptly muted as it dropped between two peaks, and the night was silent again.

Leyla switched on the flashlight and changed the dressing on Ed's wounds. Some of the stitches had torn through the soft flesh, and the surrounding skin was mottled every colour of the rainbow and so tender that even to look at it made it hurt more.

"How far to the border?" Ed asked through gritted teeth.

Hakimullah shrugged. He seemed to have only the most rudimentary understanding of time and distance. "Not far."

"Will we make it before daylight?" It was good country for moving at night, but when daylight came it would work against them. They would be far too conspicuous.

"Inshallah, we will."

"Let's go, then."

Wearily, they climbed to their feet and set off again. They were tired now, and the short break that had helped their lungs had stiffened the muscles in their legs. Ed set off at a good pace to show them he was strong enough to make it, but after a while he slowed and fell behind. He found it difficult to hold his arm up, but if he let it hang it throbbed even more. He wondered if it was septic. He'd seen wounds go septic very quickly in this part of the world.

He put the thought to the back of his mind and concentrated on putting one foot in front of the other.

Less than an hour later they stood above a valley with a thin grey strip of river running through it: Durand's arbitrary line. On the far side of the river was Afghanistan.

There was the faint pinkish tinge of light in the eastern sky. Ed cursed their bad luck. Hakimullah spoke for the first time since they last stopped, turning back to Ed. His face was drawn and tense.

"We have to cross here now, without delay," he said, "or hide, and wait until night comes."

"We can't wait another day," Leyla said when Ed had finished translating for her. "We need to get you to a hospital."

"On the other side the path is narrow and there are many mines," Hakimullah explained.

"What is he saying?" Leyla demanded.

"We have to walk in his footsteps on the other side."

"Why?"

"Russian helicopters dropped a lot of mines in these valleys."

She was appalled. "I don't believe this."

"It's okay, he knows the way through. And because there are so many mines the Pakistanis won't expect us to cross here. It's the best chance we've got. It's going to be okay."

Scrambling downslope through the loose rocks and stones, Ed slipped and fell and knocked his wounded arm, and the pain was so great he curled up in a ball. Leyla lifted his face from the ground and cupped it her hands. She kissed his forehead and his cheeks.

"I love you," she said. "I don't care about what happened before."

He smiled, but he didn't say anything. There was no energy in him to spare. She helped him up and gripped him around the waist, and he leaned on her for support. At the bottom of the ridge they left the cover of rocks and stumbled across an exposed gravel plain. If the helicopter came back now, it was certain that they would be killed.

When they reached the river, they hesitated. The old man's granddaughter was the first in. She plunged in to her waist and battled against the current. Hakimullah was next, and then Leyla and Ed. She gripped him around the waist and held him upright. It was freezing, the glacial water cutting through their bones like steel. Ed managed to keep his arm out of the water, but he felt his resolve draining away as the cold penetrated.

The girl splashed ashore and paused at the top of the bank to help the rest of them. Ed sank to his knees on the gravel.

"We can't stop here," Hakimullah said.

Ed nodded and Leyla helped him, slowly and painfully, to his feet again.

Hakimullah took the lead. They walked in single file following a barely discernible path. Ed gripped the back of Leyla's wet coat with his good hand. Once the old man knelt down and pointed to a shape in the gravel within a foot of the edge of the path. It was a sycamore-shaped piece of plastic, its seed pouch full of liquid explosive. It was a Soviet PFM mine, scattered here a quarter of a century before. Ed imagined many more of them lying hidden in the gloom. Hakimullah set off again, and they followed, fearing that each step might be their last.

After ten minutes Hakimullah stopped and said, "We are through the minefield."

The path climbed up out of the valley on a winding track between outcrops of rock, and they were shielded from view as the leading edge of the sun rose above the ridgeline behind them.

At the top of the track they saw a herd of goats, their fur matted with mud, and beyond them the outline of buildings clinging precariously to the rocks and a twist of smoke in the frigid air.

53

The Code of Life

Ed lifted the shaking cup to his mouth. He was still shivering uncontrollably and it burned his chapped lips, but as the hot tea travelled down his throat and into his gut he could feel it warming him to the core.

They were sitting huddled around an iron pan full of burning firewood in a *hujra* at the centre of the village. It was a squat building made out of boulders set in mud, and the earth floor was covered in rushes of reeds. Large parts of the room were in shadow and, though it was difficult to be sure, Ed estimated that there were more than a dozen men of various ages spread out against the walls and in the corners.

Leyla was on one side of him and Hakimullah on the other, with the village headman facing them across the fire. He was related to Hakimullah by marriage, and the two old men spoke with solemn familiarity while staring into the embers. On a rough-hewn shelf in the corner of the room there was a VHF radio, and every now and then it crackled into life. Men from the local Taliban were searching the valley for them, calling out to each settlement in turn.

"What happens now?" Leyla whispered.

"Hakimullah has invoked Pashtunwali," Ed replied in a low voice.

"What does that mean?"

"He is asking for asylum," Ed explained. "He wants them to protect us against our enemies."

"Why should they?" she asked.

"It's the code of life: courage, revenge, hospitality, and generosity to the defeated. It's always been this way."

"Are we the defeated?"

"Not yet," he said with a weary smile. "These people are no friends to the Taliban. The headman is complaining that they come and steal their livestock. And they take young girls from the village in temporary marriages and discard them when they get tired of them. He says the girls are no use after that."

Leyla shook her head. "It's so screwed up."

"Hakimullah is urging him to take a stand," Ed told her. "There's a chance for us."

A man's voice on the radio interrupted them. It was frighteningly loud.

"They're getting closer."

After another five minutes, the headman turned his attention to Ed. He had a wizened face the colour and texture of a walnut, and his beard was completely white.

"Will you fight?" he asked.

Ed nodded. "Yes."

The headman got up and reached up into the gloom amongst the rafters with his arthritic antler-like hands. He lifted down two Kalashnikovs, one after the other, and handed them to Hakimullah and Ed.

"We will fight with you," he said.

Ed pressed his good hand to his chest. "Thank you."

He heard the rustling of reeds as the men got up from the

floor and the click-clack of working parts as they prepared their weapons.

"What's going on?" Leyla demanded.

"He's agreed. Here, help me with this." He passed the rifle to her. "Pull on this." She used the heel of her palm to pull back the cocking lever, and the first bullet fed into the chamber. He set the rifle down in his lap and reached into his belt for the Makarov.

"Take this," he told her, giving her the pistol. "I want you to stay here. If they make it this far into the village, it's over for us."

She stared at it as if it terrified her. "What do you want me to do with it?"

"They're bad men, Leyla."

Her eyes were wide as saucers. "You're scaring me."

"Don't let yourself be taken alive."

Tenderly, he touched the side of her face and then drew her to him. They kissed tenderly.

"Thank you," he said. "I love you."

Using the gun as a crutch, he climbed to his feet and followed the men out of the building and into the bright morning light.

Ed crouched in the stark shadow of a rock at the top of the trail, just outside the village. It was a bright morning without a cloud in the sky. Soon it would be ferociously hot. Hakimullah was somewhere close by, and the other men of the village were spread out in the rocks around him.

He was listening as hard as his concentration allowed. His arm was throbbing, and he felt light-headed. His mouth was dry, and he needed a drink of water. He wished that Leyla were beside him. He didn't want to die alone.

Somewhere up ahead he heard the soft slap of sandals and

the patter of dislodged stones. A shape flitted between two rocks, a twist of turban in the morning breeze.

He opened fire. Three round bursts.

Someone nearby started firing as well. Then they stopped.

A momentary hiatus: everyone conserving ammunition.

He heard the sound, like a cork popping, of an RPG leaving its launcher. In a moment a ball of smoke and dust and shattered rock swelled up behind him. He was pattered with flying grit. Raising his head, he caught a glimpse of one of the Taliban rolling across the trail.

Ed surged upwards and around the rock with the rifle butt in his shoulder and the barrel rising into the path of the Taliban, who was rising from the crouch that he'd landed in. Close enough to make eye contact, a stiff unwashed beard and kohl-rimmed eyes. Ed pulled the trigger. The Taliban's body heaved.

There was firing all around him. Another RPG warhead exploded amongst the rocks, and another cloud of dust billowed. It was impossible to see the trail or the sky overhead. Ed struggled back up from cover to cover, pausing to fire at the Taliban coming up the trail. Behind a boulder, he found one of the men from the village sitting down, trying to pick rock chips out of his flesh. He had an expression of intense concentration on his face.

Ed thought he heard a helicopter. His first thought was that the Pakistanis must want him dead very much. He took the magazine from the villager's rifle and reloaded his weapon, jamming it between his knees before slowly and painfully pulling the cocking handle.

Then he heard a machine gun firing, close by. He crawled to the edge of the boulder and risked a glimpse. The dust was beginning to clear. He saw movement on the trail and fired. He slumped back into cover. The injured villager had stopped moving. Ed didn't have the strength to get himself back into the village. This was it, he realised, the ground where he would make his stand.

He smiled. *The Weald of Kent.*

June 1940. Churchill's last stand: *We will never surrender.*

He dried his trigger finger against his shirt and slipped it back into the guard. He was ready.

The machine gun opened up again, first near Ed, pummelling the rocks and shredding the dirt in a maelstrom of sparks and rock chips, and then, drifting towards the rising sun, it found the advancing Taliban—in an instant their bodies whipped like tattered flags in a high wind. Within a few seconds, the assault was broken, the surviving fighters retreating down the trail.

Ed let his rifle drop to his side. A large black man in combat fatigues emerged out of the smoke. He was wearing a helmet and carrying a rifle.

Ed didn't recognise him at first.

"Jonah?"

Jonah knelt beside him. "How are you doing?" he asked.

"Just fucking dandy," he managed.

Jonah reached across him and felt for a pulse at the neck of the villager beside him. He shook his head and closed the man's eyes.

"Is she okay?" Ed demanded. "Leyla, I mean, is she okay?"

"She's fine."

He felt a wave of relief.

"Medic!" shouted Jonah. "You're the one that needs attention."

"How did you know how to find us?" Ed asked.

"We were listening in on the Taliban. We knew you were out here somewhere. When they announced they were going to attack the village, we knew it must be you."

"I thought you wanted me dead."

Jonah laughed.

"It would have been tidier," he conceded, "but who wants tidy?"

54 ◆◆

The Finger of God

"They make a desert, and call it peace."
Tacitus, *Agricola*

Khan paid no attention to him at first, a boy pulling at his sleeve. The market was full of beggars. He was choosing mangoes for Mumayyaz.

"Sir?"

Irritated, Khan turned on him, raising his cane to strike him. But something made him pause. The boy was small, dirty, and barrel-chested with a narrow, pinched face and a glob of snot on the end of his nose. He was wearing a filthy black coat that was far too large for him. There was something strangely familiar about him. Khan had seen him somewhere before. An odd thought struck him: this was what Noman must have looked like, before the army fashioned him into a man.

"Do I know you?" Khan demanded.

"Yes indeed, sir," said the boy, politely.

"How?"

The boy opened his coat, revealing row upon row of shiny steel ball bearings like chain mail. Khan remembered him from dinner with the one-legged mullah on the banks of the Kabul

River on the night before bin Laden was killed. The boy had sat just out of reach and watched them eat.

"What do you want?" Khan said, softly.

"It is time."

"What do you mean?"

"Time for the death of Pharaoh."

Pharaoh? Was that how they saw him?

"Now?" Khan asked.

The boy nodded, solemnly. His right index finger curled around the trigger switch. He began to recite from the Koran: *"And the guilty behold the fire and know that they are about to fall therein, and they find no way of escape . . ."*

Khan realised that the boy was right. There was no point running, no point sounding the alarm. It would only start a stampede. *Really, there was nothing to be done.* Khan looked around him at the bustling market, and the sights and smells assailed him, the crowded stalls with their chaotic ever-changing vibrancy and the warren of alleyways slipping away in all directions, the sacks of spices—saffron, turmeric, cumin, and halved burls of nutmeg—the bolts of brightly-coloured cloth, the mottled stacks of fruit, the aroma of dust on the warm breeze, and beneath it all, the sly whiff of rotting fish. And people everywhere. He loved this place. This verdant valley. This teeming city. He imagined it moments from now as a slaughterhouse of legs and arms and torsos with glistening loops of entrails and a torrent of blood. It was depressing, really. He found that he had nothing to say. He knew he should be making peace with God, but the truth was, he did not believe in God. There was just this world and nothing beyond it.

He would not wake up in Paradise.

He looked down at the boy and saw that his face had become a mask. The boy's eyes were shocking. They looked through him and beyond him to some place of pain and torture, to some inward hell that Khan would never experience and could not even imagine.

"Go on," Khan said, closing his eyes. He realised that he'd wasted his final moments watching a child relive his life when really he should have been reliving his own.

The boy squeezed the trigger.